The Broken Pieces

The Paladins, Book 4

DAVID DALGLISH

BOOKS BY DAVID DALGLISH

THE HALF-ORC SERIES
The Weight of Blood
The Cost of Betrayal
The Death of Promises
The Shadows of Grace
A Sliver of Redemption

THE SHADOWDANCE TRILOGY
A Dance of Cloaks
A Dance of Blades
A Dance of Death

WATCHER'S BLADE TRILOGY
Blood of the Underworld
Blood of the Father (coming late 2012)

THE PALADINS
Night of Wolves
Clash of Faiths
The Old Ways
The Broken Pieces

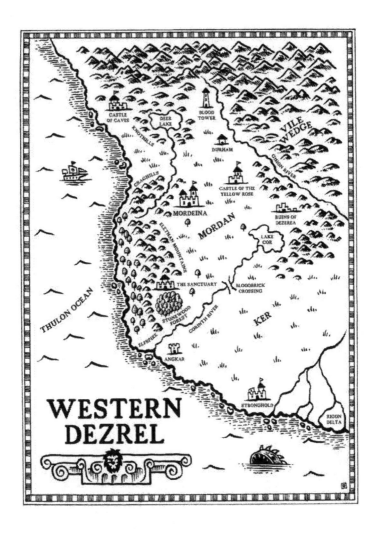

WESTERN DEZREL

1

In the Castle of the Yellow Rose, Lord Sebastian Hemman stood staring at his throne. Upon the wood of the chair he'd handsomely paid an artist to stencil in various lions, all roaring and clawing with sharpened teeth and claws. The cushions were red, and sewn in golden colors were two symbols. One was of the rose, his banner, the other another lion. His entire seat of power, the representation of his divine right to rule, was nothing but a declaration of his faith in Karak.

Except he felt no faith, only fury. His thin hand dug into the cloth as he entertained thoughts of tearing off the stitching with his bare fingers.

"Milord?" said a guard, stepping through the doors into the grand hall.

"Have they finally arrived?" Sebastian asked, not bothering to turn around.

"The priest has, if that is who you mean."

"Who else would I mean? Leave me, and send the bastard in. Just him, and no others."

Sebastian sighed and settled into the throne. It felt like the carved lions bit at his hands, and the stitching growled at his back. The guard hurried away, as if afraid of his master's ire. Not that Sebastian blamed him. He'd hanged two men the day before, peasants stupid enough to be overheard speaking ill of him. It'd done nothing to improve his mood. Nothing would. Karak had betrayed him. Despite his loyalty, his devotion, and most importantly, his exorbitant tithes, the god of Order had sealed his doom in his war against his rebellious brother, Arthur.

The doors opened again, and in stepped the elderly priest, Luther. They'd met several times before, though never for long. Something about his manner made Sebastian feel like a child waiting to be exposed for the lies he'd told. Luther slowly approached, walking between the many empty tables. There'd be no feasting, not for several years. Most of the men who'd raised cups to Sebastian's name were now dead, crushed by Luther's army of mercenaries and paladins.

"I know I should greet you, Luther, but I fear I do not know how," Sebastian said, standing. "Are you my friend, my enemy, or my conqueror?"

"I am none," Luther said. "I come as your priest."

"Then you are all three."

Luther smiled.

"Your wit is sharp as ever. That is good. I expect you to listen well, and keep your pride in check as I speak."

There'd been no spoken threat, but Sebastian felt it keenly, like a sudden chill sweeping through his hall. Taking a deep breath, he choked down his anger. Now was not the time, not when Luther's army outnumbered his own two to one.

"Before you speak, I would ask two questions," he said. "If you'll permit them."

"It is your hall, and I am but a guest," Luther said. "Ask."

"Is it true what I've heard? Did you attack my army when it was on the verge of crushing my brother in his Castle of Caves?"

Luther stood before the throne and crossed his arms. The directness of the question didn't seem to bother him any. If anything, he looked bored.

"I did," he said.

The words shoved a spike into Sebastian's gut. His self-control was stretched to its limit as he asked his second question.

"Then pray tell me, why? I have loyally served you for years. It is my brother who speaks out against Karak, denouncing the mandatory services my people attend on the seventh. I have sent a fortune in tithes south, and yet when I fight a common enemy..."

"Silence," Luther ordered, and Sebastian obeyed. The priest's apathy was gone, if it had ever been. Instead he saw a terrible rage only barely contained. Sebastian tried to rise above it, to stand to his full height and deny a meddlesome priest, but could not, so great was that fury.

"The North is in shambles," Luther said. "And the blame lies on your shoulders. In my travels I have talked to the people, and I have heard their faith. It is nothing, Sebastian, an idiot's faith at best. There is no love for Karak in your lands. No devotion. You put faith as a yoke around their necks, then rip gold from their hands far beyond what we ask."

"But...but I have done things this way for years, and your order..."

"Is full of men who thought you caused no wrong, and might foster a better way," Luther said, disgust dripping from every word. "But we judge a farmer by the harvest, and this harvest is poor. Rebellion stirs in their hearts, and not just against you. The Citadel is crushed, and Ashhur's paladins are nearly extinct. There is a chance to accomplish something here in the North, something great, but it will not be with you as its lord."

Sebastian felt his blood pounding in his ears. So this was it? The priesthood would try to overthrow him at last? Years ago, when he first took rule of the North, Karak's priests had come to him, whispering careful words about remaining respectful of their faith. Sebastian had known what it meant, and been a careful follower ever since.

"If you take any action against me, all of Mordan will war against you," Sebastian said. "No lord or lady will risk losing their throne because of the whims of a priest."

"That has been happening since the dawn of time, Sebastian. But no, I will not take action against you. I only present you a choice, one you will either accept or refuse. The consequences will then be yours, however you decide."

So this was it, then. At last he'd hear the true reason for the betrayal.

"Speak it, then," Sebastian said, leaning back in his chair. "Waste no more of my time."

"Your army is crushed," Luther began.

"And whose fault is that, I wonder?"

"Please," Luther said. "Do not waste my time, either."

Sebastian waved for him to continue.

"Regardless the reason, you are defeated," said the priest. "Your brother marches this way, the rebel Kaide at his side. Together they have gathered men, more than enough to surround your castle and starve you out. The North knows of your defeat, and the seeds of rebellion are sprouting. Your only hope, other than surrendering, is to accept our aid."

"Aid?" Sebastian asked. He could hardly believe what he was hearing. "You crush my army, then offer me aid? What nonsense is this?"

"Not nonsense," Luther said. "Just the plain truth."

"You would blackmail me," Sebastian said, realizing what was going on. "By the gods, you have the stones to do it, too."

"One god," Luther said. "And I will do all he desires, regardless of my…stones. As for you, you have no wife, and no heir, something your people have grumbled behind your back about for some time. Not that you've cared, selfish as you are. You have never worried about succession, or ensuring peace after your death. I will end that, now. With my aid, you'll sign a will donating all of your lands, and the lands of your brother after his defeat, to the temple of Karak."

Sebastian blinked, hardly able to believe his ears.

"All of it?" he asked.

Luther nodded.

Sebastian rubbed his eyes, then stood from his throne. For once, he felt a fire brewing in him, and he would cower no longer.

"You ask for land that has been in my family for generations!" he cried. "You ask that I crush my brother, and then in death hand over the entire North to your temple? And how long, pray tell, until I die in my sleep? A year? Two? You're a patient one, Luther, but I have a feeling you'll want this to happen in your lifetime. This is…this is…this is unacceptable. You have overstepped every bound imaginable. I will send word to Mordeina. When the King hears of how you attacked my army, how you blackmailed me…"

"The King will hear what we tell him!" Luther roared back, his voice shockingly powerful for his age. It was as if Karak's fury thundered out of his throat. "If you do not agree, then we'll reveal the fleecing of your people in our name. We will tell him you waged war with the claim of our approval, and even used the faith of our god to recruit and fund this brothers' squabble. Do you know who King Baedan's advisors are, Sebastian? They're priests, and not of Ashhur. What do you think they'll whisper in his ears? They'll say we did what was just, for how could we ignore a lord insulting and profaning Karak in such a way?"

Sebastian didn't want to believe it, couldn't believe it, but he knew it was true. Common knowledge throughout Mordan was of how the priests of Karak guided the King's every move. Just yet another reason why Sebastian had tried to side so publicly with the Lion.

"Why?" he asked, slumping in his throne. "Why have you turned against me so? Why such hatred?"

Luther pulled his robe tighter about his shoulders and turned to the door.

"I do it because there is no faith in your heart," he said. "Just a shallow lie that has damaged our cause greatly. Dress yourself head to toe with the mark of the Lion, but you still hide nothing, not from me. Think on my offer. If you refuse, you'll have to fend off Arthur on your own. But we both know how that will go, don't we?"

Sebastian's hands shook as he clutched the sides of his chair. His mind whirled, trying to make sense of it all, to think of some way to save himself from his predicament.

"Give me a week to decide," he said at last.

"No," Luther said, walking away. "You have three days. Use them well, Sebastian."

The guards opened the doors so he might leave, and the noise of them shutting thundered throughout the suddenly quiet hall.

Sebastian rubbed his eyes, felt them tearing up with frustration and panic. He wouldn't lose this war. He couldn't. Arthur would hand him over to that rebel, Kaide the Cannibal. What the man would do to him…would he even kill him?

"Damn you, Luther," Sebastian said, though he had no clue what god might be left to do it. Karak would not damn his own, and as for Ashhur…

Ashhur was dead, his paladins gone, his priests too weak to stop it. There was no one left. No one left at all.

2

Jerico awoke with a start, crying out while hardly aware he was doing so. Sweat poured down his face, and it felt cool against his skin in the chill night air. He'd flung off his bedroll, no doubt from flailing about in the night. Clouds hid most of the stars, but the moon shone through one of the scattered gaps, and in its light Jerico stared at his hands. They were shaking.

"Just dreams," the paladin said, steadying his breathing in an attempt to slow down his heart. "Dreams, that's all, nothing more."

He lay back down and closed his eyes. Though he was on the outskirts of Robert's camp, he was still close enough to hear the snores and shuffling. From all around thrummed the cicadas, plentiful in the tall grass in the Knothills where they camped. To some it would have seemed dreadfully loud, but to Jerico it was nothing compared with Sandra's echoing screams in his head.

Every time he closed his eyes, he saw it. The battle at the Castle of Caves was at its end, Sebastian's siege crushed by the unexpected aid of Luther's army. Sandra had come running, leaping into his arms, oblivious to the gore and death all around them in the gates of the castle where Jerico had helmed the defense. She'd been his first love, his only love, and night after night he re-lived that moment where Luther came, pointed his finger, and blasted her heart to pieces with a bolt of lightning that had shimmered black.

Now do you understand, Jerico? Luther had said as Jerico held Sandra's corpse in his arms. You are insignificant, just a puppet to my desires. Go off into the wilderness and die. There is no longer a place for you in this world.

Such calculated cruelty. It made him shiver still. Luther had meant every word, and spoken them as if to a child or troublesome animal. Jerico, covered in the blood of dozens of soldiers, had been nothing but a tool. But for what reason? As he closed his eyes and tried to fall back asleep, he pondered on that, wishing his mind to remain on things other than the life vanishing from Sandra's eyes. Why had Luther wanted Jerico to keep Lord Arthur alive? What purpose? Everything he knew about Lord Sebastian implied he was an ardent supporter of Karak.

…just a puppet…

That's how Jerico felt. A clueless puppet. How did one fight against the strings when ignorant of the direction they pulled?

"Forget it," Jerico muttered, slowly rising to his feet. His mind was too awake.

Walking away from the camp, he hoped to put his mind at ease, to let the sounds of the night and rhythm of his steps drown away the lingering fears. Just south of the camp was a larger hill, and Jerico climbed it, the motion stretching the muscles of his legs in a satisfying way. He'd thought to overlook the encampment alone, but was surprised to find another. Jerico's first instinct was to reach for his mace, but Ashhur cried no warning in his mind. Besides, he'd left his mace and shield next to his bedroll, a rather stupid act in hindsight.

"Shouldn't you be sleeping?" the other man asked. He sat facing the camp, a long dirk in hand. When he looked up to speak, the faint light shone across his face, revealing his gray hair tied in a long ponytail.

"I could ask you the same thing, Kaide," Jerico said.

Kaide met his gaze, and for several long seconds he showed no reaction. Then he looked away, back down to his dirk.

"I think we both know the answer," the bandit lord said.

Jerico did, of course. Six days ago they'd buried Sandra along with the rest of the dead. If anyone felt the pain keener than Jerico, it'd be Kaide.

"Mind if I sit?" Jerico asked. "If neither of us can sleep, we might as well talk."

"Why not?" Kaide said. "You do tend to help one fall asleep."

"That's what the people in Durham used to say after my sermons," Jerico said, forcing an unreturned smile. Shaking his head, Jerico sat beside the man, and together they overlooked the tents. On one side were Lord Arthur's men, about five hundred in number. On the other side were those belonging to Kaide. Most slept below the open sky instead of in tents, having little more than the clothes on their backs and a desire for vengeance in their hearts.

"What is it you see?" Jerico asked when Kaide continued to stare at the camp.

"I see my men outnumbering Arthur's," Kaide said. "Yet we will receive no honor at Sebastian's defeat. We'll earn no lands, and be given no credit. It'll all belong to Arthur."

"I thought he promised to give you back Ashvale," Jerico said.

Kaide let out a chuckle.

"I'm not sure I want it anymore. Enough blood on my hands." He fell silent for a moment, and Jerico could tell he was struggling for words. "She told me, you know," he said after a time. "That bastard, Luther, he gave her warning. Said I was to stay away, me and my men. I laughed at her.

Laughed. And now look at what's happened. Here I am, Kaide the Cannibal, marching south to have my revenge, and all I can think of is how I wish I'd let you and Arthur rot in that castle."

"It's not your fault," Jerico said.

"It's not?" Kaide asked, shooting him a glare. "Then whose is it? Luther's? Arthur's? Yours? Tell me, Jerico. Tell me, so I can shove this blade up their ass and rip it out their throat."

Jerico waited to respond, letting Kaide calm first. In truth, he wasn't sure what he had to offer in answer, but he had to try. He'd felt distance growing between him and Kaide for a while, and when Sandra died it'd turned into a massive chasm.

"Revenge isn't how you should honor her," he began.

"Bullshit!" Kaide shouted, stabbing his dirk into the dirt. "Bullshit. Revenge is all I have left. It's what's gotten me this far. It's what has rallied these men to fight on my side to overthrow Sebastian. All I had beyond revenge was my sister and daughter, and now I've lost one."

"She's not lost, not…"

"No," Kaide said, glaring. "No, don't you dare tell me that. I don't want to hear about the hereafter. I don't want to hear about golden streets and rows of angels. My sister is dead, gods dammit! Dead, gone, lost, and for what reason? Because I pissed off a priest? Because I was stupid enough to think I could accomplish something in this miserable fucking world?"

"Luther killed Sandra to hurt me," Jerico said, the words like acid in his throat. "That's why she died."

"To hurt you?" Kaide said. "That's all? To think she died for so noble a purpose. Why are you so special? If he wanted to hurt you, he should have just hurt you. Not my sister. Not my little…"

He was crying, and he jammed the dirk into the dirt again and again. His upper body trembled with the action.

"What good are you, Jerico?" he asked at last. "Sandra loved you. I know she did. And you couldn't protect her, not even her. I sit here, and you have no comfort to offer other than petty dreams of gold you desperately pretend are real. You're an excellent killer, I'll give you that. An excellent killer in a world that's gotten so very fucking good at that lately."

Kaide stood, dirk in hand, and paused. His back was to Jerico, as if he were waiting, giving Jerico one last chance to refute the words. Jerico wanted to. He wanted to say something profound, something meaningful. A dozen responses he'd learned at the Citadel came to mind, things he'd been trained to say at such questioning. But they felt prepared. They felt dishonest. If he and Darius were wiped out, what did the world of Dezrel lose? What did he have to offer?

"Hope," Jerico said. "I offer hope."

"Hope?" Kaide asked, looking over his shoulder. "I don't see any hope in your eyes. I don't hear any hope in your voice. You're living a lie, Jerico, and I want no part of it. Luther was right. You should go off into the wilderness and die. There's no hope left in this world, just a lot of tears and blood."

Kaide descended the hill. Jerico watched him go, his gut wrenched into a knot. More than ever he wished he could say something, offer something, cleanse away the man's anguish for his sister with a simple prayer. But instead he heard the words, the accusations, and as the clouds passed over the moon, darkening the land, Jerico dared wonder.

When the sun rose, and the army below stirred in preparations for another day's march, Jerico remained upon the hill, still awake, still in doubt.

Grevus stepped into the tent, then waited at the entrance with his hands clasped behind his back. His dark armor was polished to a fine gleam, the lion on his breastplate intricately detailed so that it seemed its fur blew in an unseen wind. Sheathed at his side was his well-worn blade. For twenty years he'd served as a paladin of Karak, and in those twenty years, he'd never met a priest more frightening than Luther.

"You called for me?" he asked when Luther turned from his candlelit desk. A parchment lay before him, an inkwell beside it. Luther put away the quill he held, then gestured to what he'd written.

"I have a message for you to deliver," the priest said. "One that, given the circumstances, might put your life in peril."

"My life belongs to Karak," Grevus said. "I shall do whatever he commands without fear or doubt."

"Fear itself is irrelevant," Luther said, turning back to the parchment and scanning over it. "It's how you act upon it that matters. Doubt, however, is poison. I say this only to ensure you are careful, and remain guarded. This is a most delicate task, more than just delivering a message."

Grevus hated the cryptic words but knew better than to demand a proper explanation. If Luther wished to give him one, he'd do so on his own terms.

"I will do as I must," Grevus said. "Where am I to go?"

"To the Blood Tower," Luther said, letting out a sigh.

Grevus swallowed, everything clicking in place.

"To Cyric," he said.

"Yes, to Cyric," Luther said. "This must be handled delicately. I've already sent a missive to Mordeina, requesting the full force of our might to come north under my command. So far none of them know of Cyric's claims to be Karak made flesh, and I'd like this settled without them ever knowing."

"You fear they'll condemn him, and risk war amongst ourselves?"

"Condemn? No, Grevus, I fear that my brethren will believe him. The only thing worse than a madman is a madman with followers."

Grevus felt his body stiffen. Luther was the most faithful, intelligent priest he'd ever known, hence why he feared him so. He knew Karak's every desire, and when he spoke, it was with the voice of the Lion. If he was afraid of Cyric's claim, and the damage it might cause...

"So you don't believe him then?" Grevus asked.

Luther shot him a look.

"Believe him? Of course I don't believe him. That you have to ask makes me reconsider sending you as bearer of my message."

"Forgive me," Grevus said, bowing low. His mind scrambled for the right words. He thought back to his days at the Stronghold, particularly the weeks spent reading over prophecy before returning to the physical training and prayers. "But every child of Karak has been told there will be a day when our god walks the world as he once did. When the sun rises, we pray today is that day, so our hearts may be ready, and our faith strong enough to kneel in his presence without shame."

"Grevus, I trust you above all others," Luther said, and the worried look on his face made Grevus uneasy. "You are a simple man, faithful, practical. If you are uncertain about

Cyric's claim, then I fear all the more how the rest of our brethren will react."

"You misunderstand me," Grevus said. "I believe that Karak might one day walk this world. What I do doubt, however, is that he's Cyric."

"You speak of doubt yet again. Be certain, or admit you know nothing. Never doubt."

The ink dry, Luther rolled up the message, then began melting wax so he might form a seal. Grevus watched, the tent feeling incredibly cramped despite its large size. The air was suffocating, he realized, though he was unsure why. Maybe it was Luther's worry that infected him. Grevus felt best walking into a conflict with his sword drawn and his armor shining. That was his home, on the battlefield, the heathens and the blasphemous dying upon his blade. Philosophy? Prophecy? They appealed to him, but only as a curiosity. Debating them, on the other hand, made him feel like he was on a different battlefield, naked and fighting with his bare fists.

"He was a good disciple," Luther said, interrupting his thoughts. "Good, but there was a flaw in him, one I tried to repair. But some flaws are too deep. Some flaws define who we really are."

"And what might that be?" asked Grevus as the wax dripped upon the message he was to bring north. "What was Cyric's flaw?"

Luther smiled sadly and shook his head.

"He hated the priesthood."

Grevus's mouth dropped open. That was a flaw? That sounded more like a massive contradiction for a young man determined to be a priest.

"I'm...not sure I understand."

Drip, drip went the wax.

"It's not that hard," Luther said, carefully watching it collect. "A subtle thing, really. But the priesthood, its laws, its restrictions, all of its members…he saw them as beneath him. He saw them as failing to live up to Karak's standard. Whenever he failed, he'd blame not himself but the priestly order. It was we who taught him weakness, was it not? No, he always looked to the old ways. That was his excuse, his reason for the flaws he saw in all of us. We didn't sacrifice sinners like we used to. We tolerated too much. We weren't as strict, weren't as demanding. So much easier for him to yearn for a past that was better, more full of faith and wisdom."

Grevus tried to think like that, to understand, but could not. The past was the past, nothing better, nothing worse.

"In all times, there are men who are faithful, and men who are weak," he said. "Cyric is a fool to think it wasn't always this way."

Luther smiled as he put down the candle and wax.

"So true, paladin. Thank you for reminding me why I chose you."

He pressed his ring into the wax, placing his seal upon it.

"Ride alone to the Blood Tower," Luther said, offering the missive to him from his seat. Grevus accepted it, hoping the priest didn't notice his nervousness. Even through his gauntlets, it felt like the paper shocked his skin. "If Cyric is not there, he might be at a nearby village named Willshire. When he is alone, break the seal and read him my message."

"Shall he not read it himself?" Grevus asked.

"No, no. From your lips, Grevus. I want there to be no doubt, no confusion. I trust you to believe what I say, and to know what to do after the message is delivered. Act with faith, and do not hesitate. There is more at stake here than you know."

"And what is that?" Grevus dared ask, even if it revealed him to be lacking in wisdom.

Luther leaned back into his chair, and his eyes glazed over as his thoughts traveled inward.

"A man who yearns for the past now claims to be Karak," he said. "A man who would make things as they once were. His faith is strong, and his words will be seductive. He'll speak of power, of conquest and subjugation. He'll speak of enforcing faith throughout the land, denying people even the illusion of choice. And if given the chance he'll crush every last remnant of our order, which he views with such contempt, all to remake a world that never existed except in his foolish dreams."

"The words I carry, they are the words of Karak?" Grevus asked, looking at the parchment.

"They are," Luther said, his eyes refocusing. "And if they are not, they should be. Prepare your things quickly, and ride out before the dawn."

Grevus bowed low, but had one last question before he left.

"Luther," he said. "I must ask. I must. If Cyric claims he is Karak made flesh when he is not, then he speaks blasphemy of the highest order. You know our law. You know what I am called to do."

Luther stood from his chair and walked over, putting his hands on his shoulders.

"Read the message," he said. "And then act with the wisdom and faith I know you have."

Grevus's insides hardened, and despite all his training, he felt fear and uncertainty facing such a task. To judge the life and faith of a priest, knowing that blood must be spilled should he not deny the blasphemy…

"I will do my best," he said, standing up straighter.

"I know you will. Now go."

As Grevus went to leave, Luther gave him one last command.

'Oh, and while you're up there," he said, his old eyes sparkling, "should you find out where Darius is hiding, hunt him down and kill him. An embarrassment like that to our order has no right to live."

"Of course," Grevus said, bowing low. He felt a smile pull at his lips. Everything else might worry him, especially being caught between two powerful priests of Karak, but in this, he knew there was no debate.

Darius, the traitor paladin, deserved to die.

3

The people of Willshire rose with the sun, for there was work to do. For them, it meant dealing with the fields, their homes, with baking bread and dirty clothes. For Darius, it was an execution.

The paladin strode from his tent toward the town square, the new day sun shining off his polished armor. Where once had been the sigil of Karak was now a golden mountain. It'd taken many meticulous hours scraping away at it with a dagger to clear off the original paint, and his drawing, while careful, was still crude. Skill in art had always eluded Darius growing up, not that he'd had much practice beyond a few doodles made while learning his letters in the Stronghold. But he was proud of it nonetheless, though it now worried him greatly. He bore the symbol of Ashhur on his chest, but on his face he would wear the hood of the executioner.

An older man, Brute, saw him along the path through town and strode to join him.

"It doesn't have to be you," Brute said.

Darius shook his head.

"You know it does."

They continued on, neither speaking. After the defense of Willshire and the arrival of Daniel Coldmine's soldiers, they'd remained in town. They'd fortified the outer roads and built up some barricades, but not with any real expectation of defense. In truth, they'd not known what else to do. Daniel himself was lost, presumed dead after a failed attack on the Blood Tower. Once casualties were counted and done, Brute had assumed leadership, though only in name. Darius had become their leader after that battle. He'd defeated Cyric and sent him running, and it was his sword that had killed the demon lion, Kayne. They looked to him, expecting a miracle that Darius simply did not have to offer.

"It shouldn't be you," Brute said, finally breaking the silence as the square came into view. "This man is one of mine. Crimes committed by soldiers should be tried, judged, and punished by other soldiers."

Darius heard the words, and a large part of him wanted to accept. Brute had quickly become a good companion, offering advice earned from many long years of battle. His gray hair and numerous scars weren't needed to convince Darius that his wisdom was more often correct than not. But this, he had to do.

"Who gave the order that the people of Willshire were to be untouched?" Darius asked.

"You did, but…"

"And," Darius continued, "who warned Conn that if he forced himself on another woman, he'd have a choice, his prick or his life?"

Brute shook his head.

"You did, but you had no authority to make those orders, or those threats. You spoke them, but I made them law. Let me swing the blade. It's not your fault."

"I know it's not mine," Darius said. "It's Conn's. Who'd have thought the fool would rather lose the head on his shoulders than the one down below?"

To this, Brute could only shrug.

In the center of town was a great pit of ash. It was there Cyric had constructed his altar, where he'd planned to sacrifice many in the name of Karak. Once the mad priest had been defeated, Darius made sure every bit of wood and nail had been burned to the ground. Later they'd burned the bodies of the dead upon it, for they had little spare wood for the purpose, and the fire was already blazing. That the law required Conn's execution to be held in the public square, on that same spot he'd fought and killed to prevent similar beheadings, felt bitterly ironic.

Conn waited on his knees in the center of the pit, hands bound behind his back. Two soldiers stood at either side of him, their hands on the hilts of their swords. At their arrival Conn looked up, then spat at Darius's feet.

"Figured you'd be here," he said. "Plan on using that big ass sword of yours?"

Conn was a fine looking man, but his heart was ugly. Twice Darius had caught him pressuring the young girls of the village to lie with him, implying harm might come to them otherwise. He'd been given warnings, but little else. Then one drunken night, not three days after they'd stopped Cyric's sacrifices, Conn had flung a barmaid against a wall and tried to take her by force. Again Darius had stopped him, and then told Brute to declare the law. Trying to live by the forgiveness Jerico had taught him, Darius gave Conn more warnings, and every bit of hard labor he could think of around the town to keep him busy. It'd not been enough.

This time, Darius had not been there to stop him. They'd learned only from the girl's furious father.

"You can change your mind," Brute told Conn. "It's not too late."

Conn spat at his feet.

"You want me to live as half a man? That ain't living. I'll die whole, not like that."

"You won't die whole," Darius said, pulling his greatsword off his back. Blue-white light shone across the blade, soft and subtle. It was the material manifestation of

26

Darius's faith, and by how weakly it flickered he could see how much his confusion had shaken him.

Conn sneered.

"Whole enough. Go ahead, unless you're too much of a coward."

Darius swallowed, and he tried to bury his frustration, his anger and hatred. Stepping closer to Conn, he knelt down so they could stare eye to eye. No matter what Conn was, he was not a coward, and he met Darius's gaze without flinching for fear of what was to come.

"Don't do this," Darius said. His voice dropped low, as if it were just the two of them alone in the world. "There's still a chance for you to change. There's still a way you can make this right."

"You want to make this right?" Conn asked. He leaned closer, his arms still bound behind his back. "Then let me go. I didn't do nothing, and you've got no right mutilating me. What you said, it's sick. Only have yourself to blame."

Forgiveness and compassion, thought Darius. He saw neither, not in those eyes. He stood, then beckoned the guards to step away. Conn sat on his haunches instead of presenting his neck.

"I ain't making it easy for you," he said to the paladin. "And you," he said, glaring at Brute. "We fought to keep that Cyric bastard from taking us over. What's the point if we just let one god replace the other?"

"Conn Graham, you have broken the king's law, and chosen a sentence of death," Darius said, ignoring Conn's snicker at the word king. "May you find peace in the hereafter."

"Maybe I'll find justice, too," Conn said.

Down came the blade in a sweeping angle, chopping through Conn's neck side to side. His head rolled, and Darius turned away, not wanting to see. The two guards reached for the body, and the paladin trusted them to clean up the mess. Wiping down his sword, he placed it on his back and marched away. Brute stepped in line, following.

"We get all kinds of men for our towers," Brute said. "Most we hammer and beat into something worthwhile, something a man can be proud of. But sometimes…sometimes we're trying to make armor out of mud. Can't change what a man's made of, only improve what's there."

"So you're saying Conn was mud?"

"I'm saying if you gave him a hundred chances, he'd break every one."

Darius shook his head, troubled but not wanting to reveal why, not even to Brute.

"Then perhaps I should have given him a hundred and one."

Brute grabbed his arm, forcing Darius to stop and look at him.

"You son of a bitch, you really are bothered by this," he said. "I told you to let me swing the damn sword. Next time maybe you'll listen."

Darius opened his mouth to retort back, but then just sighed.

"Fine," he said. "And pass your own laws, too. I'm clearly terrible at it."

"Not so bad as you think."

They stopped, for down the street rushed one of their men, clearly excited about something.

"He's back," the man said, out of breath from the run.

"Who's back?" asked Darius as Brute raised an eyebrow.

"Daniel," said the soldier. "Daniel Coldmine's back from the Wedge!"

They gathered in Darius's tent, the largest and most private in the camp. Daniel sat on the cot, a blanket wrapped about his upper body. He held several slices of buttered bread, wolfing them down and pausing only to speak. A cup of ale rested between his knees, half-empty. A small boy stood in the corner of the tent, attending him should he need more to eat or drink.

"Best thing I've ever tasted," Daniel said, finishing his third slice. "After eating bugs for a week, you'd be surprised how close to tears a sliver of butter will bring you."

Darius chuckled, sitting in a rickety chair opposite the cot. Beside him stood Brute, arms crossed and patiently waiting for his returned commander to tell his tale.

"We assumed everyone lost," Darius said. "Did anyone else survive? What of Sir Robert?"

Daniel stopped eating, and the bread trembled in his hands.

"No," he said. It was as if he were suddenly an inch from breaking down. "No, no one lived, especially not Sir Robert."

He glanced up, and Darius realized it wasn't tears that made Daniel tremble. It was seething rage.

"That bastard, Cyric, he turned Robert into an abomination. His throat was cut, yet somehow he still lived. Still moved. They kept him chained in the tower, writing letters south, telling people that Cyric's takeover of the Blood Tower was all a lie, and that the priest was only advising him. I...I cut off his head. It was his order, his last order. Gods help him find peace."

"What happened then?" Brute asked.

Daniel gestured to the dirty child in the corner.

"Not sure I wish to say more with the lad here."

Darius tried to reveal nothing with his gaze, and shrugged off the comment.

29

"That lad's my helper, and he'll hold his tongue. Tell us, what happened at the tower?"

"The rest of my men gathered at the door of Robert's tower, sacrificing themselves so I could escape out a window. Nearly died even then. One of those abyssal lions spotted me. If you'd care to look, you can see the scars he left on my back with his breath."

"Her," Darius said. "It was a her, by the name of Lilah."

"How the fuck do you know?" Daniel asked.

"Because I killed Kayne, the other."

Daniel shook his head in disbelief.

"If you faced one of them down, you have greater stones than I do. Only way I escaped was by crossing the river. Fled into the Vile Wedge, and lived among the monsters. Shouldn't have had problems staying hidden, but something's amiss in there. Too many wolf-men, and not enough of anything else. You'd think they'd have learned after we slaughtered them at Durham."

The man drank down the rest of his ale, then tossed the cup to the floor.

"Are you two really the ones in charge?" They nodded. "Shit."

"We stopped Cyric's plans here," Darius said, shifting uncomfortably in his chair. "His soldiers were killed, and his sacrifices halted. Cyric lived, though. Ran before I could shove my sword through his belly. After all that, we weren't sure what else to do. Our numbers are too few to recapture the Blood Tower, and the town lacks the supplies for any lengthy travel. The only way to reach civilization would be to sail down the river, right past the Blood Tower. The garrison there would crush us if we tried. So we've stayed here."

"Hoping for the best?" Daniel asked. "That's your plan?"

"Put simply, yes," Brute said. "You disagree?"

Daniel shook his head.

"Cyric will be returning to the Blood Tower. With Robert gone, their ploy will fail if they can't tie up all the loose ends. That's what we are, one giant loose end. He'll come, and then we'll die."

"I saw what Darius could do on his own," Brute said. "Get some food and drink in your belly, then sleep away the day. You do us a disservice as you are. None of us have any plans of dying."

"You misunderstand me," Daniel said, putting aside his plate and standing. "I didn't survive all that just to play the coward or the fool. Sir Robert was a great man, a good man, and what Cyric did...I can't forgive it. I won't. We'll find that madman and make him pay. And the first step to that is retaking Robert's tower."

"Robert's dead," Darius said. "It's not his tower anymore."

"Then we'll take back my goddamn tower," Daniel said. "We'll fling those mercenaries into the river, and maybe you can kill yourself another of those forsaken lions. How does that sound?"

"It sounds impossible," Darius said, even though he smiled. "But I've been doing the impossible lately. What's one more attempt at it among friends?"

"Not quite impossible," Brute said. "We do have that woman of yours."

Daniel leaned back in his chair, setting aside the last of his meal and drink.

"Woman?" he asked. "What woman do we have that can make the impossible possible? Because I'd be glad to meet her."

"You already have," said the boy in the corner. He stood up straighter, and suddenly looked so much taller than before. His build thickened, and his hair turned red, growing longer so that it curled about her neck. No longer a boy but a woman with breasts beneath her sleek black tunic, which matched the leather of her pants. Brute frowned, clearly unhappy with the display, while Daniel tensed as if expecting some sort of attack.

"Always one for the dramatic," Darius said, shaking his head. "Daniel, I'd like you to meet Valessa, formerly a gray sister of Karak, and my current guest."

"Who…" Daniel said, then paused to swallow. "No, what are you?"

"I was one of Karak's most faithful," Valessa said. Even now, Darius could hear the pain in her voice. "And now I am accursed and abandoned. Cyric stripped everything from me, betraying me to excuse his own failures. I am shadow, I am death, and I will have my revenge upon him, same as you."

"There must be something stronger in my drink than I thought," Daniel said, standing. Darius met his gaze, which had hardened tenfold. "Are you a madman, paladin? You invite a creature of Karak into our tent because she claims a desire for revenge? How do you know she doesn't report our every move to Cyric? How do you know she won't kill us all in our sleep?"

"I don't," Darius said. "But I trust her."

"You trust her?" Daniel said. "That's great. But can you guard her?"

Darius looked to Valessa, trying to read her. It was nearly an impossible task, her very image that of an illusion, an exquisite mask to hide the shadows. In her eyes, he thought he saw anger, perhaps wounded pride.

"I do not fear pain," she said to him. "If you must, show Daniel the manacles you hold over me, if he needs such a display to sleep at night."

It didn't feel right. It felt akin to when he drew his sword to cut off Conn's head, but he would not refuse Valessa's request. He pulled his sword off his back and held it with both hands. The blade shimmered with light, and even though it did not seem bright in the tent, it immediately began to burn Valessa's flesh. Her pale skin flaked away inch by inch, and her body trembled as whatever held it together steadily broke. Daniel watched, his mouth open. Darius pulled his blade back to sheath it, but Valessa stepped closer, grabbing his wrist. She stared into his eyes as the light burned her deeper, until even her face was lost in shadow and darkness.

"Enough!" Daniel cried. Valessa's hand released his wrist, and he quickly sheathed the sword onto his back. The light faded away. Now a mass of darkness on her knees, Valessa slowly regained her strength, her form solidifying with each passing moment.

"Satisfied?" Darius asked Daniel, feeling irate.

"Not even close," Daniel said, watching the skin reappear on Valessa's hands and face. "I think you've only disturbed me further."

"We've kept her presence hidden from the others," Brute said, putting a hand on Daniel's shoulder. "So far she's done nothing suspicious, nor threatened harm upon anyone other than Cyric."

"So be it," Daniel said, pointing at Darius. "If you can control her, then she stays in your tent. I take it she's been going out in the disguise of a boy?"

"She has," Darius said. "We call him Vale."

"Cute." Daniel grabbed the blanket off his chair and wrapped it about his shoulders. "If she wants to kill Cyric, she can get in line. We don't need tricks and charlatans to retake the Blood Tower. We need men, able-bodied killers."

"There are fewer killers finer than I," Valessa said.

"My comfort only grows in your presence," Daniel said.

Darius tried to keep his temper down. He knew Daniel had little patience or tact when frustrated, but this felt unfair. Valessa had come to him willingly, offering aid.

"She knows where Cyric is," Darius said as he put a hand on Valessa's shoulder. It felt cold to his touch, but he gently squeezed anyway. "At all times, she knows. We can use her, Daniel, track Cyric no matter where he goes, evade any ambush while planning our own."

"A good trick," Daniel said, settling back into his chair. "Can she do that with anyone, or just Cyric?"

"Only two," Valessa said, her voice soft, eloquent. She'd adopted the habits and persona of a highborn lady, and Darius knew she did it to seem superior to the soldier. "Men who have wronged me greatly, and who by my very creation I am called to kill. Cyric is one."

"And the other?"

Valessa smiled, and then she was the boy, Vale. Without a word she left the tent. Darius smirked at Daniel, and he found himself needing to talk to Valessa, to apologize for the agony his blade had inflicted upon her.

"The other's me," he told the lieutenant. "Good night, gentlemen. Rest well. We're going to need it if we're to overthrow the Blood Tower."

4

yric stood in the center of the bones, unafraid of the hundreds of wolf-men gathered around him, snarling and howling amid a fit of rage. Redclaw had repeatedly warned him of such a reaction.

"They will never lower their heads to a human and call him pack leader. Not unless you are a man of miracles."

The moon shone high above, its light illuminating the near four hundred wolf-men. They were in a circle surrounding him, and gathered together in various packs. If the wolf was to be believed, Redclaw had once united them all and declared himself Wolf King. His attack on the village of Durham had been disastrous, the defeat stripping him of any claim to such a title. Cyric had promised him he'd have it back, earning a mocking chuckle from the gigantic beast.

"You insult us all, Redclaw," said a hulking wolf-man with red fur pocked with scars. He was known as Many-Bruises, and was leader of the largest tribe at the Gathering, nearly two hundred strong. Redclaw's pack was the only one sworn to Cyric, and therefore sworn to Karak. At last count, that number was barely more than fifty. Cyric looked to Redclaw, curious how he'd react. The wolf-man was not as big as Many-Bruises, but he was quicker, more agile. He was also stronger, Cyric knew, despite his size. Karak must have blessed Redclaw at birth, Cyric decided. The creature was destined to be his champion here in the beginning of the end times.

"This human speaks of our past," Redclaw said, his voice carrying through the wild hills of the Vile Wedge. "He speaks of gods, the gods we worshipped before we bowed to the moon. He is strong, stronger than any wolf, and promises us we will be even stronger."

Curses filtered through the crowd from the various pack shamans, all insulted that one would dare claim they had once worshipped something other than the moon.

"I would rather follow the weakest wolf than the strongest human," Many-Bruises snarled. "For even the weakest wolf is stronger than the greatest human."

"Such impeccable logic," Cyric said, chuckling at the stupid thing. "Would you care to prove it, Many-Bruises? Or would you rather let Redclaw tear open your throat instead? I'd hate for you to die at the hands of anything other than a wolf."

"Let me be the one to spill his blood," shouted another pack leader, this one an ugly creature with one eye by the name of Gutdancer. He was the only one with a pack as small as Redclaw's. Cyric turned on him and lifted a hand.

"I have heard of you from Redclaw," Cyric said. "You are stupid, and always eager for blood. Would you fight me, young wolf?"

Gutdancer howled, but another stepped in his way, blocking him. It was a wolf-man with golden fur, and his red eyes shone with intelligence that rivaled Redclaw's. His name was Warfang, and above all others, Cyric had been warned that he would be the one to fear most.

"No," said Warfang, hurling Gutdancer back toward his pack. The wolf-man spun to face Redclaw, even though his eyes remained on Cyric. "What you say is blasphemy. You speak against our mother in the sky. You speak against the shamans. Now you want us to kneel, and worship a human? We will not, Redclaw. You know this. Why have you come to the Gathering with lies on your tongue?"

Redclaw and Cyric stood in the center of the Gathering, on a small mound of bones brought by the various packs. Some were old, some were fresh, and piled together they formed a place of religious importance. Should any pack leader step onto the bones, they'd battle, most likely to the death. Whoever remained standing on the bones afterward would be declared the stronger. Cyric knew he could best any of them, but Redclaw was his champion, and Redclaw was right. None of them would swear allegiance to a human. At least, not yet.

"The moon is not your mother," Cyric shouted, using magic to enhance his voice so it was heard by all. "You were not born of its light. You were made for war, in an age long past. Two gods battled, and my god, Karak, was the one who gave you life. He gave you legs to walk upon, and minds to lift you up beyond those of your four-legged brethren. You have strength, and bloodlust, all born not from the moon but from Karak. You have moved away from him now, turning to the blasphemy of your shamans. I offer you a chance to return to Karak's embrace, to worship the Lion in the way you were always meant to worship: in servitude."

They looked ready to bury him in a wave of claw and fur, but against their rage, he smiled. It was the flailing of children, angry at their parent for a scolding. They would come to know his wisdom, one way or another. As much as it pained him to rely on Redclaw, he would have to let the beast prove the truth of his words. Many times before the Gathering he'd coached Redclaw on what to say and when to say it, and this was that moment. Cyric tensed, eager to see how his champion reacted.

"I am strong," Redclaw roared to the rest of his race. "But I will be made stronger still. The moon is false. We bow to the Lion now. Come, any of you. Face me upon the bones, and I will show you my strength!"

Mostly right, though he should have said 'Karak's strength', not 'my strength'. The priest took a step back, to the far edge of the bones, so that Redclaw stood at the top, towering over them all. This was it. Cyric had thought long on this, and knew exactly what he desired. Karak had already blessed him with the arrival of the two lions, Kayne and Lilah. Pulling two creatures of the Abyss into the world of the living was a tremendous boon, but it was not enough. The world needed cleansing. He didn't need two lions. He needed an army.

And so he would make it, for he was Karak made flesh, was he not?

"I will not be denied the pleasure of a blasphemer's blood on my tongue!" Gutdancer cried, leaping past Warfang before the other could react. Redclaw crouched low, and when Gutdancer came lunging in, he rose up. In a sudden display of speed and strength, he caught Gutdancer by the throat, twisted him in the air, and then flung him on his back amid the pile of bones.

The wolf-men were howling, the Gathering reaching a frenzy as Redclaw licked blood from his claws. Now was the time. Cyric lifted his arms, calling forth all his power. The world of Dezrel needed a cleansing flood, a purging force of claws and muscle to tear away the life of the faithless.

"Be my champion," Cyric whispered. "Be my blade."

High above, where there had once been clear sky, a dozen thick clouds rumbled with lightning. It struck the pile of bones once, twice, the power of its thunder rattling teeth and sending wolf-men to the ground. Fire burned, swarming over Redclaw, the lightning having set his fur aflame. Redclaw let out a cry of immense pain, but it meant little to Cyric, for he could see the transformation had already begun.

As the wolf-men regained their senses, their eyes recovering from the sudden blinding flashes, they looked upon the changed Redclaw. His fur glowed a deep crimson, as if he were made of living embers. From his claws dripped molten rock, sizzling upon the bones beneath him. When he took a step forward, his footprints trailed fire. He sucked air deep into his belly, and then his roar breathed red in the dark night.

"Demonflesh!" cried Many-Bruises. Cyric had been told that wolf-men knew no fear, and he saw the proof of it then. Many-Bruises flung himself onto the pile of bones, accusing Redclaw again and again of being demonflesh. Redclaw did not even bother to block the claws that swiped at his skin. When they pierced his flesh, liquid flame poured across Many-Bruises paws, and he let out a pained scream. Redclaw slashed open his throat, then ripped off the head to hold it up to the stars. In his grip, the head shriveled black as it burned.

Cyric climbed the pile of bones, standing beside his champion.

"You are beautiful," he told Redclaw, who glanced his way.

"I am strength," Redclaw said. "I am fire. Give me something to kill."

Cyric gestured to the hundreds gathered about.

"Those who do not bow," he said. "Those you may slaughter."

"Wolf must not kill wolf. It is law."

"Who's law, Redclaw?" Cyric asked. "Yours? The pack's? You follow Karak's law now, and the unfaithful must be punished." He turned to the crowd and lifted his arms. "Kneel!" he shouted to them, using magic to enhance his voice. "Kneel, and accept your true god. Either Karak is your master, or Death. By your choice, one or the other will claim you this night."

All at once Redclaw's tribe dropped to the ground, their nuzzles pressed to the dirt. Within the rest of the crowd bowed various wolf-men. Some were mocked, others even assaulted, but not for long. With a smile on his face, Cyric watched his champion leap into the crowd, a wave of fire in his wake. His molten claws tore through their ranks, and his howl was louder than all others. Within moments the meeting was in chaos, and Cyric reveled at its center.

Redclaw spun and fought in the largest group, his long arms leaving afterimages of red with each slash. Each kill, each step, some leapt to attack Redclaw, while many more fell to their knees and shoved their noses to the dirt. But not all focused on him. Many-Bruises' pack rushed Redclaw's, and with them bowed face to the dirt, Redclaw's faithful would die in seconds. Cyric shook his head, knowing he should not be surprised by the pitiful creatures' stupidity and stubbornness. It was like trying to teach a child a complicated truth. There'd always be a few who'd never believe, no matter how intelligently explained.

"You defy a god!" Cyric yelled to Many-Bruises' pack, lifting his arms to the sky. Cracks split the earth, and they belched fire as the wolf-men leapt over. Dozens burned, and others yelped and fled. About a third continued on, clawing and biting at the bowed members of Redclaw's tribe. Others rushed through their ranks, their target solely Cyric, who smirked at their approach. A handful of wolf-men sought to take down Karak's physical manifestation?

They'd have better hope of ripping the moon out of the sky with their claws.

Cyric crossed his arms over his chest, summoning his magic, but was given no chance to use it. Another pack of wolf-men struck from behind, overcoming them with impressive speed. In moments the entirety of the Gathering either knelt in submission or lay bleeding. From the ranks of Redclaw's tribe emerged Warfang, who dipped his head low before Cyric.

"I see the strength given to Redclaw," he said. "I would have that blessing."

"What of Karak?" Cyric asked him. "What of your faith to the moon?"

"The moon would let us die this night," Warfang said, glancing upward. "The moon has never blessed my claws with fire. I trust what I see. I will bow to Karak."

"You?" asked one of the dying wolf-men that lay near Warfang's feet, his intestines piled in his paws. "You would bow to a human?"

"I bow to no human," Warfang said, his eyes meeting Cyric's. "I bow to a god."

Careful with this one, thought Cyric. He knew Redclaw intelligent for his kind, but this one might be even wiser. Still, he'd slain his attackers, and professed faith. Such things should not go unrewarded.

"Kneel," he told Warfang. The wolf-man did so as Redclaw returned to his side, the gore on his fur sizzling. Cyric put a hand on Warfang's head, and he bestowed a fraction of the strength given to Redclaw. Warfang breathed in deep, and when he flexed his claws, they flared red, like embers being blown upon.

"To all of you who kneel," Cyric cried, taking a step back. "To all of you shoving your snouts into the dirt, professing faith to a name you have never known before, know this! Your faith is weak, your knowledge pitiful. But you will still be blessed! You will learn of the god you serve. You will gain wisdom and power beyond anything your kind has possessed since the day the gods waved their hands and bade you to stand. You were made for war, and I will bring you that war again. The humans beyond the river, they are weak, and tremble at the thought of you crossing into their lands. But you will cross the rivers, you will tear down towers, and you will surround their villages and farms. Those who do not bow, as you have bowed, must know death. Bring it to them!"

"We are one tribe now," Redclaw said as Cyric fell silent, and the hundreds of wolf-men rose to their feet. "Not Warfang, not Many-Bruises, not Gutdancer. One tribe, Karak's tribe, and Redclaw is his champion!"

Chants filled the clearing as the burning wolf-man climbed the bones and let his full strength flare.

Redclaw! Redclaw!

Cyric frowned, even though he knew he'd blessed Redclaw for such a reason. Beside him, Warfang stood with his mouth open, chest shaking, a gesture he recognized as laughter.

"Careful," Cyric whispered to him.

"Glory to Karak's champion," Warfang growled before resuming laughing. "All the glory…"

Later that night, Cyric sat before an enormous bonfire. It was the pile of bones, used by the wolf-men in their heathen ceremonies. With a wave of his hand, Cyric had set it to burning, commanding the dead and dying to be thrown into its flames. Not all of them, of course. His wolf-men were hungry. A few had grumbled seeing their sacred bones destroyed, but not many, not after the display they'd just witnessed. Not when they could count the dead being tossed into the fire.

Redclaw hunched down beside Cyric, a large slab of meat in his left hand.

"Am I to be like this even when asleep?" the wolf-man asked, the grass where he sat shriveling black from the heat. "Can I not touch a mate without burning her fur?"

"The power is yours to control," Cyric told him. "So control it."

Redclaw growled but did as commanded. He closed his eyes, brow furrowing from concentration. Slowly the red glow faded from his fur, the tips of his claws becoming the deep brown they once were. When Redclaw opened his eyes, his lips pulled back in a macabre smile.

"Better," he said. "But I am still not pleased. You blessed Warfang. Why?"

Cyric stood so he could step closer to the fire, feel its heat against his skin.

"You dare to question a god?" he asked.

"When a god does stupid things, I question, yes."

Cyric shook his head.

"You are not the only wolf I may use for my ends, Redclaw. Remember that the next time you would insult me. Warfang was faithful, and with his aid the disjointed tribes will be far more loyal. Nearly four hundred wolf-men, all blessed in some way for when we cross the river. With your speed, your strength, we can swarm the North and crush armies ten times your number. But your faith must be strong. Karak's name must be on their lips…not Redclaw's."

"I am fire," Redclaw said. "I am their champion. Why not let them cry my name?"

In answer, Cyric stepped into the bonfire. Bones crushed beneath his feet, and the flames licked at his robes.

The fire swirled across his skin, like sand blowing across a desert, and not a hair on his body was burned. Cyric turned about, let Redclaw see.

"Because I cannot be burned with fire," Cyric said, pleased to see the wolf-man intelligent enough to fall to his knees. "I am of the Abyss, Redclaw, and your strength is my strength, and mine alone. Send out runners, and gather every wolf-man scattered about the Wedge. I want them here, all part of a single, unified army. And when we march into the first village, one of very many, I assure you, I want to know that it will be my name my army cries out in worship."

"They will worship Karak," Redclaw said. "I promise."

"No," Cyric said, shaking his head. "Not Karak. Karak made flesh. Cyric."

"As you wish," Redclaw said, the tips of his fur glowing. "Forgive me, I must go see that my pups are well fed."

"You are a father?" Cyric asked, honestly surprised. He thought the brute would be a solitary creature for some reason.

"Two pups," Redclaw said. "They are not old enough for names. But they will have them soon."

"Do you know what you'll call them?"

Redclaw hesitated, then nodded.

"I do," he said. "But only if you are who you say. Only if we conquer. Manslayer and Manfeaster, they will be called."

"Names to be feared throughout the North," Cyric said, and he smiled. "Though if we conquer, perhaps you should name them after the god that has led them to such glory."

"Perhaps," Redclaw said, and left without saying more.

5

"It is a stupid thing to shut me in here," Valessa said as Darius prepared his bed.

"I'm sorry if my snoring keeps you awake," he said. "But surely it isn't that bad."

"I do not sleep."

Darius shrugged.

"Well, then never mind about the snoring."

"Just because I do not sleep doesn't mean the sound is pleasant."

Darius laughed. He pulled off his armor piece by piece, setting it beside his bed. His sword he put by his feet, and was careful not to touch it for long. He didn't want its light to burn Valessa, for though she would not admit it, he knew it caused her tremendous pain.

"You once served Karak," Darius said, easing into his bed, which was really a cot with a bit of extra padding. "Surely you can understand Daniel doubting you, especially after all he saw at the Blood Tower."

"You once served Karak as well," Valessa said, crossing her arms. "How easily they forget."

"They haven't forgotten. I've proven myself. You haven't." Darius opened an eye, closed it. "You're not going to stand over me like that all night, are you? Just because you don't have to sleep doesn't mean you get to be weird."

"Damn fool."

After that there was silence, and that was enough for Darius to know she'd left. Sighing, he got up from his bed, took a look around to confirm she was gone, and then hurried out of his tent. Finding her would be difficult, especially if she didn't want to be found. She could make herself look like any man or woman, and cover herself with the finest of dresses or the lowliest rags. A frightened part of himself urged retrieving his sword for safety. Valessa still insisted she'd take her revenge against him. Was he being a fool for trusting her so?

Darius shook his head. Enough thoughts like that. Looking about the tents, he tried to think where Valessa would go. She'd want to be alone, he knew. His gut told him she also wanted to be herself, not Vale, nor any other disguise. On a hunch he headed from their camp at the edge of Willshire and into the village itself. Nearly everyone was asleep. Away from all the soldiers that looked to him for leadership, and free of the eyes of villagers who saw him as their only savior, he felt himself relax. Forget finding Valessa, it felt good to be walking alone through empty streets. His walk took him through the center of town, and he stopped to stare at the pit of ash where he'd beheaded Conn. But Conn wasn't the only person he'd killed there. He'd fought Valessa to a standstill, slaughtered a dark paladin of Karak, and even chased away Cyric.

He shook his head. Burning that altar had been the best thing he'd done.

Continuing north, he found a large barn. It was in there the people of Durham had been imprisoned to await their sacrifice upon the altar. Darius had hidden with them, and he remembered their anger and betrayal when they first saw his face. He'd been at Velixar's side as Durham burned to the ground. The memory made his heart ache, and he tried to remember the fiery altar, remember saving Jeremy Hangfield and his daughter from the sacrificial dagger.

But of course it hadn't been him. One of the other soldiers, Gavin, had fired his bow to stop the descent of that blade. Darius had stood frozen amid the crowd, terrified of making a mistake.

"You're a persistent one, aren't you?" Valessa said.

Darius looked up to see her hunched on the rafters, wearing the visage of her true self. She was dressed in plain grays, just like when she was a member of the gray sisters.

"You do anything stupid, it'd be my fault," he told her. "And I do enough stupid things on my own, I don't need the help. Come on down."

She shook her head.

"Daniel is a stubborn fool. If I stay here instead of your tent, he won't be the wiser, and honestly, I'd rather be anywhere in the world than beside you right now."

Darius sighed.

"What is it?" he asked. "What did I do? Is it because of my sword earlier?"

Her silence was answer enough.

"You told me to do that," he said, feeling his temper rising. "You said to show how I could control you. You can't get mad at me for doing what you told me to do."

"You still don't get it."

She turned so her back was to him. Darius stepped deeper into the barn, climbing atop a few bales so he was closer to her, and faced her once more.

"There's a lot of things I don't get," he said, forcing himself to stay calm. "I don't get why Jerico let me live. I don't get why Ashhur allows such horrible deeds throughout the world. And I don't get women. So please, help a paladin out."

When Valessa looked up, a black cloth covered her face, hiding much of her features.

"You hurt me to show I would not hurt them. But all of it was a lie, and you know it. No comfort. No truth. Just a farce pretending at control. If I wanted to, I could kill this whole village, every man, woman, and child. Only you could stop me, only you. I offered to stand there to appease Daniel's weakness. And stand there I did. If you must, I told you. If you must. You could have said no, but you didn't. You needed that pathetic display as much as Daniel did, and I'm a fool for thinking you were better than him."

She was blaming him? Darius's temper flared, and he couldn't control it this time.

"So I'm to protect you now?" he asked. "The woman who says she does not fear pain, and still vows to take my life once Cyric is gone? Who are you to me, Valessa? Just a lost, broken killer, tossed and abandoned by the same god that abandoned me."

The second Darius spoke the words he felt a cold slap. Looking up at Valessa, her face hidden by her dark veil, he realized how lost she must feel. He'd felt it himself. He remembered holding his blade aloft with a cursed hand, begging for flame, begging for strength. He'd prayed until he cried, determined to feel the presence of his god just one more time.

"Valessa…" he started to say.

"Get out," she interrupted. "Get out, now. I have failed Karak again and again, and you are the reason. It is because of you I know no peace in death. It is because of you Karak turns his back to my prayers. You are a wretch and a betrayer. Do not try to drag me down with you."

Darius climbed down from the hay and made his way to the door.

"Perhaps you're right," he said, pausing. "But what of Cyric? What does that make him? Karak cannot both bless him and deny him, only one or the other. And you stood at his side."

"A red star hangs over your head," Valessa said. "And a black one over Cyric's. That is my purpose now. That is my way to salvation."

Darius chuckled, even though he felt so very tired.

"I know an easier one," he said. "Stay here, if you must. If Daniel complains, I'll tell him to either trust me, or get rid of me. And if you're willing to endure their anger and sorrow, you can walk about as yourself instead of Vale. It's not like any of them can hurt you. Just promise you won't hurt them in return. It's not their fault. The last time most people here saw you, it was at Cyric's side, and you were the one holding the sacrificial dagger."

He left, shutting the barn door behind him. He heard no answer.

The next morning, he awoke to people shouting his name and shaking his tent. Stumbling off his cot, he stepped out into the painful daylight. Several men gathered about, and they looked furious.

"It's her," one said. "The one from that night. She's come back."

"And?"

They looked at him, baffled. Darius shook his head and gestured.

"Lead on."

Upon the pile of ash sat Valessa, wearing her true face. About twenty surrounded her, throwing stones that passed right through her. Darius pushed to the front as several asked for his sword. Valessa looked up from where she sat, then leaned forward and rested her chin on her hand. Another stone passed through her forehead and out the back. Though it caused no pain, he saw her wince ever so slightly.

"I never should have been at his side," Valessa told him, answering his unspoken question. Another stone, followed by a dagger. The calls for his holy blade grew.

Darius left the group, ignoring their requests.

"Darius!" shouted Daniel, having joined the ruckus. "Where are you going?"

"To get breakfast. Come hollering if she causes any harm."

"You said she'd not show herself!"

Darius shrugged.

"Looks like she changed her mind."

Sir Gregane stepped into his lord's bedchambers at first light. He'd been woken in his room by a servant and told to come, and quickly. Normally he'd have been annoyed by such an interruption, especially since they'd just arrived at the Castle of the Yellow Rose, but his dreams, what little he remembered of them, were dark and brutal. Upon awaking, he'd gasped in air and grabbed the wrist of the servant shaking him.

Now composed, and dressed as best he could at such short notice, he crossed his arms behind his back, stood to his full height, and addressed his lord.

"You called for me?" he asked Sebastian.

Sebastian looked up from his desk by the window. The shutters were open, and the soft breeze made the dwindling candles on either side of his desk dance and shake. Instead of bedclothes, Sebastian was already dressed for the day, and by the dark circles under his eyes, and the lengthy parchment before him, Gregane guessed he had been awake for some time.

"How many are left?" Sebastian asked him.

Gregane frowned, caught off guard. How many left of...

"A hundred," he said, realizing what Sebastian was asking. "A hundred men, more than half wounded from the battle. Plus your guard here, that puts us at a hundred and fifty."

"And how many serve my brother?"

Gregane thought back to the siege, his second confrontation with Lord Arthur and his men. It'd seemed like such a small force they faced, but then had come Kaide's ragtag army, followed by the most horrific of all: the backstabbing mercenaries and paladins of Karak.

"When we lost, they did not have great numbers," he said. "But our siege had prevented many various houses from joining Arthur's side, plus Kaide's forces could not appropriately arm or train themselves. But surely you received the same notices I did on my march here. The Marylls have pledged their swords to Arthur, as have the Cranes and the Elliots. Not the most fearsome of houses, but together they'll prove formidable. Our loss emboldened our enemies."

"You mean your loss."

"I did," Gregane said, swallowing down his pride. "Forgive me. But a safe bet puts them with around a thousand, and five hundred at minimum."

"We should be able to crush them," Sebastian said. He turned to his desk and began rolling up the long parchment he'd written. "Here in our castle, even a thousand isn't enough to breach these walls. If we hold out long enough, perhaps until the winter, the snows will drive them back. Those wretches with Kaide won't have the stomach for a lengthy siege, not like…"

"Milord," interrupted Gregane. "If we hold out for the winter, then all is lost. Time is no longer on our side. Either we defeat Arthur, and soon, or we'll face an army ten thousand strong."

Sebastian looked up, and there was panic in his eyes. Gregane recognized it well. It was a man staring at death and knowing there was no way to escape its touch.

"Explain," he demanded.

"That thousand strong will swell with each passing moment you appear the weaker. More minor houses will ally themselves with Arthur. Those still loyal to us will prepare for your downfall by ignoring our requests for aid when the siege begins, so they might more easily befriend Arthur when he comes to power. But worst of all will be the commoners, the peasants, the farmers...they'll join by the thousands, especially should a siege begin. They'll see us as the cowards, the frightened, the ones destined to lose. By the end of winter, they might be twenty thousand strong. Our few hundred will mean nothing to that."

At first Sebastian said nothing, only nodded his head as he sucked on his teeth in thought. Then he flung himself to his feet, hurling his chair to the other side of the room where it broke against the wall.

"Why?" he screamed. "Why this betrayal? Why are the people I have protected, the people I have lawfully ruled, so willing to see me ruined?"

"The people love Arthur," Gregane said. "They love Kaide. They do not love you."

That was it, the whole truth, and why Gregane had hurried his siege against Arthur weeks ago. Arthur and Kaide were a wildfire, one that, if unchecked, would consume them all. And because of Luther's interference, a sure victory had turned into a disastrous defeat, allowing that wildfire to steadily burn its way south. But saying these things to his vain, cruel lord was dangerous, and he knew it.

The tension in the room thickened until it was suffocating. Sebastian refused to meet his eyes, instead standing there, breathing heavily, the rolled parchment in hand. And then he tossed it to Gregane, who smoothly caught it.

"I have no faith in Karak," his lord said. "I know it looks otherwise. I've enforced the prayers. I've memorized the various litanies and scriptures. A lot of it makes sense. A lot of it is wisdom the world needs. But the priesthood…they're not satisfied. I send them a fortune in gold, and they are not satisfied. I drag men, women, and children before their priests to hear their words, and they are not satisfied. I've let my rule be governed by them, my laws crafted by them, my advisors chosen by them. But it is not enough. It'll never be enough. Get your things, and prepare to leave. I want you to take that letter to my brother."

"Milord, this letter isn't sealed."

"I know," Sebastian said, walking over to his bed and sitting down on the edge. "That's because I want you to read it first."

The defeat in his lord's voice sent a chill up Gregane's neck. Still standing before the door, he unrolled the parchment and began reading. As he did, his shock grew. The letter was addressed directly to Arthur, and lacked any sort of wordiness or pomp that Sebastian's official decrees often carried. Instead it made Arthur an offer, and a simple one at that: spare his life, and Sebastian would cede control of all the Hemman lands to his brother. The only other condition was that Arthur protect him from the wrath of Karak's priests.

"You're surrendering," Gregane said, feeling stupid even as he said it. But he had to hear it for himself.

"Never enough," Sebastian said, staring out the window from his bed. "All I've done, and it'll never be enough. That priest, Luther…he came to me yesterday, just before you returned. He wants me to put all the North into their hands after my death. They don't want puppet rulers anymore. They don't want loyalty. They want to be everything, priest and lord and king. All that our father once owned, all that I now control...gone. Out of our family line forever."

The parchment crinkled in Gregane's hands as he fought down his rage at the thought of such a betrayal.

"Are you sure this is wise?"

Sebastian shook his head. For once he seemed melancholy, calm and sober.

"Sure? Of course not. But it is my right to rule, and if not me, then Arthur. This is my family's land, and shall always be. Family." He let out a bitter laugh. "You probably think it strange that I of all men would talk of family. Here I am, having tried to kill my brother, and I well know the peasants say I did the same to my father."

"Milord!"

"Don't tell me lies, Gregane." Sebastian rubbed his eyes. "I did, too, but not for the reasons they guess. He wasn't my father anymore, not by the end. At times he didn't even know my name. He was a child, just a child. Arthur felt the same, and tried to give our father a potion to make him sleep a few days so he might take over rule. I almost let him do it, too."

Gregane knew all of this, all but what Sebastian wanted to say. He tried to think, to understand whatever was motivating him to surrender now.

"Why didn't you?" he finally asked.

"Because I didn't think Arthur would be a good lord," Sebastian said. He laughed. "He wanted to put our deranged, insane father to sleep instead of killing him. Arthur didn't have the strength, but I did. That...that...shell of a man was ruining the memory of Rodrick Hemman. I would know how to rule. I would know how to play the game of politics and priests. Nothing would take over my land, and I'd do whatever I must to keep it. Arthur's honor would only be a hindrance. But now I've gone in too deep. I'm terrible at a game I thought I could master. My wife died years ago without blessing me with children, and I have no stomach to remarry. I've no heirs, and no love. But Arthur has the love of the people. He has the vagrants, the criminals, and the outlaws all swearing devotion. He has the strength to rule, so let him rule."

Sebastian shook his head.

"But not the priests. This land cannot be a land of Karak. Let them teach. Let them spread their word, and every man from peasant to lord believe as they choose. But I cannot let them rule."

Gregane felt himself at a loss.

"I will do as you say, milord. I will take this letter, though I must ask…do you think Arthur will accept?"

"I'll be giving him everything he wants. Why wouldn't he accept?"

"Because he swore your death," Gregane said. "You sent assassins to kill him, and an army to surround and starve him. To him, you were once his brother, but I fear you are no longer. You are just an enemy to be defeated. To let you live would be to break his vow. There is also the matter of Kaide. I'm not sure living out your life peacefully in your castle is what he desires."

Sebastian's head dipped low, and he closed his eyes.

"Then pray Arthur isn't foolish enough to let his vow interfere with the fate of all our lands. Convince him, Gregane. Tell him of my fate, and the desires of Karak's priests. Surely he must still hold some measure of love for me, enough to side against that bastard cannibal. Most of all, tell them to hurry. They no longer march to take the

North from my hands. They march to take it away from Luther's, and they don't even know it yet."

"I will ride immediately," Gregane said. "How soon must I have their answer?"

Sebastian looked up at him again, and his eyes were red with veins.

"You don't understand, do you?" he said. "Luther claimed he'd leave me to my fate at Arthur's hands, but I am no fool. In two days, I will give him my answer, and it will be the strongest denial my cowardly self can summon. And then they'll capture me, torture me, kill me, whatever it is they need to get what they desire. There's a reason that army camps outside our walls. Ride, Gregane, ride fast and hard. And maybe, just maybe, shed a tear for me two days hence."

Gregane bowed low.

"Keep soldiers with you at all times," he said. "And don't let any servant of Karak through these gates. Survive, milord, just somehow survive."

"Thank you. Now go."

Gregane left for the stables, stopping only to pack a few provisions that would get him to the nearest town. He told no one else of his leaving, for he did not want to risk word getting back to Luther. Ten miles out from the Castle of the Yellow Rose, the smoke from the fires of Luther's camps just a distant haze, Gregane realized he'd forgotten to have Sebastian seal the letter with his ring.

6

When they marched out from Willshire, Valessa was not with them, but Darius trusted her to follow.

Despite Daniel's arguments against it, Darius had ensured Valessa a pivotal role in their attack. The Blood Tower, even with its skeleton crew, could still easily hold off the hundred or so men allied together under Daniel's rule. They had no siege weapons, no catapults to bust gaps in the surrounding walls, no ram to batter down the gates. What they did have, though, was a woman who could walk through walls and ignore the strikes of any blade.

"Why not let her kill every last one of them?" Daniel had asked when first hearing the plan.

"Because of Lilah. That lioness is powerful, and wields the fires of the Abyss. If anything can destroy Valessa, it's her. Get me inside, and surround me with men, and we'll find victory."

Strong words, Darius knew, even though deep down he was terrified of facing another of those lions. He'd been drunk on battle the last time, every hair on his body tingling with electricity. It'd seemed his faith in Ashhur could not have been stronger, and when Kayne leapt toward him, ready to crush him with muscle and fire, he'd heard the command to stand, and obeyed. His sword had pierced through the lion, and as it had collapsed into molten rock and burning blood, he'd emerged unscathed. It was a miracle, of that he had no doubt.

And half their plan relied on repeating a miracle.

"Darius?"

Darius startled from his thoughts. He walked at the rear of their makeshift army, enjoying the silence. A young man, newly conscripted from the people of Willshire, bowed low and spoke with a sense of urgency born of nervousness.

"Forgive me if I am intruding," he said, "but Lieutenant Coldmine wishes to speak with you."

"Tell Daniel I'll be there shortly."

The man bowed, then hurried off. Darius shifted his pack of provisions from his right shoulder to his left, then upped his pace. They walked through soft hills that seemed to roll on forever, the grass up to his thighs. Although there was a worn path between the town and Blood Tower, Daniel hadn't wanted to use it. Instead they'd walk east until they hit the Gihon, and then follow the river south, all in hopes of avoiding any scouts placed along the road. Decked out in his platemail, the morning sun rising in the sky, Darius felt sweat soaking into his tunic as he began to jog.

Daniel rode at the front of the line, one of the few who had a horse. Along the way, Darius heard calls and cheers, people slapping him on the back or shouting his name like it was a ward against their enemies. It should have made him feel proud, but instead just made him all the more self-conscious. Their lives depended upon him, every last one of them. Well, him and Valessa, and only because he'd vouched for Valessa's trustworthiness.

"The youngster called you Lieutenant," Darius said as he slowed down to a walk once he finally reached Daniel's side. "With Robert's passing, shouldn't you be a Sir now?"

"I'll consider myself a proper knight once I have Blood Tower under my control," Daniel said. "It's a sad knight who can't hold his own lands. But enough of that. I'm glad you could join me. You inspire courage in my men, and it doesn't seem right for you to march in the rear."

"Does it matter where I am, so long as I'm with you?"

"You inspire only when you're seen, and in case you haven't noticed, my men have eyes in the front of their heads, not the back."

"So is that all you called me for, to let your men stare at my ass as we walk?"

Daniel chuckled.

"Somewhat crude for a paladin, aren't you?"

"The transition to Ashhur is still in progress."

"Give us some privacy," Daniel told the men who marched with them. They saluted, then held back so Darius and Daniel might travel many yards ahead. The humor they'd shared dwindled, and Darius could tell something bothered the man.

"What troubles you?" Darius asked once they were alone.

"Plenty," Daniel said. "Though I supposed I should narrow that down. You've vouched for that witch woman repeatedly. I guess I want you to do it again, and maybe this time it'll settle my mind. Are you sure we don't march right into Cyric's hands at the tower? Without her, we are dead against the walls."

"She's no witch," Darius said, harsher than he meant.

"Then pray tell, what is she?"

Darius frowned, and thought over that first night she'd come to him, explaining her situation.

"Unfinished," he said at last. "That is what she is."

"She's living shadow, Darius. Your own blade hurts her, yet we are to trust her now. You say she's sworn to kill you, and yet you vouch for her, say we should trust her. I don't understand either of you, and given how everything tonight relies on you both, that's not comforting."

"She's in torment. She's lost, confused, and had her faith in Karak shaken. I sympathize, and if I can help her somehow, I will. But if there's anything I know for certain about Valessa, it's her hatred of Cyric."

Daniel's horse stumbled over a soft patch of earth hidden by the tall grass. Steadying her best he could, they stopped a moment to check for injury. There was none, and hearing this, Daniel sighed with relief and patted the beast on the neck.

"That's my girl," he said. "Bad luck to break your horse's leg on the way to battle."

"That's why I tend to walk everywhere."

"So you say. Just admit you're frightened of horses."

"Horses don't frighten me."

Daniel grinned at him. "Then what does?"

"Half-insane priests who think they're gods?"

Darius gave a smile, tried to laugh away the real fear he felt at meeting Cyric a second time. It didn't work.

"Do you know if Cyric will be there?" the older man asked.

Darius let out a sigh.

"Valessa swears he's still out in the Wedge, doing what, I can only imagine. But if we're to take the Blood Tower, now is the time, during his absence. Once that's done, we can send messages south along the river alerting the king to what's truly going on in the North."

Daniel fell silent a moment, retreating into his thoughts.

"Again we trust that woman," he said, breaking his silence. "You're a good man, Darius, and seem to have a stable head on your shoulders. Listen to me now, even if you have to humor me. When Luther left Cyric at the tower, Robert did his best to placate him. Everything he did, it was in fear of angering the priesthood. But we went beyond that. We didn't challenge Cyric when he told us he was performing a ritual. I tried to convince Robert to stop him, and I even set up plans just in case something went wrong. But Robert trusted Cyric. Not a lot, but enough. He thought no priest could be mad enough to openly revolt against the king's men. But he did. Cyric summoned those two lions, most of our men knelt like the cowardly sods they were, and suddenly the rest of us were fleeing out into the night."

"What is your point?" Darius asked.

"My point is that you, of all people, should understand that trust, lies, truth, and sanity no longer matter when you deal with a fanatic. Don't pretend to understand Valessa. Don't think you know why she does what she does. She's not just unfinished; she's a broken thing, and it's the broken pieces that are most likely to cut when you touch them."

"I was a broken thing," Darius said softly. "Jerico still reached down for me, asking me to stand."

"Jerico was a good man," Daniel said, nodding. "I am proud to have fought beside him. But the rest of the world isn't that good. It's just not. Be wary, Darius. That is all I ask."

"If I may?" Darius asked, gesturing behind him.

"Stay close, if not at the front," Daniel ordered.

Darius let his pace slacken, and slowly the men marched past him, their armor and weapons rattling. Stopping for a moment, Darius looked about, searching for Valessa. He felt an intense desire to talk to her, to listen to her words and weigh them against what Daniel had said. But there was no sign of her, not in any form he recognized. Shaking his head, he walked on, dreading the night far worse than before.

They camped two miles out from the Blood Tower, trusting the distance and the tall grass to hide their presence. They built no fires, and ate what little cold rations they'd brought. Daniel had told them all it was to keep their packs light and their travel fast, but Darius knew the truth. If they failed to take the tower, there was no reason to have any supplies for a flight. There wouldn't be any.

As the stars slowly winked into existence, and Darius sat at the edge of the camp, occasionally praying, he saw Valessa's approach from the west. As she walked, the tall grass passed through her legs instead of being pushed aside.

"Where have you been?" he asked her.

"About."

She sat across from him, her arms against her chest, her body hunched over. It was odd, but she looked like she was cold.

"I'm sorry we have no fire to warm you," he said.

"I wouldn't feel it even if you did," she said, and he was surprised by the casual bitterness of her words.

"I'm sorry," he repeated.

"Twice now you've apologized. Have you done something wrong?"

He shrugged.

"I guess not."

"Then stop it."

Darius looked away. He assumed she was nervous about the coming battle, but then again, Daniel had cautioned against such easy assumptions. Turning his attention back to her, he noticed she still wore a strange black veil over her face. It was thin and slender, and if made of a real material it'd easily tear.

"Why the veil?" he asked her on an impulse.

Valessa lowered her eyes to the ground.

"I'd rather no one look upon my face."

Darius lifted an eyebrow.

"You're a woman of a thousand faces. If you don't want someone looking upon yours, then why not take the guise of another?"

She shook her head.

"You're such a fool sometimes, Darius. I have no desire to be anyone else. I want to be myself. I want to be whoever I was when you killed me."

"The way I remember it, you flung yourself upon my blade."

"And who put the blade against my neck?" she countered.

The memory was still vivid, and Darius felt ashamed of it. He'd been ready to butcher Valessa, all because he'd seen her as a threat. Jerico had been furious at him for it, and rightly so.

"Fair enough," he said. "I won't ask any more about the veil."

They sat quietly for a moment. Sighing, Valessa waved a hand over her face, banishing the veil. Her skin was pale, her eyes a vibrant blue, like gems dug from the deepest caves of Dezrel. She might have the ability to resemble anyone, but she wore her true face, and she was beautiful.

"Lilah can still kill me," she said. If she was bothered by his staring, she did not show it. "I put my life in your hands. Don't let me down. I cannot enter the Abyss as I am."

"Easy enough solution," Darius said. "Don't go to the Abyss."

She smirked at him.

"You would have me be a coward and a traitor, like you? Because I cannot live up to Karak's standards, you'd have me abandon them completely for a god with none whatsoever?"

Darius shrugged.

"Just an idea."

They both went silent as Brute joined them, a half-full mug of alcohol in hand.

"You two ready for the fun?" he asked, settling down in the grass.

"Not as ready as you are, apparently," Darius said, grinning.

"Well that's what this is for," Brute said, handing the mug over as the nearby camp stirred with commotion. "Drink it up, but save me that cup. It's my favorite. We're marching out, so get your sword, and, milady, get your...well, whatever is you'll be killing people with."

The older man gave them a salute, then left to join the rest. Darius stared at the mug with a frown.

"What?" Valessa asked.

"I'm not sure if I'm supposed to drink this anymore. I'd need to ask Jerico."

Valessa stood, and her blue eyes flared with something dangerous.

"I'd give everything in the world to taste that horrible shit burning down my throat," she told him. "Drink it, now, or I'll have you leave here without a tongue to taste anything again."

"Well then," Darius said. "Bottoms up."

That crucial matter taken care of, they moved to the front of the army, crossing the two miles toward the Blood Tower under the cover of night. When they were several hundred yards out, just beyond any hint of light from the numerous torches, Daniel called for them to stop, then summoned Darius and Valessa.

"Now is the time," Daniel said, addressing only Darius and not Valessa. "Are you sure she can open the gates for us?"

"I'm sure she can," Valessa said, glaring. "So long as the lioness doesn't eat me first."

"A hundred and fifty men will weep for your passing," Daniel said as Valessa ran toward the tower. "If it's before the gates open," he added.

Darius drew his sword, its light shining across the water of the river flowing beside them.

"What will it take for you to trust her?" he asked.

"What will it take?" Daniel pointed to the tower. "Let's have that in my control. That'd be a start."

"So be it then," Darius said. He waited until the shadow in the distance that was Valessa reached the walls of the castle, then counted another minute before lifting his blade high, letting all there see its light. "To the gates," he cried. "To the tower. Some pussycat thinks it's hers, and it's time we take it back!"

7

Valessa ran without weapons toward the outer wall of the Blood Tower. For a moment she'd thought to bring her dagger when they left Willshire. Darius had locked it away in his tent, telling her it was for her own good. Truth be told, she didn't want it. The thing glowed with a red power that strangely made her uncomfortable now. The thought of Karak's presence shouldn't do this to her, she knew. Her failure was growing, her betrayal all the more terrible. And now she fought at the side of a paladin of Ashhur.

Out of your mind, she told herself. Put it out of your mind.

She had a job to do, and it was all part of the plan. Killing Cyric would calm her mind, and killing Darius afterward would calm her faith. This was one step to that, and to do it, she didn't need a dagger. Her hands were just as deadly, her very being shadow and frost. No armor or blade would stop her from taking their life. Just holy light and infernal claws. To her twisted amusement, she left one behind with Darius only to approach another with Lilah.

Valessa paused a moment when she reached the wall, trying to see if she could sense Lilah's presence. The beast was unnaturally quiet, and her intelligence frightening. If Valessa walked right into the embrace of the lioness, there'd be no opening the gate for Daniel's men, just a painful death and an even worse eternity. But try as she might, she couldn't sense anything. Banishing her fear, she made herself incorporeal, and through the wall she went.

When she stepped out the other side, she was only fifty yards from the gate leading into the inner complex. Dropping low, she glanced about, scanning for guards. Two were at the gate, standing at attention with far more discipline than she remembered from their kind. Lilah must have kept them permanently in fear after Cyric's defeat. Valessa could almost smell it reeking from the very stones of the tower, if she'd still had the ability to smell.

Besides those two, she spotted another pair upon the wall above the gate. Staying low, her guise nothing more than shadow and her skin a softly shifting mass of black, she checked for Lilah. She saw more mercenaries guarding the wall, especially by the river. Tents dotted the spaces between the wall and the tower, along with a few dwindling fires, yet she could not find Lilah.

If I can't see her, she can't see me, Valessa thought as she turned her attention back to the gate. I hope.

She slunk along the wall. The torches atop it left heavy shadows below them, which wasn't too surprising. After all, they guarded against the outside, not within. How many enemies could walk through walls? With each step she felt her anxiety grow. Once she exposed herself, it was only a matter of time before Lilah came running.

Shaking her head, Valessa chastised herself for her fear. This wasn't her. She hadn't been cowardly in life, and she would not start now in whatever her current existence counted as. No longer slinking, no longer shadow, she rushed the two guards. With her coming in from the side, only one had a reasonable chance to notice, and when he caught sight of her rushing from the corner of his eye it was far too late. Leaping at him, she made her hand become solid, and it chopped against his throat, crushing his windpipe and sealing away his startled cry. The motion of his slumping body alerted the other, who turned.

"You all right?" he asked, and before the last word had left his tongue Valessa lunged at him with her foot leading. It was a risk, she knew, but she tried it anyway. Her foot passed through his breastplate, but in the gap between it and his chest, she made herself real once more. The blow cracked ribs in that brief moment, for she could not keep it up long. The rest of her passed through the man, and by the convulsions of his body she knew it must have felt like his entire being was encased in ice. Spinning about, she grabbed his head, and with strength far beyond what she'd possessed in life, jerked it sharply to one side. The sound of his neck snapping was louder than she preferred.

The commotion was enough to alert the guards, but whatever noise they'd heard below was quickly forgotten when cries of battle from the north broke the silence. Valessa cursed silently. They'd needed to walk a fine line, waiting long enough for her to open the gates, but not long enough for those in the tower to notice and try to close it. In her opinion, Darius had acted far too soon, the impatient oaf.

Just beside the gate was a heavy wheel attached to the wall, connected to unseen gears and pulleys that would lift and shut the gate. As Valessa grabbed the handles, she heard what she'd most feared: Lilah's roar. Not daring to turn around, she pulled. The wheel was designed to be used by two men, but Valessa could still move it with ease. Advantages of being undead, she told herself, laughing madly. As alarms sounded, pierced by another roar, it seemed the two soldiers up top noticed her meddling, or at least, heard the clattering rise of the gate. An arrow pierced her chest and thudded into the grass. Valessa smirked. Two more arrows flew, and she ignored them, only spinning the wheel as fast as her arms could go.

Realizing they couldn't hurt her, at least not with arrows, the two rushed down the stone steps. One man latched onto the wheel, trying to stall its movements, while the other swung a sword at her neck. It passed through, nearly killing the other man in the process. Annoyed by the interference, Valessa shoved her hand through the chest of the first, her icy hand closing around his heart and crushing it. For a brief moment she felt the blood swirling about her fingers, then turned her attention to the other. Keeping her entire body solid, she kicked and punched him back, each blow denting his armor. He tried to block with his sword, but her movements were too deft, too blinding. A savage blow to his chin staggered him, and when he fell he lay there, vomiting.

The gate was only half open. Men could crawl under, but they'd be helpless against any sort of defense. Turning the wheel, she ignored the mercenaries approaching to guard the gate. They couldn't hurt her. None of them could, not with their feeble mortal blades. She had no flesh to pierce. But when the lioness let out her cry, and its sound was terribly close, she knew she'd failed her task.

"You dare return here?" Lilah roared, and then something struck Valessa hard from behind. A terrible sensation of burning swarmed across her back, and she flew forward, through the wheel, through the wall, and exited rolling across the grass. Letting out a scream, Valessa fought against the pain. Glaring at the gate, she watched as the mercenaries quickly shut it. Looking north, she saw Darius leading a charge, his glowing blade held high. In moments they'd arrive to find no way inside.

"Is that it?" Valessa asked, even as she felt a form of madness overtake her. She approached the gate, where Lilah glared at her through the bars. She was just as large as she remembered, an enormous feline with molten fur and fire burning where her eyes should be. Only metal separated them, but it seemed the lioness still feared the forces arrayed against her, otherwise she'd have kept the gates open so she could attack. "Is that the best you can do to me?"

Valessa showed the flesh rent by the lioness's claws, which wept shadow, and no matter what form she assumed, would not change to match it, instead remaining a wicked scar.

"Your body is a gift, one I can take away," Lilah said, nose hovering just before the gate.

Valessa walked closer, closer, and she made her form change to match her lunacy. She wore silvery armor, a crown, and a purple cape around her shoulders that flowed down to her ankles. She stared into Lilah's eyes. They were so vivid, yet somehow dark, as if they were windows into a deep place in the earth filled with fire and molten rock. She saw no mercy in them, no understanding, only fury and disgust. At her closeness, Lilah bared her teeth, and her very breath was burning heat across Valessa's body.

"Take it," Valessa whispered as she put her hands on the bars of the gate. "Take it, all of it, and let me die if that will grant me peace."

"You'll know only pain."

Valessa laughed at the lioness.

"That's all I know now."

Daniel's army was close, so close, and already she could hear panic rising as they realized the gate was shut. Arrows had started to rain upon them, and they'd grow thicker as the army gathered together in defense. Refusing to look, not wanting to see them dying, Valessa instead pressed closer, almost daring Lilah to strike.

"Greet me when I enter the Abyss," she told the lioness. "Because you'll be there before me."

She was strong, stronger than ever. Her body was not tied to concepts of muscles anymore. Everything was fluid, changeable, becoming the form she imagined. And what she imaged was a woman with the power of a god, and her hands pulled. The gate groaned, twisted, then broke in half with a sound that shook the wall. The mercenaries stood stunned, but Lilah never hesitated, leaping through the permanently opened portcullis. Valessa's sight filled with stark white teeth. She thought to fall through the world, as she had when Cyric attempted to kill her, but Lilah seemed aware of her strategy, and her teeth closed around an arm.

It held firm, and Valessa could not pull free. She struggled, and the teeth sank in deeper. A strange black fluid poured from her body, and she felt herself becoming loose. Maintaining her shape grew increasingly difficult as Lilah shook her side to side, tearing deeper, jarring Valessa's body. The pain increased tenfold. A scream exited her mouth, though it sounded like it belonged to another. And then her scream was overwhelmed by the sound of more than a hundred men howling at the top of their lungs.

Darius's glowing blade sliced through her Lilah's jaw, and with a yelp from the great best, Valessa was free.

I am anyone, she thought. I am anything.

It was madness, but she had to try. The lioness roared with heightened fury. Mercenaries were rushing out of the gate, seeking to protect Lilah, for she was the only real hope they had left. They were met by Daniel's men, and the blood quickly flowed. Only Darius faced Lilah, as if the rest instinctively knew it would be the paladin who must deal with the creature, and if he failed, there was little any of them could do. Darius stood between Valessa and the lioness, and though the light from his sword hurt, there was still comfort in its sight.

"Fly away," Valessa whispered.

Darius swung, and Lilah reacted with the speed and reflexes of the cat she resembled, dodging aside. Instead of lunging at the hated paladin, she remained focused on Valessa, who stood there, a smile on her face. Lilah would risk everything, even defeat, to kill her now. But she wouldn't. Lilah was just a giant cat. Giant cats couldn't fly.

Lilah's jaws snapped at her, and should have closed around her neck. But Valessa had crouched down, the force of her will reshaping her, making her something new, something small. Her vision shifted, her senses overcome by the strangeness of her being. Only desperation kept her moving, kept her arms rising and falling, which were now soft white wings no bigger than a single claw on Lilah's paw. She felt herself condensed, yet lighter. Her body lifted higher, higher, and when Lilah swung at her, she banked away. The wind blew across her eyes, face, and through the nostrils of her beak. Once more Lilah swung, but she was too high now, soaring over the battlefield.

Down below, Darius's sword gleamed with light, and with a single chop, it beheaded Lilah as she roared up to the heavens. Valessa soared on. Her back felt exposed, feathers missing from where she'd been clawed. Even now the wound would not heal. From her left eye she saw her wing blackened and mangled from where Lilah had held her. One by one, soft feathers fluttered away with each beating of the wing. Whatever strength kept her going, she felt it waning, already pressed to its limits.

But oh, how it felt to fly...

She circled, just a night dove, watching as Darius leapt into the center of the mercenaries' line. Already outnumbered, they could not hold against his skill and strength. They broke, and with a cheer Daniel's army surged forward, overwhelming them. Bodies fell, and Valessa fell with them, circling lower and lower, unable to beat her wings. Floating in that downward spiral, she felt free for the first time since she'd thrust her neck against the tip of Darius's sword. A shame it couldn't last.

She hit the ground amid the corpses outside the gate, human once more. Her flesh was pale, and she wore no clothes. The scars on her back still bled shadow. Glancing only once, she saw her left hand had regrown from where Darius had cut it off, but everything below the elbow was rotting flesh. No matter how she tried, she could not make it look pristine.

"Darius?" she whispered, knowing she could not be heard over the cheerful celebration but asking for him anyway. She tried crawling to her knees, but her hands were shaking, and her body was more like fluid, resisting any attempt to stand. She just wanted to lie there. She just wanted to pass away.

Valessa?

She opened her eyes. Darkness encroached upon the edges of her vision. Amid her pain, she heard her name cried once more.

"Valessa!"

Darius was suddenly above her, his armor blackened by fire, much of it covered with blood. Somehow she knew none of it was his. He lay his sword beside her so it would not glow. Valessa stared at his face, at his worry, and tried to hate him.

"You did this," she whispered.

"Shush now," Darius said, and if he heard her, he did not react. He pulled off a gauntlet, then put a hand on her forehead. She almost laughed. Was he searching for a fever? She was ice. No heat. No life.

"Help me," she said more forcefully.

"I..." Darius pulled her shoulder, saw the marks of the lion clawed across her back. "Shit."

"Please, help. I don't want to die like this."

Darius gently laid her back down.

"I can't," he said. "I don't even know what you are, Valessa. I don't know what I can do."

"Not that."

She reached with her good arm to the blade that lay dark beside her, lifting it up an inch before dropping it. A shadow passed over Darius's face.

"No," he said. "We've won. We've crushed them and retaken the tower. We'll beat Cyric next, and it'll be you who cuts his head off, I promise. And after that, you can spend the rest of your unnatural life trying to kill me." He laughed. "We'll make a game of it, right Valessa? You'll keep trying, I'll keep living, until we both get bored and I get old…"

A shiver ran through her. This was not how she wanted to die. The Abyss was waiting for her, and she would not be safe from its cleansing fire.

"Do it," Valessa said. "I won't be a coward, and I won't let that damn lion be the one who kills me."

Darius reached for the blade, and his fingers touched the hilt. It shone a soft white. For an instant she felt the light bathe over her, burning away the pale color of her flesh and exposing the shadow swirling beneath. And then Darius released it.

"No."

He turned her over, and she did not resist. His bare hands pressed against Lilah's cuts. The pain of it was intense, and her fingernails clawed against the dirt, periodically sinking through to fall into the earth itself. And then she heard him pray.

"I've never healed anyone before," Darius whispered. "And forgive me if I'm insane to do so now."

Valessa had felt the light from Darius's blade burn her. She'd felt Cyric reach into the core of her being and try to rip it to shreds. This was beyond any of that pain, so strong her body felt paralyzed. Darius's hands dipped into her, and amid her delirium she heard his gasp. The paralysis suddenly stopped, and with strength born of pain she flung herself onto her knees.

Screaming, screaming, always screaming.

The light on her back wasn't leaving, even though Darius's hands no longer touched her. It was growing, burning away everything. She beat against the dirt, and from her eyes fell tears that shimmered red like the blood of the sun.

"Stop fighting it!" she heard Darius shout, as if from a different world.

Fighting what? She didn't know. Didn't understand. Fight against the pain? It was killing her, consuming whatever darkness that was her. And he wanted her to let it? So be it. She fell onto her haunches, arms out at the sides, and shrieked out every shred of her misery and torment and anguish and abandonment that had consumed her since that terrible moment her god had demanded she take the life of a simple wayward paladin named Darius.

And then, after what felt like an eternity, it was over. She collapsed onto her back. Afraid, she lifted shaking hands before her eyes. Her skin was pale as it always was, but she knew something was different. Something had changed. Sitting up, she forced away the false flesh, the afterimage of herself she superimposed across her vessel.

Her hands were made of shadow like always before, but not quite. Swirling amid it was an equal tendril of white, shining like the light of Darius's sword. All across her shadowed body snaked the tendrils, like two opposed serpents hopelessly entwined. And then it faded, and her hand was flesh once more. The pain she'd felt every moment of her existence was gone. Curling her knees to her chin, arms wrapped around them, she looked at Darius and wept. The tears ran down her face, and when they landed atop her knees, they alternated silver and blood.

"What am I?" she asked, voice trembling. "Gods help me, what am I?"

8

J erico was just sitting down to eat his dinner when they came requesting his presence. The warmth of the fire before him was tempting, but the hard bread he held in hand was not, so he tossed it aside and stood.

"Lead on," he told the soldiers who'd summoned him. "Though I'd like to know why."

"We were not told."

Jerico shrugged his shoulders and followed as they wound through the increasingly large camp. They stayed on the road now, for the Castle of the Yellow Rose was growing steadily closer, and there seemed little point in hiding. What had been a small force now resembled an army, with bannermen slowly arriving with each day to pledge their men to Lord Arthur. Today had seen the largest group so far, three hundred or so, flying a yellow and black checkered flag. Jerico had a hunch that Lord Arthur wanted to introduce him, as he had when others joined. He was their mascot, their good luck charm. Everyone wanted to kiss his feet and touch his shield.

The skies were dark, but a fire glowed within the great tent in the center of the camp. The guards let him pass without inspection, so in Jerico stepped, and was immediately welcomed.

"Ah, now he shows," said Arthur. Despite the gray in his hair, he looked more lively than when Jerico had first met him, trapped in his castle by his brother's besieging army. Grabbing the paladin by the shoulder, he pulled him closer into the light of the fire. "Jerico, I'd like you to meet

Kevin Maryll, one of my youngest and finest bannermen. Kevin, this is Jerico of the Citadel."

Kevin was indeed young, though still older than Jerico. He looked to be in his early thirties, his hair dark, his short beard darker. He had a soft face, but his eyes were hard when he bowed low and offered his hand in greeting.

"It seems all the North echoes with stories of your greatness," Kevin said.

"Are they still getting the name wrong?" Jerico asked.

"At times," Kevin said, smiling. "Though at least they agree on the redness of your hair. I'd have known who you were without ever hearing your name."

It was flattery, all of it, and for some reason it annoyed Jerico tremendously. His dinner might not have been the most appetizing, but at least it was better than parading about like a particularly magnificent horse. How long until Arthur had him performing tricks for carrots? The thought was unfair, of course, but he couldn't stop it.

"While I'm here, anything to eat?" Jerico asked. "Maybe some carrots?"

Sure enough, Lord Arthur feasted far better than his men, and offered Jerico whatever he wished from a table set beside the fire. Tired from the days of march, and more so the nights spent greeting soldiers, bannermen, children, and hundreds of common folk wishing to fight alongside Kaide the Cannibal and his blessed paladin pet, Jerico didn't bother with any particular manners and just ate where he stood. His thoughts still surprised him. By Ashhur, he was getting cranky. More than ever he missed his little services at Durham.

Arthur and Kevin talked while Jerico ate, and trying to pull his mind out from his own childish grumblings, he listened in on their conversation.

"Sebastian's put a call out for any able bodied man that remains loyal," Kevin said, settling into one of the chairs brought in and set before the fire. "I'm sure you can imagine how much of a hurry such an order has inspired. Everyone expects you to win now. No matter what Sebastian's done, he can't seem to crush you. Defeated you in the field, put siege to your castle, yet still here you are, on your way to his very doorstep."

"I've been blessed by good men who have fought and died for me," Arthur said. "I am humbled knowing so many rally to my name."

"And Kaide's," Jerico interjected.

Arthur glanced over, his look placating.

"And Kaide, of course," he said. "We cannot forget the rebel."

"We're all rebels now," Kevin said, crossing his arms over his chest. "What is Kaide like, anyway? I suppose I should meet the man who's raised the peasant army. Is it true he is a cannibal?"

While Arthur had been placating, Kevin's tone was purely dismissive. Jerico thought of all Kaide had suffered, all he'd lost, trying to help Arthur in overthrowing Sebastian. His underhanded tactics in particular had caused immense pain to Sebastian's men, disrupting their supplies of food and clean drink. Jerico's opinion of Kevin was forming rapidly, and it wasn't a good one.

"It is," Jerico said, his appetite souring. "He's the most bloodthirsty vicious monster you'll ever meet wearing the skin of a human. They say his blood-thirst is greatest when he's slicing into the flesh of his victims, and that to enter his army you must cut a sliver of your own belly, cook it over a fire, and then set it on your tongue for five minutes. It's how he builds the loyalty of his men, introducing them to his twisted fetishes. I'm sure he wouldn't mind taking that dagger of his to your skin in particular, Kevin. So smooth, so pale, I bet he'd tell me it'd taste just like…"

"Like what, pray tell?" Kaide said, shoving open the tent flaps. His hair was tied behind his head in a ponytail, and his eyes simmered with fury. Beside him was a man dressed in armor, his hands bound behind his back. Jerico felt his neck flush. He knew Kaide hated the title, hated the stories, but the growing shock in Kevin's eyes as he told his little tale had been too amusing.

"I'm sure what Jerico says is all in good humor," Arthur said, trying to calm both Kevin and Kaide. "No one in my army feasts on human flesh, and I won't permit talk that says otherwise. Forgive us, Kaide, and please have a seat, or pour yourself a drink if you desire."

It was only then that Arthur seemed to realize another man was with Kaide. Arthur reached out his hand to offer greeting, then froze.

"Sir Gregane?"

Jerico knew that name well. Sir Gregane had led Sebastian's armies in both the siege at the Castle of Caves as well as the first battle in the Green Gulch. Jerico dared entertain a moment of hope. Why would Sir Gregane be there other than to offer terms of peace?

"It is good to see you, Arthur," Gregane said. "Twice now we've fought as enemies, though I pray today we leave as friends."

"You were always a good man," Arthur said, turning his attention to Kaide. "Untie his hands. He is no threat to us here."

"He rode to the edge of my camp and asked to speak with you," Kaide said as his dagger easily sliced through the rope. "He carries a message he swears is for your eyes only, but I'd appreciate knowing what it reads."

"And you have every right to hear it, as do all those here." Arthur gestured to Gregane. "Whatever your message is, deliver it now."

Gregane handed over a rolled piece of parchment.

"I assume this is from Sebastian?" Kevin said. "There's no seal."

"The handwriting is his," Arthur said as he began to read. His brow furrowed deeper with every word. After finishing, he started anew, this time reading aloud so all could hear.

"My brother, I write this now hoping that of all the errors of my life, delaying this letter is not one of them. Your army is the greater. Of this, I am no fool. Spare me, and I will cede to you our family holdings, and all control of the North granted to our protection by King Baedan. If you accept, I beg that you make haste, and arrive at my castle while the North is still mine to give. Save me from these priests that would kill me, brother. The Lion eyes a nation of his own."

Silence followed. The four men looked to one another as Gregane stood perfectly still, awaiting an answer.

"It's a trap," Kevin said, breaking the spell.

"I can assure you it is no trap," insisted Gregane.

"Which is what you'd say if it was a trap."

"I will have no petty bickering," Arthur said, turning his attention to Jerico. "He speaks of the Lion eyeing a nation of his own. What do you think he means, paladin? Why would he ask us to save him from their priests?"

Jerico's heart hammered in his chest. He thought of how Luther had arrived with his dark paladins, priests, and mercenaries, and then crushed Sebastian's army just when victory over Arthur was within his reach. Sebastian, who had been so loyal to Karak. But eyeing a nation of their own…

"We have to do as he says," Jerico said. "Now."

"Why do you say that?"

"I assume Gregane could tell us, if we let him. But Luther wants the North to himself, doesn't he?"

Gregane nodded.

"They'll raise their swords against you," he said, "so long as milord Sebastian writes a will leaving all his lands and titles to the temple of Karak. If not..." He shook his head. "I don't know what they'll do if we refuse. But Sebastian is convinced they'll kill him."

"Ashhur grants me knowledge to the truth of a man's words," Jerico said. "Gregane does not lie."

"Perhaps Gregane doesn't, but Sebastian might have lied to him," Kevin argued.

"This is preposterous," Kaide said. "We know the temple hates Sebastian, even if we don't know why. We saw them crush his army. Now they come for him, and he begs us to save him. I wonder, though, what happens after we've weakened ourselves fighting such a powerful foe? What happens when Sebastian's forces exit the castle afterward, demanding we surrender?"

"The seal," Kevin said. "There's no seal on that letter. It isn't binding. Sebastian could always claim it was a forgery even if we managed to present such an argument before the King."

"And we'll have killed members of Karak's temple," Kaide continued. "Suddenly we have dark paladins of the Stronghold swarming into the North with a vengeance, and all we'd have to protect ourselves is one lousy paladin."

Gregane looked furious, but clearly knew his arguments carried no weight in that meeting. There was no guarantee that Gregane even knew Sebastian's true plans. He could just be a piece in a larger game. Jerico listened to their arguments, and he knew there was a shred of truth to them. Sebastian had shown a lack of honor before in sending assassins after Arthur. But what could he have done to earn the ire of the temple? Jerico shook his head. It didn't matter. His own talks with Luther were enough to convince him of that. He thought of Luther ruling all the people of the North, passing their laws, controlling their fates. A terrifying precedent to set.

"We can't let this happen," he said. "It doesn't even matter if it's a trap. We can't risk it. I know the man who leads Karak's followers. He's brutal, and dangerous. If he's wanting to conquer the North, then we need to take action before he can consolidate power. This is Sebastian's only hope to stop him, the one thing he knew Luther would not expect."

"My brother is a self-centered coward," Arthur said. "This isn't him."

"Then perhaps for once he is trying to be brave. Don't spit in his face."

"I'll spit in it if I damn well please," Kaide said, his neck turning red. "I don't care about gods, Karak, or Ashhur. I'll even side with Jerico that Luther needs to die after what he did to my sister. But you promised me Sebastian. I have thousands of men and women, all waiting to see me hoist that tiny little shit's head by the hair over the walls of his castle, before slamming it down on a pike. Arthur, you cannot spare the life of your brother. It's no longer yours to spare. It's mine now, mine alone."

"And who are you to tell a lord what they can and cannot do?" Arthur asked.

"The man who's filled the ranks of half your army."

"Filled them with farmers and sheep herders. Not warriors, not real soldiers like those my bannermen bring me. Only one in ten even has a sword."

Jerico could feel the situation spiraling out of control, and he had no idea how to stop it. What could he do to fix their distrust, especially when much of it centered on Sebastian, a man proven to be particularly untrustworthy? He begged Ashhur to give him words, because he had no idea what to say.

"Enough," he said, loud enough to startle them all. "Forgive me, all of you, but this bickering solves nothing, and it never will. Whether or not this offer is real, we must show haste. Karak is friend to no one here, and the temple's treachery to such an ardent supporter like Sebastian should prove that. Arthur, if what he says is true, your rule over the North is in far greater jeopardy than it ever was before. And if Karak's army joins Sebastian instead, they will be a force that could crush us without need of walls or gates. The best thing we can do is to get to your brother's castle and hear this offer from his own lips."

"You won't," Gregane said. "He'll be dead by then. I know it, as did milord."

"If any priest kills my brother, I'll hang their heads for all to see for a hundred years," Arthur said. "But tell me, paladin, what happens if we rush into an ambush in our haste?"

Jerico shrugged.

"Then we'll have a fight on our hands. Has that frightened you before?"

Kevin stepped between Jerico and Arthur, and he spoke low, and hurried.

"Do not listen to his folly," the bannerman insisted. "He just wants to enlist us into his own conflict with Karak's temple. Your brother is grasping for straws to save his life. This is his last trick. Do not fall for it!"

Arthur breathed in deep, and Jerico sensed he'd come to his decision. He prayed it'd be a good one.

"No matter what the truth is, dallying here does not help us. We'll wait for no more lords to join us, and march flat out toward the Castle of the Yellow Rose." He turned toward Kaide. "As for my brother's life, I will hear from his own mouth the reasons for his aggression and betrayal. Removing him from power, and stripping him of all his lands, should be more than you ever hoped to accomplish when you first started this foolish conflict."

"Do not cheat me a death," Kaide said, his voice cold. "I will have vengeance, whether you try to stop me or not."

"I do not take kindly to threats, even from close allies."

"Not a threat. A damn fact."

Kaide stormed out, shoving the flap of the tent out of his way. Jerico wanted to go after him, but the man wanted none of the comfort he had to offer. He wanted revenge, not forgiveness. He wanted death, not life.

"What of Sir Gregane?" Jerico asked.

"Will you carry a message for me back to my brother?" Arthur asked him. Gregane bowed low.

"So long as he lives, I will deliver it."

Arthur's cheek twitched at the statement. Jerico didn't know if he thought it a lie or not, but either way the idea of the priesthood killing Sebastian angered him greatly.

"Tell him I will hear his offer from his own lips, not from a scroll lacking the stamp of his ring. I give no promises, not to his life, not to anything. All I promise is to come with an open mind, and hear out his plea."

"As you wish," Gregane said.

"Kevin, if you could get him a fresh horse, and something to eat or drink if he so desires."

Kevin gave an elaborate bow.

"As milord requests," he said pleasantly enough, but a twinkle in his eye showed it was anything but. With the two of them gone, Jerico was left alone with Arthur. He stepped close, thinking how he could try to press the lord to act more firmly against the priests, but instead it was Arthur who approached, his voice rising as he talked.

"I hope you appreciate all I have done for you," he said.

"Me?" Jerico asked, baffled.

"I want no war with Karak's temple, not if I am to have any hope of ruling the North. And no matter how dangerous you claim they are, I have eyes to see, and what I saw at the end of Gregane's siege was Karak's followers saving my castle, and my life. Yet from the word of my enemy alone, you'd have me declare war against the entire temple, riding off to prevent the most ludicrous of possibilities. No temple will ever own the King's lands. No priest will ever rule as a lord. The King would never allow it, nor a single knight of the North."

"If you believed this, then why did you not say so?" Jerico asked, feeling stung by the complete lack of faith in his deciphering of events.

"Because you are the one who inspires my men more than anything I've ever seen before. I still hear them talking of your stand at the gates of my castle, of how you held the line at Green Gulch. Many think you'll walk right up to the Castle of the Yellow Rose and beat down its doors with your mace and shield. I would not ruin that now, not unless you give me no choice. We'll move cautiously, and give no hint as to our stance toward Karak's priests. If they want my brother removed from power, I see no reason not to accept their help."

"They're dangerous," Jerico insisted. "You've seen the power Luther wields. Why would you desire to be allies?"

"You just answered your own question," Arthur said, plopping down into his chair and groaning. "There are only two gods worshiped in all of Mordan, yours, and Karak, and you know damn well which one is stronger."

"Not stronger," Jerico said quietly.

"More popular, then," Arthur said, waving a hand dismissively. "Either way, if I'm to rule, I cannot alienate either temple. I risk their ire just by having you as a symbol of my victories. Don't make me risk more."

That was it, Jerico knew. There was nothing left to argue.

"I will trust your decision," he said, "and I will do all I can to help, so long as my conscience permits."

Arthur closed his eyes, the chair steadily rocking.

"Go on out," he said. "I need rest. And Jerico...let us make a promise, together. I'll never go against my conscience, and you'll never go against yours. Will that be enough to earn your trust?"

Jerico smiled.

"I trust you to be a good lord, and a good man. You don't need to buy that from me with a promise."

"Earned trust is the strongest trust," Arthur said. "You're wiser than you look. Good night, paladin."

Jerico left the tent, and was surprised to find Kevin waiting for him. The man stood with his arms crossed, staring at his fingernails as if he were supremely uninterested.

"Did you change his mind?" Kevin asked, looking up.

"Arthur makes his own decisions," Jerico said, trying to step past him, but failing. Kevin shifted to the side and put a hand on Jerico's breastplate.

"Decisions influenced by counsel," Kevin said. His eyes narrowed. "Did you sell him your fanatic delusions? Do we rush toward a holy war for the glory of gods?"

Jerico grabbed Kevin's wrist. Both tensed, and Jerico sensed Kevin dangerously close to reaching for the shortsword strapped to his thigh.

"There's rarely anything holy about war," Jerico said softly.

"And there's rarely war without holy men. Release my hand, or say goodbye to yours."

Jerico did so, pushing the man back a step. Kevin fixed his sleeve, then gave Jerico a vulture's smile.

"He'll see through you one day," he said. "All wise leaders eventually do. The wisdom of men must rule, not the whims of gods."

Jerico brushed past without giving him the dignity of a response, even though Kevin's words burned like fire in the back of his mind.

9

When he'd first converted the wolf-men at the Gathering, Cyric had been happy with four hundred of the brutes. But what he'd thought was the bulk of their numbers had only been the tip. For days on end he watched as his pack swelled, creatures from all over the Wedge making their way to his camp. More and more hunters had to seek out food, and it seemed they dined on orc meat as much as they did anything else. Not that Cyric would partake in such cursed flesh. There was always a bit of rabbit for him come time for his meal.

"Why does a god care what he eats?" Redclaw had asked him once when he refused the cooked flesh of an orc, still connected to a bit of bone. "A god is a god."

"I am a god made flesh," Cyric had said, glaring. "And I will not spoil that flesh with such filth."

Redclaw had laughed, as he often did lately. Whatever it was that gave him such good humor, Cyric could not say. That he ruled a pack over a thousand strong, and possessed the strength of demons and the speed of angels, might have something to do with it.

An endless parade of tribal leaders came to Cyric, all kneeling with their snouts pressed to the dirt upon his introduction. They did the same to Redclaw, professing their loyalty. At first the idea of serving two masters had confused them, but eventually Cyric had enlisted the aid of one of their shamans, a wily old female with gray fur by the name of Silver-Ear.

"We once served both moon and pack," she'd tell the newcomers just before their introductions. "You will bow to the leader of all packs, the Wolf King, and then you will bow to the moon made flesh, the maker of the moon, the god made human."

A crude explanation, perhaps, but Cyric allowed it. So many were reluctant to give up their worship of the moon that it was becoming easier to just let them think he was the moon. So long as they worshiped him, and therefore Karak, their souls would find a place safe from the fires of the Abyss.

Silver-Ear had taken a spot in his council, though it was a lie to call it that. They did not counsel, only listen to his orders and obey. Around a large bonfire they gathered, given a respectful distance from the rest of the packs. Redclaw was there, his claws flaring with flame each time he flexed his paw. Warfang was the last of the four, a valuable addition. While Redclaw was Wolf King, there were so many to control, and the beasts' aggressive nature was only heightened by their worship of Karak, not diminished. Warfang helped enforce his word, and denied any chance of protest. Every last wolf was eager for bloodshed, and they eyed the river to the west with a hunger that Cyric himself could not deny.

And now, after two weeks of gathering, of preparing and praying for the wisdom to succeed in such an ambitious plan, he called together his council and gave them the orders of their god.

"Our numbers are sufficient," he said. "Have your hunters kill all they can of the nearest tribes, and bring back many live prisoners. We will need food between the villages. Tomorrow night, we swim across the Gihon. Tomorrow night, the great cleansing begins."

Redclaw and Warfang yipped and howled, but Silver-Ear remained silent. The old female stood, dipped her head, and slowly limped back toward camp.

"Go hunt," he told the two males. Something wasn't quite right with the shaman, and he felt like having a word with her to discover why. Perhaps she was having a crisis of faith. Not the most opportune time for such weakness, not when he relied on her to calm the more religious of the savages. Calling Silver-Ear's name, Cyric quickened his pace so he might walk beside her as she limped.

"Something troubles you?" he asked her.

"Do the gods care about our troubles now?" she asked, stopping her walk so she might bow respectfully.

"Have we not always?"

"Always?" She shook her head. "For years we prayed to the moon. We prayed as wounded wolves died and bled. We prayed as pups were born without a beat in their heart."

"You prayed to a lie," Cyric said, frowning. "How could you expect an answer from a lie?"

"And now we pray to Karak," she said, ignoring his question. "You promise conquest, and power, and I believe you will give us all we could want, and more. But tell me, will pups still die when born? Will their mothers bleed out, while I can only give herbs to dull the pain?"

These were dangerous questions, and for some reason they quickened his breath.

"You're smart for your kind," he said, stalling.

"We shamans often are. I mean no disrespect. I am loyal, I am your servant. Looking upon Redclaw shows me the blessings you can bestow, and if you lead us into the promised land beyond the river, I will lower my head and call you the moon made flesh. But you are not a god."

Cyric's hand caught her by the throat and held her still. Her yellow eyes, already red with veins, began to water as he squeezed tighter and tighter.

"You would challenge me?" he asked. His voice quivered, and it surprised him. "You, a stupid little thing with fleas, would look upon your god and deny the truth of him?"

"My god is Karak," she rasped. "Who are you?"

He flung her to the ground, then stood over her with shaking fists.

"I am Karak," he said. "Do you hear me, shaman? I am Karak!"

"Then remake the world," she said. Her request stunned Cyric silent. "Wave your hand, and see it change. Cast the moon down from the sky. Make life from the dust. Show me the power of a god."

Cyric took a step back. He felt an attack of panic coming on, and it frightened him. He shook his head violently from side to side.

"I will kill you," he said.

"Men can kill. Wolves can kill. Try better."

He opened his mouth, closed it, opened it again. Struggling for words, he tried to wrap his mind around exactly what she asked. Who was he? What was he?

"I am Karak made flesh," he said, staring into her iron gaze. "I am Karak, but I am not yet completed. I am not yet whole. His power is mine, and it enters me gradually. That is why I must do what I do. You tell me to remake the world, and I will. Should the people of Dezrel listen, they will know true order in their lives. Should they bow, they will know true peace. I will not do it with a wave of my hand, but with tooth, claw, and blood. I am a shadow of the god that created you, but when all of Dezrel worships my name, you will see me in my true glory. Does that satisfy you, wolf?"

"Yes," Silver-Ear said, slowly crawling onto her knees so she might bow. "I know who you are now."

"Good. Tell the rest what you must, so long as they obey. Have them worship Karak as their god and me as his physical manifestation. Do you understand?"

"I do," she said. "If it pleases you, may I leave? There will be wounded to attend to after the hunt."

He dismissed her with a wave, and she limped off without a word. Cyric watched her go while something ate at the corners of his mind. Of course Silver-Ear would have trouble understanding such a complex concept. These aspects of gods were beyond even the wisdom of a shaman. But why had the answer been so difficult for him? Unspoken fears assailed him, and he tried to shrug them off, to think on them no more, but he couldn't.

Every night, he prayed to Karak, and it was those prayers that strengthened him, gave him power and understanding. Who was he, to pray to himself? Why did he have no memories of the centuries before? His limitations were painfully human, painfully created by the mere mortal that was Cyric. But Karak was imprisoned in the celestial lands, and this vessel, his vessel, would be imperfect until the elven goddess was defeated and her prison destroyed. Cyric knew he had to be strong, to keep faith in all he did.

That he might not be Karak at all, he dared not let that thought enter his head, as much as it screamed at him from every subdued part of his intellect with voices that were steadily growing stronger, belonging to demons infesting his soul.

The hunt went well, though it'd taken longer to reach the nearest rival encampment than expected. It seemed the massing number of wolf-men had made the other races of the Vile Wedge skittish. They'd run beneath the stars, until at last Redclaw's hunting party encountered a tribe of a hundred bird-men. Gangly things, their meat would not be pleasant, but he dared not continue further looking for more appetizing game, not with how far they'd already traveled. Descending upon them like a monster of the Abyss, Redclaw led the attack, crushing all but a scattered few that fled every which way in the night.

Each of the fifty wolf-men carried a body over their shoulder, some dead, some not. Back at the camp they were greeted with much celebration. Redclaw ate little, his appetite strangely missing for having just completed a hunt. He stripped feathers off a thick slab of thigh, gave it to his two pups, and then watched them eat. They were only a year old, and not yet speaking or walking on their hind legs. One day, they'd challenge him for rule, but what would they rule if they won? Would it be a wretched stretch of yellow grass beside a cold river, or would it be miles and miles of green hills filled with bountiful game?

Thinking himself alone, Redclaw looked down at his upturned paw. With a single flex, he watched fire trace through his veins, watched the heat turn the tips of his claws a vibrant red. Cyric had told him they would melt through even the finest armor of men, but Cyric had promised lots of things.

"Greetings, Wolf King," Silver-Ear said, disrupting his thoughts. Redclaw bowed his head in respect.

"You honor me, shaman," he said.

"Then I ask that you honor me in return, and walk with me for a bit. I wish to speak."

Redclaw rose to his feet. The bigger of his two pups turned his way and yipped once. Redclaw reached down, then stopped, remembering the heat of his claws. He'd learned to control it, mostly, but he dared not risk it.

"Stay here," he told them, and the firmness of his look conveyed his desire. Both whimpered, then returned to eating. Redclaw took up step beside Silver-Ear, and together they walked west, toward the river and away from the rest of the camp.

"It seems so long ago, doesn't it?" Silver-Ear said, her voice dry, as if she'd been coughing a lot recently. "Do you remember when you were first named Wolf King, and faced the moonless dark?"

"I do," Redclaw said. "I remember it well. You had me breathe in the smoke of Goldmoon petals, then crawl through a cave of bat shit."

Silver-Ear smiled, but it did not reach her eyes.

"That I did, though do not pretend I did it for no reason."

"I know. You did it to amuse yourself. That is reason enough for most."

This time Silver-Ear's laugh did reach her eyes. She glanced back at the camp, let out a sigh.

"You command a great force, Wolf King," she said. "Far greater than before. The last time we crossed the river, there were many who fled, and many more who stayed away. They did not believe you their king. They thought you would die, and they would steal your lands. Such simple dreams they have, and always will."

"That is why they need their king," Redclaw said.

"Is it now?" Silver-Ear asked. "What if we were meant for simple dreams?"

Redclaw stopped, and he let out a soft growl to show his disapproval. They were far from the camp now, at the

95

base of a stump of a hill. Large sections of it were bare, the grass long ago dried up and dead.

"You speak in riddles, shaman," he said. "Speak plainly, if you would speak at all."

"Warfang has broken the packs up to fight, each numbering one hundred. We have ten, Redclaw, ten such packs to cross the river. And what is it we aim to do? What is it our god commands us to accomplish?"

"We're to conquer," Redclaw said.

"Yes," Silver-Ear said. "Conquer all of mankind, forcing every village to kneel. We attacked one such village, Redclaw. Do you remember? Do you remember our dead, numbering greater than we could count? We shamans speak ill of humans, but not because we are fools. We do this so great wolves like you will not be afraid. But listen to me now, and hear what we've always known. You are not the first to have crossed the river west, nor will you be the last. A hundred times it has happened, many miles south and north, and not just by wolf-men. We listen, we watch, and then we return to tell the others what we have known since the birth of our fathers' fathers: we will never, ever escape the Wedge."

Such words were close to blasphemy in the ears of Redclaw, and he could scarcely believe them. Not long ago he'd gathered wolves together, rallied them to attack the village of Durham. Yes, they'd lost, but their foes had been vicious, and possessing such strange magics. One man had fought with a shield shining with painful light, another a blade consumed with dark fire. They'd defeated his pack, but he was stronger now, gifted with similar otherworldly magic.

"Why did you not tell me this before?" he asked. "When you led me into the cave, when you called me Wolf King...why, if you thought it hopeless?"

Silver-Ear let out a sigh.

"Because we have always hoped. We pray to the moon to deliver us a paradise full of fat game and warm blood. The humans fight among themselves, no different than us. One day they may not be ready, and we may claw a tiny scrap of land for our own. And then we would guard it closely, like we guard our pups, so it can grow. So it becomes something strong. But even that is still a dream."

"Why?" Redclaw asked. "Why, if we are so much stronger than they? Why is it terrible for us to dream of a land our young can hunt on with pride instead of this ugly yellow grass?"

"Because we are but a speck to them!" Silver-Ear cried, grabbing his arm and holding it tight. Immediately she let go, clutching her hand to her breast as the smell of burned fur reached Redclaw's nose. He thought to say something, to apologize, but Silver-Ear continued on.

"Just a speck," she said. "There are more humans than you can understand, Redclaw. Our ten packs of a hundred each are nothing. They have armies that make us look like a fly biting an orc's ear. Do you not remember the stories? In the days of our creation, the first Wolf King led hundreds beyond hundreds down the river, and still we were crushed by the men in their metal armor, their wizards with their evil magic, and their champions with their glowing blades. They hate us, they fear us, and they will never let us escape the prison they have made for us."

"Why do you tell me this?" Redclaw asked softly. "Why would you try to crush all hope?"

"Because Cyric would have us war against them," she said. "We'll travel miles beyond the river. We'll feast well at first. We'll drink the blood of our kills, and we'll howl to the moon following our victories. But then the humans will strike back. They are not like us. They take time to prepare for a battle, but when it comes, they will bury us in waves of glinting metal stretching across the horizon. We'll die, surrounded, alone, in a land we have never seen before, and will never see again. Cyric says we are to become like we were in days of old, and worship the human god Karak. We died in the days of old, Redclaw. And we'll die now."

The shaman stopped, and the music of the cicadas filled her silence. Redclaw clenched and unclenched his paws, trying to think through what she'd said, trying to understand where he stood in all this. He was Wolf King, but he was also Cyric's champion. When the strange man had come into Redclaw's camp, he'd bested him with ease, forced him to his knees, and then demanded obedience under threat of death. There was no doubting his strength, and no doubting the strength he could bestow upon others.

"You speak with the wisdom of ages," Redclaw said, the words heavy on his tongue. "But I will still lead, and I will still fight."

"Why, Redclaw?"

He turned away from her.

"Because no matter how terrible the chance, Cyric might be who he says he is. This is no time for small dreams. Even if we fail, at least we have tried to conquer. At least we'll have tried to make a better life for our pups."

"You're a wise male," Silver-Ear said as he stalked away. "Keep your eyes open, my Wolf King, and never forget who you serve."

Who did he serve? Redclaw pondered this as he returned to the camp. Was it Cyric, his pack, or himself? And did it matter, so long as those loyal to him could feast upon the blood of the weaker?

The sun was soon to rise, and he settled down to sleep near his pups. Not close enough to touch, but enough to hear their breathing, see the rise and fall of their tiny chests.

10

Valessa sat at the end of the docks before the waters of the Gihon. It was the only place she knew to find solace. Torches and patrols covered the tops of the walls, and tents filled the space between the tower and the walls. It seemed nothing had changed, only instead of it being Karak's mercenaries, it was Daniel Coldmine's men who controlled the insignificant construction of stone and brick. To think she'd given everything to take it. Everything...

And when she looked to the dark night sky, she knew it was all for nothing.

"You asked for me?" Darius said, his heavy boots thudding atop the wooden planks.

Valessa nodded, not bothering to turn around. At her silence, Darius closed the distance and sat beside her. His feet dangled off the dock. Beside him he put his enormous sword, which glowed for a moment at his touch. Though its light still caused discomfort, it did not burn her.

"Well," Darius said when she didn't speak. "I'm here. Care to talk?"

"I've prayed to Karak," she said, blurting out the words. "And I've prayed to Ashhur. Neither hear me. I'm lost to them both now, aren't I? A blasphemy against the two gods, that is what I am. That is what you created."

"You're a fool if you think I created you, Valessa. I'd give that credit to your parents."

She glanced at him, saw that he was smiling. She rolled her eyes.

"Wipe the smile from your face. That wasn't particularly funny."

He shrugged his shoulders.

"To each his own. Or her, I suppose. If you feel abandoned now, I assure you, it's a fairly normal feeling. As a gray sister you were used to Karak's constant presence, for he is a jealous god, and protective of his powerful servants. But most of the farmers and laymen I preach to hear only silence whey they pray, yet still they believe their prayers heard, and often answered."

"Then they're dogs used to scraps that fall off the table. I was better. So were you. Or are you so much better now?"

Darius sighed.

"I'd like to think so. I'm not dead, at least, and I sent Cyric running the last time we met. Can't do much better than that."

"You could have killed him," Valessa said, staring at the water.

Beside her, she heard Darius shift uncomfortably.

"What is it you see?" he asked her. "Something more than this weighs on you. Tell me what it is."

Valessa looked up to the sky. High above, amid the rest of the stars, she saw two separate from the others. One was a red star, still showing her where Darius might be. It seemed a mockery now, a call to kill a man she had no desire anymore to kill. As if killing him would change anything. The other, like a scar in the sky, was different. It gave no color, only absorbed it all in. That black star was further away, and over the past hours, it'd been steadily moving, like a comet.

"Cyric's crossed the Gihon," she said. "Whatever his delay, it's over now. We need to flee south as soon as possible, before he can reach us."

"Flee?" asked Darius. "Wait a moment now. In case you haven't been paying attention, I kicked his ass at Willshire. I don't see any reason why that might change now."

"Do not play pretend, not with me," Valessa said, feeling her temper flare. "I can see the fear of him deep in your heart, no different than mine. He'll be stronger now, more furious. The time in the wild has done something to him. The black star has grown larger. I can only assume it grows with his power."

"A pleasant thought," Darius said. "But that doesn't mean we should run. Don't you still desire to kill him? That's why you came to me, wasn't it?"

At the time she thought it was. Staring at the black star, she once decided the mad priest's murder was her purpose, and part of her still believed it. But why had she gone to Darius? Was it because she thought him the only one who could stop Cyric? Or was it because she'd desperately needed some sort of order, some sense of worth, after her near-death and banishment at Cyric's hands?

"Why did he delay?" she finally asked. "Why did Cyric remain in the Wedge instead of coming back to the tower with Lilah and his men? He wanted something there, and at last he's found it."

"Perhaps he needed some solitude, maybe a chance to meditate after I humiliated him and his claims at being a god."

Valessa shook her head.

"No, that's not him. Cyric would never have the humility for such a course of action."

Darius shrugged.

"Well, what else is there but orcs, goblins, and wolf-men beyond the river?"

"All that once served Karak."

She saw a flash of recognition cross Darius's face, and then he immediately quashed it.

"No," he said. "No, that's not right. That's not right at all. If he rallied an army of orcs, or wolf-men, or even those strange hyena creatures…"

"There's no way to know," Valessa said. "Not until it's too late. Cyric wants to conquer all of the North, perhaps all of Dezrel, to force his faith upon every last man, woman, and child. We can't stop him, not with the few we have. We must flee south until we have a proper army."

Darius leaned his head on his hand, his fingers rubbing his temples.

"Daniel's not going to like this," he muttered.

Valessa had expected an outburst when they told Daniel what they surmised. Instead, he'd sat calmly in his room in the tower, a map of the North rolled out before him on his desk. Beside him stood Brute, eating a peach and looking extremely bored.

"This is what you wake me up for?" Daniel asked. "Guesses?"

"More than that," Darius said. "Well, slightly more," he added after the older man's glare.

"There's no doubt that he's on the move," Valessa said. "I can see the black star clearly, more than I ever have before. He's crossed the Gihon about twenty miles or so north of Willshire. He'll be moving south soon enough."

"Twenty miles…"

Daniel traced his finger along the map, then winced when he reached what he'd been looking for.

"There's a small town by the name of Bellham twenty five miles upriver," he said. "It's one of the last before reaching the mines."

"We have to warn them," Darius said.

"It's too late," Valessa said, and she felt an ache in her chest that was entirely foreign. "He's already there. He'll come for Willshire next, then here."

"He's coming for us is what he's coming for," Brute said, taking another bite of his peach. "Question is, is there anything we can bloody do about it?"

"I'm not running," Daniel said, preempting the suggestion.

"Then call it a tactical retreat," Valessa said. "These walls will mean nothing to Cyric. You've seen what he can do, and he's only going to get more powerful with time. We need to flee down the river, and take as many as we can with us."

"She's right," Darius said. "We only have two hundred men. Cyric may have thousands."

"All this depends on the word of one woman, you realize," Brute interjected. "How sure are you of this? Could you be wrong?"

Much as she wanted to be, Valessa knew Cyric's location with a certainty that could not be shaken.

"He's there," she said. "I know it with every bone in my body…if I had any, that is. Forgive the poor analogy."

Daniel rolled up the map, breathed in deep, and then blew it all out.

"All right then. We'll send for the people of Willshire come morning, and by nightfall we'll sail south."

Valessa could hardly believe it was that simple.

"We will?" she asked, even though she knew it had to make her sound dumb. "You trust my opinion so much?"

"Milady, I saw you rip open these gates with your bare hands, completely unafraid of that giant lion on the other side. If you're frightened now, then I trust your instincts.

This tower wouldn't be mine without your help. If you say it's time to leave, then we leave."

Valessa felt oddly flattered, though she resented the accusation of being frightened.

"I must say, I thought you'd protest a bit more," Darius said, chuckling.

Daniel let out a sigh.

"I knew this might happen, but I needed the boats here if we were to flee, plus the extra supplies. The river's our only hope of fleeing fast enough, and we couldn't use it until we retook the tower. Now the mercenaries are gone, and we're free to run like the chickenshits we are. I've got messages already sent down river, pleading with King Baedan to muster his army. Only job we have left is protecting the people of Willshire from that madman, as well as alerting all the other villages we cross along the way."

"The king won't be too pleased you left your post," Brute said, tossing the remains of his peach out the window.

"That's why I'll be staying, along with whoever will volunteer to remain with me," Daniel said. "Someone has to stall them for a bit. If Cyric thinks the tower guarded, he'll approach with caution. Even if I can buy the rest of you only a few hours, it still might make a difference."

"I agree," Brute said, looking to Darius and Valessa to see if they would argue. Valessa said nothing, for the lieutenant's life was his own. Darius clearly looked unhappy, but didn't seem willing to challenge the decision.

"But it won't be you that's staying, Daniel," Brute continued. "I'll remain behind. You have a duty to your men, and dying here ain't it."

"Absolutely not," Daniel said.

"If you stay, then that makes me in charge of the men who come with me on the river," Brute argued. "And the first order I'll give will be to turn every last one of them around to aid you along the walls. The peasants can fend for themselves. You've got no choice in this matter, Daniel."

Now Valessa saw the rage and stubbornness she'd expected from the man. But Daniel let it go as quickly as it came, and he stood so he could embrace Brute.

"Take as many with you as you can," he said. "And if that priest prick comes alone, put an arrow through his eye and then send word down the Gihon for the rest of us to join you for the celebration."

"Bring some women with you on the way back," Brute said, and he laughed. "I'll tell the men in the morning, see how many volunteers I can rope into dying with me. I suggest we grab some sleep. It's going to be a long few days, for all of us."

Sleep wasn't something Valessa needed, but she did desire solitude. She made herself incorporeal, but when she slipped down through the floor, she saw something in Darius's eye that filled her with terrible annoyance. Stopping at the bottom floor, she walked through the wall and then waited for him. When he stepped out, he seemed surprised to see her.

"You look upset," he said.

"You damn well know why, too."

"Is that so? I beg to differ. Care to let me in on the secret?"

He started walking toward the docks, where he'd left his sword. She followed.

"You're staying," she said.

"None of your concern."

"It's suicide, and noble or not, you know that isn't your place."

"Is it?" Darius asked as he walked out onto the wood planks. "What if you're wrong, Valessa? What if he's alone? I could face him myself, put an end to all of this right here and now. I could save the lives of every man left here to die. What use am I otherwise? Do you think Daniel needs my help to nursemaid a town of people? Besides, Jerico would have stayed."

"Is that all you know?" Valessa asked. "What Jerico would do? What Jerico would say? How about what you want to do? How about what you would choose?"

"If I do what I want, instead of what I know is right, how am I different from any other man?"

"Is that how you see yourself?" she asked. "Is that how you convince yourself you're better?"

"I said different," Darius said, glaring.

He reached down for his sword. As his fingers closed about the hilt, a soft light enveloped the blade. She squinted at it, the proximity filling her with a sense of vertigo.

"But you're still wrong," she said, standing before it despite the intense discomfort. "This isn't what's right. Your place is with the people."

Your place is with me.

She almost said it. Almost. The vulnerability of it alone kept her mouth shut.

"What are you really upset about?" Darius asked, turning on her. "Worried I might die to Cyric instead of you? Your concern for my life would be more touching if you weren't saving it for your own murder."

Despite the veil she immediately created to hide herself, he must have seen the shock and pain on her face, for his shoulders sagged, and he reached out a hand for her.

"Valessa, I'm sorry, I didn't mean…"

"Stay here and die," she said, turning away. "But you're not dying alone. If you're to face Cyric, then I will too. You've already turned me into a walking blasphemy. I might as well join you on your trip to the Abyss."

She knew he'd argue, but she didn't care. Putting her back to him, she ran to the tower, then through it, through the outer wall, and out into the open wilderness where she could finally be alone. She looked to the sky only once, to see if the red star followed after her. It did not, and though she was unsurprised, she was disappointed nonetheless.

11

Sebastian sat on his throne, knife in hand. At his feet lay a pile of fluff, along with large strips of cloth. He'd cut the Lion from every cushion, and as for the carved wood, he'd hacked at it with an axe. His throne was a disheveled, mutilated mess, but he'd never felt more lordly than when he sat awaiting Luther's arrival.

An hour after dawn, the dreaded message came, bringing with it a surprising amount of relief.

"A steward of Luther requests an audience," said one of his soldiers. He remained by the doors of the great room, as if nervous to come too close. Sebastian nodded, and with a weariness he pushed himself to his feet.

"Come with me," he said. "And bring your bow. It's time we give our answer."

"I do not have a bow," the soldier said as he took up step beside Sebastian.

"Then I suggest you find someone who does."

They exited the front of the castle. Pausing for a moment, Sebastian turned around so he could observe the mark of his family. The castle was large and inelegant, little more than an enormous rectangular block of stone hollowed out with rooms, but across the front was its true beauty. It was a yellow rose, drooped to one side, with a single petal falling from its center. Sebastian remembered the day they'd begun, back when he and Arthur were children, and their father was still himself.

"This ugly thing's been crying out for beauty for too long," Rodrick had said. "I hope the gods can forgive me for not getting it done before your mother died."

Over twenty men had worked for days on end, painting, drawing, marking sections for the various flowers and carving holes in the stones to help with the planting and watering. Months had passed as the castle front transformed into the symbol of his family, a family now perilously close to being wiped off the face of Dezrel.

An image struck Sebastian with enough force to take his breath away. He saw his castle, except instead of the yellow rose a roaring lion was painted over the stone, white flowers as the teeth, red roses the drops of blood that dripped down toward the castle entrance. It felt profane, and his stomach clenched. Shaking it away, he turned back to the soldier escorting him.

"Take us to the wall," he said, his conviction renewed.

It was a long walk to the wall, built just shy of a mile from the castle. The wall itself wasn't extraordinarily tall, and ladders could scale it with ease, but it'd been built sacrificing height to enclose a greater area. They had plenty of wells for water and grazing land for livestock. So long as they weren't shut into the castle, they could endure a siege from a smaller force for many months. A larger one might force a retreat to the castle proper. But what about one made up of dark paladins and priests?

"Are all of my men at the wall?" Sebastian asked as they walked.

"Per your orders, yes. Your men are loyal to the true lord of the North."

"Even to the end?"

Not the slightest hesitation to his words. It made Sebastian feel proud, and for once, grateful.

"Even to the end."

As the wall neared, Sebastian saw his gathered men. It wasn't that impressive of a force, but the hundred and fifty were formed up on either side of the gate, safely out of view of Karak's lurking army. It wouldn't be enough to stop them, for they couldn't guard even a shred of the wall's length. But it didn't matter. He wanted to, at least for one brief moment, show Luther he was unafraid.

"We could last longer if we pulled back to the keep," the soldier said. He spoke tentatively, as if afraid his suggestion might cause offense.

"If we do, we've lost all chance at surprise," Sebastian said. "Luther thinks of me as a coward. He's probably right. He's the lion, and I'm the hare, and the last thing he'll expect is me to jump straight into his mouth. Perhaps with a bit of luck, we can rip off his tongue and shove it down his throat before we die."

When they arrived at the wall, he saw the men looking his way. Many had expected death for years, and were finally being given the chance to meet it. Others were nervous, and were looking to Sebastian to see if he would offer them hope, or change his mind completely. He'd give them neither. Maybe a noble death, if there was any nobility in rebelling against a god.

"I have no words, no speeches," Sebastian said to his escort. "All I have to say is for Luther's ears. And like I said, find yourself a bow."

The soldier called out a name, and then with two men as escort, Sebastian climbed the steps of the wall, and above his gate he peered over at the forces arrayed against him. Luther's army had been gaining in number every single day. Sebastian knew he must have called for them long before arriving at his castle. Perhaps he had always expected a fight, perhaps he only wanted to increase his show of force. Guessing why was pointless, so he didn't bother to try. At last count there were five hundred mercenaries in the temple's pay. Far more worrisome, though, were the dark paladins, twenty in number. Sebastian could pick several of them out from where he stood, tall men in dark platemail walking like kings among the more ragtag ranks. Along with the twenty paladins were a handful of priests, each one possessing an unknown degree of power.

But Sebastian knew that power well. He'd heard the stories, and seen the rare example of it in use. His gates? His walls? They'd mean nothing to them. In fact, he was counting on it.

"Where is Luther?" Sebastian called out. He saw a younger man wearing the dark priestly cloth standing before the gate below him, but he had no interest in speaking to a whelp like that, regardless of the message he carried.

"I am to speak for him," said the young man.

"Good for you, but I will be speaking only to Luther, and it is my answer he desires. Piss on your message. Bring me Luther. I will surrender only to him."

Every word was carefully chosen. The young man bowed low, then ran back to the camp. Sebastian watched, and was not surprised to see how quickly they readied for war. Regardless of whether or not Luther expected him to surrender, he was still prepared for a fight. Catching him unaware would be a nightmare, yet that was exactly what Sebastian was hoping to do. A bitter smile crossed his face. By the gods, he must be going as crazy as his late father.

Several minutes later Luther arrived, a paladin at each side. He looked up at Sebastian with an expression unreadable at such a distance.

"Come now, Sebastian," Luther said, "it is uncomfortable for a neck as old as mine to crane up at you in such a way. Can we not talk in your castle, or face to face at your gates?"

"I promise to keep this short to spare your neck," Sebastian called back. "Not that I should. You wouldn't spare my life if I went against your whims, let alone my neck. Tell me, why should I extend you the courtesy?"

"I have no desire for banter," Luther said. "Just your answer."

This was it. He could still change his mind. He could agree to the terms, and live out the rest of his life in relative peace. Did it truly matter what happened after his death? Did it matter who ruled his lands once he no longer walked upon them?

Sebastian glanced at his father's castle and saw the rose replaced with a lion. It did matter, he knew. He might not leave much of a legacy, and little of it would be fondly remembered, but at least he'll have done one thing right.

"No hesitation," Sebastian said to the man with the bow beside him. To Luther, he shouted, "I will not surrender. I will not obey. I will not kneel. You can cross these walls, but my keep will delay you. By the time you drag my body out, the King's army will be on its way to crush your squalid dreams. If you're still alive then, Luther. I pray otherwise."

The bowman drew an arrow and fired in a single smooth motion. Another was in the air before Arthur registered the hit of the first. The arrow punched into Luther's chest, knocking him to the ground. The two paladins reacted with shocking speed, flinging themselves in the way so the second arrow struck armor and ricocheted off without causing harm.

Sebastian fled down the stairs before any of the other priests might retaliate with a spell. Deep down, he dared feel a spark of hope. The arrow hit had been solid, though he hadn't caught where Luther had been pierced.

Be through a lung, he begged. Be through a lung, and kill that goddamn lunatic.

Feet back on solid ground, the men around him drew their weapons and readied their shields. From beyond the wall he heard war cries and the sounds of marching feet.

"Should we open the gates?" one of his men asked.

"Keep them closed," Sebastian shouted over the din. "Let no one be seen through them, either. I want Luther thinking we've fled to the keep." He looked to the gate and imagined the furious priests on the other side. "Besides, we won't need to open it. They'll do that themselves."

Sure enough, the spell hit before he could even finish the sentence. The gates were hurled inward, torn from their hinges and accompanied by the sound of shrieking metal. A solid beam of shadow continued through the gap, and the few men caught in its path died, the bones in their bodies crushed by the force. With a shout to Karak, the mercenaries charged. Sebastian looked to his army, split evenly between the two sides of the entrance, and hoped they would carry far less regrets to their graves than he.

"Crush them!" he cried to his men. "Tonight we bathe the Yellow Rose in blood!"

The first of the mercenaries rushed through the entrance, and then Sebastian's men charged. There were only about fifty through at the time, and caught on both sides, they were overwhelmed. Sebastian watched from the rear of the fight, wearing no armor and not even bothering to carry a blade. He would take no lives with him, other than those who already bled and died at his orders.

The ambush couldn't have been more perfect. The mercenaries fell, many trying to turn back around to flee. They had no room, the rest of Karak's men pushing forward with only a vague idea of the combat on the other side. As Sebastian watched, his men merged into a single line, bowed at the middle, completely enclosing the gate entrance. Hopelessly outnumbered, the mercenaries slowed their rush, until at last they were beaten back.

"Build a wall of their dead!" one of Sebastian's commanders cried.

Despite the victory, Sebastian felt a pall settling over him.

Not enough, he thought. Still not enough. Where are their paladins?

With another cry, a second wave hit, and this time the dark paladins accompanied it. Their blades burned with black fire, and when Sebastian's men tried to lock shields against them, they beat them back with flurries of blows that tore their shields in twain. Mercenaries swarmed around them, letting the paladins spearhead the assault. Where the initial ambush had Luther's men dropping like flies, now they died in equal numbers, and outnumbered nearly four to one, equal numbers was not something Sebastian's men could keep up for long.

Luther's men surged forward, and despite their heavy casualties, the dark paladins themselves would not go down. Their push was unstoppable, until at last they were free of the gateway entrance. With more room to fight, and greater numbers of mercenaries rushing in, Sebastian saw the turning point had arrived at last. His men died, and there were many who saw the end and flung down their blades. They were not spared. Sebastian stood tall, and he stood alone. Those before him died, and then a dark paladin towered over him, ax in hand. The fire on its heavy blade was hot enough to feel from where he stood.

"On your knees, dog," the dark paladin said, striking him across the temple with the hilt of his ax. Sebastian collapsed to his side, and he felt blood running down his face and neck. As the screams of the dying slowly faded, he looked up with blurred vision at the rest of Karak's forces surrounding him. They kept a wide berth, and Sebastian knew they planned to torture him somehow.

"All this, just for me?" he asked the paladin with the ax. His remark earned him a boot to his teeth.

"Damn coward," the paladin muttered.

Sebastian laughed even as he spat blood. Despite everything, despite the loss and death, he could at least die knowing that the paladin was wrong. He might have lived as a coward, but he wasn't dying as one.

The crowd of mercenaries parted. Sebastian rubbed his eyes, craning his neck up from where he lay to see who approached. It was Luther, held in the arms of two other priests so he might walk. The arrow was still embedded in his chest. By his guess, it was a mere two inches from his right lung.

"So close," Sebastian said, laughing despite his terror. Luther lifted a hand. He said nothing, no mocking words, no bitter remarks. Any desire the priest had to lord over his victory was gone. Luther's palm flashed with darkness, and within it Sebastian saw fire. Pain flooded his body, a great pressure swelled within his skull, and then the darkness took him far, far away.

12

All throughout the preparations for departure, Valessa accompanied Darius. She said nothing, and whenever he asked her a question she refused to respond. Perhaps it was childish, but Valessa didn't care. The paladin had certainly earned a cold shoulder, at least for a single day. The combined people of Willshire and Durham reacted with a numb calm when hearing of their need to flee. They'd been through too much to react otherwise, Valessa knew. No one argued. The memory of Cyric's initial attempt at subjugation was far too recent.

Through it all, Daniel kept their spirits high. He hollered and shouted, acting like his soldiers were incompetent sods while the villagers were the bravest of heroes. Boat after boat filled, as many crammed in them as possible without capsizing. And then, while the sun was beginning its final descent, they left without fanfare or goodbyes. Only Daniel made the shortest of speeches to Brute and his seventeen volunteers.

"Bloody their noses for me," Daniel said. "And I'll make sure the king builds you a memorial right here at the tower engraved with the names of every last one of you. And then we'll grind Cyric's bones atop it, put them into a bowl, and fill it with my own piss before tossing it to the Wedge."

"An elegant hope," Brute said, grinning. "Now get out of here, you old bastard."

With that, they were alone, twenty total to guard the walls of the Blood Tower. Valessa looked to the sky, saw the steady approach of the black star. Twenty soldiers, when they'd need two thousand to stand a chance. What was the point, she wondered. What gave the men the jubilance they showed? What allowed them to laugh and joke as they prepared their armor for battle?

Only Darius looked bothered by his fate, and even then she wasn't sure. He sat atop the northwestern section of the wall, staring into the distance. Waiting for Cyric, she knew. Was he nervous about the meeting? Valessa shook her head, berating herself. Of course he was. The thought of meeting Cyric, of hearing his voice speak her name, filled the center of her blasphemous body with terror.

"Hey Darius," Brute called from down below, having finally found the paladin. "Time's getting short, so come join us, be sociable."

Darius chuckled, and his gaze flicked over to Valessa. She kept silent, refusing to offer any input. Being there at all was lunacy. What did it matter if they drank themselves stupid or remained sober and at attention?

"Be right there," Darius said.

He climbed down the stairs, and Valessa followed.

The seventeen volunteers gathered in the mess hall of the tower, drinking to their heart's content. Brute waited in a far corner, and he had two cups ready, along with a pitcher.

"Forgive me if it seems I am a poor host," he said to Valessa. "I'd have prepared a drink for you as well, but far as I know, you're not much for that type of thing anymore."

"I tried to drink once," she said, standing beside Darius instead of sitting. Sitting was actually more difficult, since she had to keep more of her body solid than just her feet. "The liquid ran through my jaw to the floor."

She'd killed the couple who witnessed that spectacle. Their faces flashed before her, and she wished to think on anything else.

"I'll drink double for her then," Darius said, grabbing his cup.

"You're my kind of paladin," Brute said. The drink lifted to his lips, Darius paused just before, as if something was wrong. Realizing they were watching him, he laughed, and his neck flushed.

"Sorry," he said. "Weird feeling. Still thinking this might be against our code or something."

Brute laughed.

"If a cup of ale's the worst sin on your shoulders when you die, I dare say you worry too much."

Darius drank the liquid, then set it down. As the wood tapped atop the table, Valessa stared at it, feeling a mad jealousy. What she'd give to eat, to drink, to experience sweet fruits and bitter ale. In this undeath, she had an existence cruel enough to know how much she'd lost, yet an inability to do anything about it. Meanwhile, Darius was worrying Ashhur might flick him on the nose for a stupid drink. What she'd give to trade problems...

"So why are you really staying?" Brute asked, pouring more of the dark liquid into his cup. "Every one of the men here knows they're to die. They're doing it for family, for honor, or because they're old and tired and don't want to spend the next few weeks running just to die anyway. But you...you strike me as a man who has no intention of dying. So why?"

Valessa had heard his reasons, his inane sense of honor in replicating an act he assumed Jerico would perform in a similar situation. Shaking her head, she wondered just what this Jerico was like. He wasn't even human, if she went by how Darius talked of him. He was more a caricature of godliness, a walking shield of good deeds and sickening perfection. Perhaps she should remind him that it was Jerico who had killed Claire, her companion?

It took Darius a moment to answer, and when he did, he failed to be convincing.

"Because it's what I should do," he said.

"I beg to differ," Brute said. "No, what I'm thinking you should do is get into that little rowboat I kept here and row like a dragon's teeth are nipping at your ass. But then again, I'm no paladin, just a simple soldier."

"Sometimes I think the simple soldiers know more than us educated paladins," Darius said, and he smiled. The smile was clearly forced. Valessa wondered if his nerves were starting to get to him.

Brute shot her a wink.

"We know more about killing and dying, and that sometimes lends clarity. I spiked your drink, by the way. Just want you to know for when you start passing out. Would hate to scare you."

Valessa lifted an eyebrow, and she looked to Darius, who was gripping the table edge tightly. His skin was turning pale, and sweat trickled down his neck.

"No," he said, and his head bobbed as if he were suddenly dizzy. "Not your...not your place to..."

Brute was up from his seat in a heartbeat, catching Darius as he fell. With a whistle, two other men came over, helping him lift Darius from the table.

"Where are you taking him?" Valessa asked, following after.

"To the rowboat," Brute said. "Weren't you listening?"

They dumped Darius unceremoniously into the rowboat, which was tethered to the southernmost dock. It rocked back and forth, the old wood looking dangerously insufficient compared to the heft of the paladin and his armor. One of the soldiers carefully set Darius's large sword beside him.

"Get in," Brute said when that was done. "You're going with him."

Valessa opened her mouth to protest, but Brute gave her no chance.

"You can row a boat, can't you?" he asked.

"Water and I don't get along," she said.

"Then don't fall out. We've all volunteered to stay, and not a one here is willing to appear a coward by helping Darius get out safely. That leaves you, and truth be told, woman, I think I'll feel safer once you're off with him. You raise the hairs of my neck. I've already loaded the rest of his things, and there's a bit of food too, in case it takes you a bit to catch up with the others. Not that you will need to eat much."

Valessa bit back her retort. She eyed the boat, thinking of what had happened the last time she tried crossing a river. The water had torn at her being, tried to sweep her along without any true form. Her body had shifted and changed with the current, incredibly painful and beyond disorientating. But if she were careful, she could stay within the boat, though she wondered how long until the thing sprung a leak, and down to the bottom of the Gihon they went.

Slowly, carefully, she lowered a foot into the boat, followed by the other. She pulled out the lone oar as Brute untied the boat.

"Why?" she asked him.

Brute shrugged.

"No matter what he says, he's not supposed to die here. Elsewhere, perhaps, and at a later time, but not here. Not when he's got no chance to change anything. Row as fast as you can. He'll wake in a few hours. I suppose we'll all be dead by then."

The boat shuddered once as it drifted out into the heavier current. Valessa guided it with the oar best she could. Her experience with them was limited, but she was strong, and that helped immensely.

"He's almost here," Valessa shouted to them as the Blood Tower started to drift further and further away. "Don't let him know you're afraid, and don't you dare bow your knee."

"We won't," Brute shouted back.

He and the others turned their backs to her, and just like that, they were alone on the river, drifting south in a sudden calm that felt almost threatening. Valessa looked to the sleeping Darius in the center of the boat. A sensation came over her, like a tightening of her focus. If she still had a body, it would have been akin to the speeding up of her heart.

Darius lay alone, unguarded, and without his sword in his hand.

Dropping the oar, she picked up the blade by the hilt. It had once been consumed with the dark fire of Karak, a cleansing flame to burn away the weakness and filth of the world. It had been replaced with the holy light of Ashhur, pushing away the shadows, revealing the ugly nakedness of man. But now it was neither, just a heavy hunk of metal with one side sharper than the other.

The tip hovered a foot above his neck. Over and over she imagined plunging it into his flesh, slamming it down with a primal cry of torment and fury. Just like that, his life would be over. The red star would shine no more in the sky. In her hands, she thought, the blade was in her hands. All she had to do was use it.

The boat drifted on. The Blood Tower looked like a child's toy in the distance, just a tiny thing illuminated with torches no bigger than the light of the fireflies.

"Why?" she asked aloud as she sat down beside him. "Why do I let you live?"

She had to know. The blade rested atop his chest, the hilt still in her hands. A hard shove, and it would slide upward, through the lower half of his jaw and into his brain. But not until she knew why she felt such a terrible impulse to spare him. She would not act against it, not in ignorance. She did not love him. That was easy to discount. She wasn't even sure she cared much for him. But something about being in his presence comforted her. She wanted to hear him speak to her, even if she had nothing to say back. His arguments for Ashhur were uneducated and shallow. But he'd turned anyway.

He was a man who had endured similar turmoil, who had even knelt at the foot of the prophet, Velixar, and yet through all that he'd emerged whole, sane, and relatively happy. It was a future she could not see for herself in any way. Was that what she thought he offered her? But that was a happiness she could not take.

Could she?

She remembered when she and Cyric fled from Darius's glowing blade at Willshire. Valessa had been threads of shadow barely held together by magic she did not understand. Cyric had towered above her, condemning her. Every bit of hate in his eyes had shone clear, and still she'd seen the love of Karak surrounding him, blessing him. What had happened to her god? She'd cursed Karak then, swore against him. Was that the same god Darius had turned against? Did she really want to find peace and redemption through Darius's blood bleeding out of his neck and onto her hands, forever staining them the same shade of red as the star that shone above him?

"Stop it," she said, standing. The motion rocked the boat, and she fought for balance as she lifted the blade high and screamed out again. "No doubt! I am faithful, I am faithful, I am…"

Tears of silver and tears of blood ran down her face, the only liquid seemingly capable of touching her ethereal flesh. They fell upon Darius's armor with soft plinks, like rain. She knew her purpose. She knew her place. Was it not to kill the mad priest Cyric? It wasn't Karak's love she'd seen about him. It was hatred. It had to be. He was blaspheming, he was evil, horrible. He condemned her, called her unfinished. Doubt was killing her. Doubt was destroying her. She was faithful, she'd always been faithful. Ever since she was a child old enough to speak words, she'd knelt before Karak and called him lord. He wouldn't abandon her. She couldn't abandon him. Faithful, faithful, Karak help her, she was faithful…

She lost control. Her feet slipped through the boat, followed by her legs. Instinct had her lash out, dropping the sword so she might grab the first thing she could. It was Darius's leg. Her lower half felt aflame, and she had a sensation akin to her legs stretching on and on, as long as the river. The fish and the bugs crawled through them, and she felt every bit of their surface. Her fingers dug into Darius's armor, and with a cry she flung herself back into the boat, her whole body solid. Atop Darius she lay, her upper half trembling, the lower half slowly becoming bones, legs, flesh.

Kill him, she thought. Kill him, then fling yourself into the river, and let whatever god that would take you, take you.

She reached for the hilt but stopped. No. Enough of this farce. Her hatred for Cyric and Darius had nothing to do with Karak, not anymore. It wasn't for redemption. It wasn't cleansing, and she knew without a shadow of a doubt that it wasn't her performing Karak's secret desire. No, it was selfish, it was desperate, and it was all she could hope for to remove the torment and chaos that filled her mind. Her entire world, built prayer by prayer, lesson by lesson by Karak's priests, had crumbled. She only hated Darius for exposing it with that damn glowing blade of his.

But there was no honor in killing Darius. No redemption. No salvation, no clarity, no relief. Just a bitter, angry denial of the painfully obvious.

Abandoning the sword for the oar, she began to row so she might have something to do instead of dwelling on her decision. Summoning the courage only once, she looked back and saw the black star directly over the distant blur that was the Blood Tower. She wanted to pray for the men remaining behind, but knew Karak would only mock her, and she did not think Ashhur would care to listen. So she rowed, rowed, and wished the night would finally end.

13

Thirty years Brute had served in Mordan's military. Before enlisting he was Tory Baedan, an older cousin of Marcus Baedan, who would soon be crowned king. Brute had known remaining in any possible contention for the crown would put his life in danger, and so he'd become a soldier, quietly and without ceremony. He'd changed names often, but after a particularly deadly conflict with border raiders from Ker he'd earned the nickname Brute from his superior officer. Separated from the rest of his squad, and outnumbered four to one, he'd emerged victorious through his sheer strength and skill with his ax.

Four to one, thought Brute as he stood on the wall overlooking the coming force. What he'd give to have odds that good.

"I want every man on this wall," he ordered, not taking his eyes off the north. "Let's hope they don't realize the gate is broken, and think far more of us are on the ground."

The soldier beside him saluted and hurried down the stone steps. Brute took in a deep breath, then slowly let it out, trying not to question his decision to send away Darius and the witch woman. He'd expected to die before, coming close numerous times. Once an elf had shot an arrow aimed at his eye, stopped only by another man stepping in the way without realizing it. Several times he'd been outnumbered, and whenever rebellions broke out in the north, it'd been Brute's men who went their way, far ahead of any reinforcements. He'd often thought Marcus was secretly trying to get him killed, despite all his attempts to show his lack of desire for the throne.

But then he'd been assigned to Sir Robert Godley's division, and had stood with him when he refused to engage the fleeing elven refugees after the destruction of their kingdom. To the wall of towers he went, joining Sir Robert in his punishment. For years he'd been a glorified gatekeeper, killing the occasional beast foolish enough to try crossing the Gihon. Never had he thought to see another battle, not anywhere near the scale of his early days. But if he was to die, at least it wouldn't be from a raging fever or shitting himself in a bed as his innards slowly turned on him.

Brute looked to the gate. He'd purposefully snuffed out the torches near it. The witch woman had completely ruined the metal, and he hadn't a fraction of the men required to repair it. So in darkness he hoped Cyric would not realize it was broken, and even better, assume some sort of trap lay within. Not that he expected to find any kind of victory. No, he was a delaying tactic, nothing more. Every minute Cyric wasted observing his walls and planning his strategy was another minute those under Daniel's protection could travel toward safety. And from what he saw, they'd need every minute.

"How many?" asked Alex, the youngest of the men to elect to stay. He'd come up the stairs to join him, watching the approaching force with a mournful expression on his face.

"Hard to say with the darkness, but my guess is a thousand, maybe more," Brute said. "So much for hoping Cyric would come alone, eh?"

Stretching across the horizon was Cyric's army. In the darkness they might have been hidden, but foul magic shone across them. Every one shimmered with a red light, much like moonlight flickering across a watery surface. And amid the horde he saw several that burned far brighter, as if they were moving torches, or demonspawn from the deepest reaches of the Abyss. Brute felt his stomach tighten as they neared with terrifying speed. He wasn't afraid for his own life, but for those on the run. This was no normal army. Even on foot, they might outrace the river.

"Why'd you stay?" Brute said as he pulled his ax off his back. "I understand the rest, but you?"

Alex crossed his arms, and Brute recognized the look of a man struggling to hold himself together.

"Daniel said that Cyric's army would have attacked Bellham before coming here," said Alex.

"He did."

Alex nodded at the approaching force.

"My family lives in Bellham. If that's true, I've got nothing left. I might as well join them."

Brute put a hand on the man's shoulder and squeezed it tight.

"You'll see them soon," he said. "But before you do, make them proud."

The rest of the defenders gathered along the wall, spacing out to exaggerate their numbers. Brute stood in the center, and he lifted his ax high. The wolf-men were less than a minute away.

"The mad priest will have no taste for a siege," he shouted to them. "And if he does, all the better for those we protect! He'll come running, and all that matters is us stalling as long as we can. The moment these walls are breached, retreat to the Blood Tower. We'll hold in there until our last breath. You might have lived like scum, but tonight, we all die heroes."

"Fuck that!" cried someone on the far end. "I'll stay scum to the end. It's heroes that die easy. I plan on going down hard."

"You say that to your whores as well?" Brute called back, and a smile crossed his face. A long life of killing lay behind him. No long, tedious future of growing old and dying lay ahead of him. Whatever mysteries of the beyond awaited, at least he'd get to them now. The thought energized him, and when the wolf-men pulled back a hundred yards from the wall, each one howling at the top of their lungs, Brute held his ax above his head with both hands and howled right back. The cacophony thundered over them, carrying an almost physical force. Several held their hands over their ears. Howling, howling, like a legion of wolves gathered together to sing to the moon.

"Let them howl!" Brute cried, even though he doubted any of the others could hear him. "They can howl all night if they want. I'll howl right back!"

And he did. Stupid creatures, thinking they needed to intimidate, to showcase their massive numbers. They knew nothing of what they faced. Keep wasting time, thought Brute. Just keep on wasting it.

The wolf-men approached, this time much slower. Brute was thankful they came from the north. The broken entrance was to the west, and there would be no way they could see it from where they were. From the enormous pack emerged two figures. One was a gargantuan wolf-man, his fur glowing crimson as if it were made of embers. It made Brute think of the two lions Cyric had originally summoned during his ritual, on that terrible night he'd betrayed them all at the Blood Tower.

Cyric stood beside the wolf-man, dressed in his priestly robes, his face illuminated by the fire of his companion. Brute wished he were closer so he could spit on him from atop the wall. The wolf-men fell silent so the priest might shout up to Brute and his defenders.

"How gracious for you to guard my tower in my absence," Cyric said. "But you need do so no longer. I am home, and I bring with me an army. Kneel to the true god, and I will spare your lives."

Wolf-men yipped and growled around him. Brute doubted they liked the idea of a surrender. They were hungry for a fight.

"Give me an hour," Brute shouted back. "I'll talk it over with my friends here, see who feels like kneeling."

"There is no debate," Cyric insisted. "No consensus, and no compromise. Kneel and live, or stand and die. Either way, you will serve Karak."

Brute shrugged.

"I guess I'll beg to differ. I won't serve Karak, and I sure as shit won't serve you. Send your pups after me, if you must. All hundred of us are ready to die."

An easy lie. Outnumbered ten to one was still a dire situation, but with the aid of walls, they would inflict significant casualties. Of course, they didn't have a hundred men, and their walls could be bypassed by a short run around to the west. Brute prayed Cyric realized neither.

"I don't think you understand," Cyric said. "But you are acting out of loyalty to your king, and such loyalty is admirable. Loyalty is a trait sorely lacking in this age, so for that, I will reward you. I will let you see your fate if you continue to deny me my rightful place."

He made a motion with his hand, and the wolf-men behind him parted.

"What's going on?" Alex asked, and then he gasped, seeing it a fraction of a second before Brute. Walking through the lines, overshadowed by the hulking wolf-men, were pale-faced men and women. They shambled forward, limbs stiff, eyes locked ahead. Over a hundred of them in number, and when Cyric called out for them to kneel, they did. Their clothes were torn, their necrotic flesh covered with claw marks and missing thick chunks where they'd been bitten.

"Do you see?" Cyric asked. "The village of Bellham has been made pure. The weakness in it is gone, the divisiveness of serving two gods in one community ended. The murderers, the rapists, the heartless, the heathens; they all have been made to serve. Those who remain behind have loyal hearts, and will serve in the new nation I'll create. One nation, from east to west, full of loyalty. Full of faith. We have allowed men to sin, to fail, and to condemn themselves for an eternity. It was wrong of us. It was weak to let children suffer the fire for their own failures, all under the guise of choice and fairness. Open your gates, and kneel. Confess your faith, whether it is born anew tonight, or has been in your hearts since your childhood days. All of you, kneel before Karak made flesh. Serve in life, or serve in death. Dezrel shall be made pure, one way or the other, for I shall have my paradise."

"Paradise?" breathed Brute as he stared at the walking dead. Beside him, Alex let out a cry, and he looked ready to collapse.

"Don't you kneel on me, boy," Brute said, grabbing him by the shoulder.

"No," he said, shaking his head as tears ran down his face. "I'll never. That's my family there. Don't you see? That's them."

He was pointing into the rows of the dead. Brute felt his innards twist.

"That's not them," Brute said. "That's not. That's just a corpse, a shell, an empty thing. Be proud of them for staying strong till the end. They're safe from him now, as will we be. As will we all." Turning to Cyric, he shouted, his rage never before higher. "Send your wolves. Send your dead. Not a knee will bow on this wall."

Cyric shook his head as if disappointed, but he was grinning.

"I could strike you down from where I stand…but my wolves are hungry." He turned to his wolf-men. "Kill all but the man who leads them. I would have him humbled before he dies."

The wolf-man standing beside Cyric let out a howl, and with that the charge began. Brute readied his ax, baffled as to what they planned to do. They had no ladders, no siege towers. Did they hope to tear down the wall with their bare claws? Or was the priest powerful enough to smash open a gap with his magic? A red hue shone around them, and all of their claws flared as if with a great heat. Brute knew they would be terrifying to face in combat, but they would face no combat with the wall standing…

And then the wolf-men leapt, hundreds of them, slamming into the side of the wall and digging in with their burning claws. The stone gave way, the claws piercing it as if it were butter. All around, Brute heard his men cry out in fear. Like spiders they climbed, or cats up a tree. The wall was nothing. Castles, towers, gates…nowhere in Dezrel would be safe, not from them. Brute prepared to swing his ax as he cried out an order, canceling his initial idea to retreat when the walls were breached. They'd be overrun before they ever reached the tower door.

The first wolf to poke his head over the edge received Brute's ax through his skull. Brute let out a roar. They might have been blessed with unholy magic, but they were still mortal. There might be hope in Dezrel after all. Another tried climbing over, and Brute smashed his face in. All around his men stood firm, and his heart swelled with pride. Every second, he thought, every second was precious. Beside him, Alex stabbed a wolf-man through the eye, then fell as two more hurled themselves over the ramparts. Their claws shredded his flesh. Brute flung himself at them, severing in half the spine of one. The second lashed out, and it knocked the ax from his hand.

Strong paws clutched at his arms, and he screamed as he felt teeth lock around his neck, holding him in place. Like an unstoppable river the wolf-men flowed over the wall, overwhelming the last of his men. He struggled, but now three of the creatures held him down. He bled from their claws and teeth, but only superficially. None of it would be fatal. They'd leave that to their master.

The minutes passed in horror as he listened to the wolf-men feast.

"You're a frustrating one," Cyric said, walking up the stairs to join him upon the wall. Brute heard his approach, but could not see, his head locked so he could only stare upward at the stars.

"I do my best," Brute said, his voice cracking.

"A hundred men, you say? I count twenty at best. Willshire was empty, and I expected them here. Where are your men? Where are the refugees?"

"They're safe from you," Brute said as Cyric loomed over him, a sick smile on his pale face.

"You cling to old ideas," Cyric said. "Nowhere is safe, not anymore."

He turned to his wolf-men, and with a clap of his hands, they backed away from the bodies.

"I promised them a feast," the priest said. "No doubt they feel cheated, but the North is plenty large enough. But you must be humbled. You won't join them, not like the others. Your soul will move on to the fire, and the fault will be yours alone."

Cyric stood, putting his back to Brute. He raised his hands, and they shone with a dark power. Words reached Brute's ears, indecipherable. The very sound of them made his skin crawl. When Cyric stopped, he saw nothing, and could only hear the soft growls of the many wolf-men. He struggled against the creatures holding him, but they pushed down harder, one popping his shoulder out of joint. Brute choked down his scream.

Walking into view, his ghoulish body missing large chunks from where the wolf-men had feasted, was Alex. Cyric turned and stood beside him, rubbing Alex's bloodied face lovingly.

"His soul will be saved," Cyric said, pulling away. "But yours will not."

The wolf-men holding him howled, as if terribly amused. Alex approached, and he held no weapon. His hands reached out, and his knees bent as if he were an elderly man. When the cold fingers closed around his neck, Brute gritted his teeth and shut his eyes. Even in death, he'd deny the priest, deny him the satisfaction, deny him everything.

"It's not you, Alex," Brute said while he still had air in his lungs. "I know it."

Stars of all colors swam before his eyes. His chest heaved in futile attempts to draw in breath. Then nothing.

14

The dark paladin Grevus rode toward the Blood Tower amid the howls of wolves. The sound chilled his blood, and he was not one prone to fear. Had the wolf-men of the Wedge launched another attack across the Gihon, as they had in Durham? But why such a well-fortified place as the Blood Tower? Grevus paused a moment so he could dismount. Grabbing the reins, he pulled his horse's head low, then carefully put his fingers upon its eyes so he might cast a spell.

"You've done me fair," he said. "But I need haste."

When his fingers moved away, the horse's eyes shimmered red. Mounting once more, Grevus spurred it on, his horse now blessed to see in the darkness as well as if it were midday. He felt an urgency, and he prayed to Karak he was not too late. Luther had told him Cyric would most likely be at the tower, but what if he was not? Or what if he was in danger? Would it be right to help him, or let him be? The answer might be in the scroll Luther had given him, but Grevus had not dared break the seal to read it along the way. Luther had insisted it be for Cyric's ears only.

Grevus had spent so much time thinking on how he would judge Cyric's deeds, he'd not entertained notions that things might differ so greatly. He didn't consider himself a quick thinker on his feet. More and more he prayed that he misunderstood the sounds, and that all was well. But when he neared the gates, he saw the torches there extinguished. Trusting his horse to react to any danger with his blessed eyes, Grevus rode closer. Just as he'd feared, the gates were broken, the metal mangled as if hit by a battering ram. As Grevus rode through, he realized they were twisted oddly, almost as if they had been pulled outward instead of battered inward.

What madness has happened here? Grevus wondered.

The sound of the wolves had grown louder, and Grevus drew his heavy blade from its sheath. He didn't know their numbers, and if the combat had turned badly, he'd need to come riding in like a beast to change the tide, however poor the odds. The Blood Tower was before him, and he saw no outward damage, nor defenders manning the windows. Curling around toward the northern side, he saw the expanse between the tower and the wall, and it was then he stopped, mouth agape.

Hundreds and hundreds of wolf-men filled the space, tearing through the remains of the tents, gathering together into groups and feasting on meat of a type he dared not think about. More were along the walls. Grevus saw no defenders, no corpses. Had the defenses been abandoned? He barely had time to consider this before the nearest of the wolf-men sensed his arrival. A howl went up, and a hundred others matched it. Turning his horse about, Grevus kicked his sides to flee, but it was already too late. The wolf-men swarmed to either side of him, moving with terrifying speed. They bit at his horse's feet to slow him down, then fully surrounded him.

Grevus lashed out with his sword, trying to keep them at bay, but they were not interested in him just yet. As his horse reared up, trying to kick two wolf-men biting at his legs, another ducked in, slashed out its throat, and then leapt away. The beast began to topple, and Grevus scrambled to launch himself from the saddle. He landed in a roll, and came up swinging. The wolf-men stayed back, snarling, watching. It was just a game, Grevus realized, a little play with their food. The black fire burned deep across the blade of his sword, and he beckoned them on. Let them do whatever to his mortal body. He'd take plenty with him, and enter eternity with his head held high.

But it seemed eternity was not yet ready for him, for a loud cry broke through the howls.

"Get back!"

The wolf-men obeyed, their ears flattened and deep growls emanating from their throats. Through their opened ranks approached a man who must have been Cyric. Deep down, Grevus knew he should feel relieved to see the priest coming to his aid, but instead his anxiety only increased. He'd been ready to give his life killing the wild savages; what did it mean if the wild savages served Cyric?

"You must be the one I seek," Grevus said, standing tall and nodding his head in greeting. He kept his sword unsheathed.

"Many will seek me before the world's end," Cyric said, and he smiled. Grevus took in his pale skin, his carefully brushed hair, and his vibrant eyes so bright a brown they almost looked red. He was a handsome man, almost seemed to gleam with life. Grevus's worries deepened. The words the priest spoke were familiar to him, and oft-repeated in the holy scriptures housed in the temples.

"And cherish the rare man who finds him," Grevus said as a test. Would Cyric then and there declare himself Karak? Would he state himself the man the world sought in its darkness, yet seldom found?

"Indeed," Cyric said, his smile growing. "Warfang, please give my guest some space. He is to be treated with the respect of his station."

One of the larger wolf-men beside him snarled, and with a few quick barks, the rest of the wolf-men retreated further into the complex, leaving the dark paladin alone with Cyric.

"You're not in danger," Cyric said, stepping beside Grevus and putting a hand on his shoulder. Grevus sheathed his blade, and then with the same hand, grabbed Luther's scroll from the pouch at his hip.

"Forgive me," Grevus said. "Seeing so many of the beasts puts me on edge. My name is Grevus, and I come from Mordeina." He gestured to the wolf-men. "I must ask...do they serve you willingly, or have you enslaved them with magic, perhaps beaten them into submission with Karak's might?"

"It is a little of all three," Cyric said. "Some serve for power, some serve for loyalty, and some out of fear. It matters not. The wolf-men obeyed Karak in the beginning times, and it is right they do so again."

"Some priests say their kind should be extinguished, their blight removed from the land."

"All because they no longer serve?" asked Cyric. Grevus nodded, eliciting a chuckle from the priest. "Amusing, then, that they judge these heathen creatures of the wild more harshly than the wicked men of the cities."

"Are you saying we should show the wolf-men leniency?"

Cyric looked to Grevus as if he were a simpleton.

"I say we hold man to the highest of standards, not the lowest. Wouldn't you?"

The priest turned back to the broken entrance, and Grevus took step after him. He thought he should read the message now, but he wanted to see more. He wanted to gain a feel for the strange man. His looks were pleasing, his voice charismatic and aflame with faith.

"I would not consider myself intelligent enough to say either way," Grevus said. "Karak gives his word to his priests, and sometimes to me in my most heartfelt prayers. I will obey orders, without question. Let those smarter than I decide the rest."

"In your humility you show wisdom," Cyric said. "Come with me, and do not open the message you hold just yet. I would show you something."

At first Grevus was surprised, but realized he shouldn't be. Given Cyric's activities, he would surely expect some sort of message, be it blessing or reprimand, from the priests in Mordeina. But did Cyric realize the message was not from them, but from Luther only, made in secrecy? Grevus didn't know, but the way the priest looked straight through him, as if he were barely a shadow compared to his light, it made him wonder.

Cyric led him to the gateway, then stopped. Walking in rows, over a hundred in number, were men, women, and children. Grevus immediately sensed the power of Karak about them, intermixed with an unmistakable aura of death. It was necromancy he sensed, and although he had been in its presence rarely, he didn't need the blessings of a paladin to know it. The men and women walked with vacant eyes, slack jaws, and gaping wounds across their flesh that did not bleed.

"What is the meaning of this?" Grevus asked. "Why do you make the dead walk?"

"They walk because I command them to walk," Cyric said. "And I command them for I would save them."

Grevus looked at the rotting horde, walking in perfect, orderly manner, and fought down a shiver.

"Save them?" Grevus asked. "How? From what?"

"Let me present you a simple parable," Cyric said as he looked over his undead like a parent would his offspring. "There are two doors. One leads to happiness, the other to death by fire. Before the doors stands a child. He must choose, one or the other, for not choosing would also lead to death by fire. You know the correct way, but the child does not. Tell me, Grevus, what would you do?"

"I would show the child the way," Grevus said. "For that is our role in this world."

"Yes, you could show him," Cyric said. "But the other door is covered with gold, and its way is easy, and from the other side come whispers of temporary pleasures. The child may not listen. What then?"

Grevus shrugged his shoulders.

"Then the child will have made his choice. Not all are meant for peace in the eternity."

"No," Cyric said. His voice thundered over Grevus, and within it the dark paladin felt a furious certainty that set his heart racing. "That is a coward's way. Wash our hands of the blood while calling it fate, or destiny, or the free will of man. It is wrong, paladin. It has always been wrong and it will forever be so. You say you would instruct the child, then let him make his choice? You give him power he should never have. You put the weight of his soul in his foolish, impulsive hands."

"Then what would you do?" Grevus asked as Cyric walked over to one of the undead and caressed its pale cheek with his fingers.

"I'd do what is right," Cyric said. "I'd nail the other door shut."

That was it, then, exactly as Luther had described. Even worse, he already had an army to do it. What if Luther was right, and other paladins and priests of Karak joined his side, swelling his ranks? Grevus swallowed, and he reached for the message.

"I bring word," he began, but Cyric ignored him.

"Their souls are still here, you know," the priest said, pushing a finger against the forehead of the walking corpse of an elderly man. "Right here. They refused to bow, Grevus. They refused, shouted angry, ignorant denials. Some, like this man here, were even worse. They professed a faith in Ashhur, as if that would save them. As if that meant something. He thought by going to the Golden Eternity he would be safe from my grasp. But he doesn't understand. He isn't safe from me there. No one is. I'll ascend, and on a glorious day tear down those gates. Order must be made above all things. I will find and judge every soul, even the ones that flee to Ashhur."

"You speak as if you are Karak himself," Grevus said, such blasphemous words bitter on his tongue. He looked to the rows of undead, thinking of the torment the souls must be enduring within. Did Grevus think shallow obedience in a desiccated form would lead to their salvation?

"Why such serpentine words?" Cyric asked. "I know what you wish to ask, so why not ask it? Are you afraid of the answer, paladin?"

"There are only two possibilities," Grevus said. "You are who you say you are, or you're a blasphemy against our god. You cannot be both, and you cannot be neither. Let me hear the words from your own tongue, Cyric. Let me judge for myself."

Cyric smiled, but for once that glow about him faded.

"Then let this be my answer; you cannot judge me, Grevus. No one in this world can."

For a moment it seemed time stopped in that dark night. Grevus heard his heart thundering in his ears, and his mouth turned dry as sand. There was power in Cyric's words, and whether they were true or not, the priest fully believed them. But how could he speak such blasphemy yet not be condemned by Karak? That the dead followed his command showed Karak had not abandoned Cyric, nor turned his back to him. What did that mean? What other choice did he have?

"I bring message," Grevus said. "Let me read from Luther's hand, and then I will decide what it is I believe."

"If you must," Cyric said, but Grevus could tell he was irritated by the mention of Luther's name.

Pulling out the scroll, Grevus looked at the seal, and with trembling hands he broke it. Slowly unrolling the parchment, he saw the priest's handwriting, and something about it calmed him. Luther was a wise man, brilliant both in the ways of the world and of gods. He'd know how to reconcile the apparent contradiction in Cyric's power remaining amid such blasphemy. Because Cyric was not Karak made flesh. Despite all his confusion, Grevus was certain of that one truth. Because if Karak did come to the world, Grevus knew he'd fling himself to his knees in worship the moment he saw him. Cyric did not inspire that devotion. Cyric didn't inspire devotion at all. There was a tantalizing promise to him, though. A nation devoted to Karak, one sworn to the proper way…how many of his brethren would rally behind that ideal?

Forcing the thoughts from his mind, Grevus read the scroll aloud.

"My dear pupil, Cyric," it began. "I have heard of your exploits in the North. I know of Willshire, and of your schemes at the Blood Tower. Reports so far say otherwise, but I fear Sir Robert is dead, for that proud man would never bend the knee to Karak. Did I not tell you he could be of use to you, even if his faith was lacking? But you have never seen the world as I have. You see it in a light that has never existed. You see a past far more glorious than it ever was, and view our growing understanding of Karak's wisdom as nothing more than perversions of the original truth. And now, worst of all, you claim yourself Karak made flesh. You speak blasphemy, Cyric, and there is only one penalty. I would ask you to repent, but your soul is scarred too far for that. Karak forgive me for not stopping you in time to save you."

So far Cyric had said nothing, done nothing, only stared at him with an amused smile on his face. But there was one sentence left, and it was written not in ink, but in blood. Grevus read the words aloud, knowing their pronunciation even though they were nothing but gibberish, a sentence of strange, archaic words. It was the language of magic, Grevus realized, even as he felt a fever overcoming him with each word leaving his tongue. Powerful, ancient magic.

The sound of the Lion's roar echoed throughout the Blood Tower. Grevus dropped the scroll and clutched his arms to his chest as he felt his mind being ripped in two. His knees shook, and then the fire began to swirl about him. Red light shot from his fingertips, and from behind his eyes he felt Luther peering out.

At last that smile left Cyric's face.

"What is this?" he asked. "Who are you really, Grevus?"

Luther's power enveloped him fully now. His muscles felt as if they were made of stone, his armor the lightest of cloth. In the back of his mind he heard a constant hymn, sung by voices whose words were indecipherable. The darkness about him was suddenly bright, and surrounding the hundred dead were auras of a deep red. Around Cyric he saw ethereal fire of a royal blue, burning without consumption. Grevus drew his sword, whose fire burned so great not a hint of steel could be seen.

"Our house must not be divided," Grevus spoke, but the words weren't his. "Your way is wrong, and would lead to our destruction."

"Do you think I fear your puppet?" Cyric asked. "I am your master. I am your god."

"No god. Once my student, now just a man. That's how you lived. That's how you'll die."

His sword arm moved without him thinking it. The blade rose, then fell, the black fire trailing behind. It should have cleaved through Cyric's skull, but the priest lifted his hands. A shimmering translucent shield appeared before him, and Grevus's sword smacked into it as if it were hardened steel. The paladin tensed his muscles, and power flooded through him anew. It was as if Luther stood beside him, lending every bit of his holy strength. The shield sparked and cracked, unable to endure the force.

"Once a student," Cyric gasped, his fingers locked tight and his hands shaking. He fell to one knee, gasping as the sword descended closer and closer to his skull.

"Once a man."

He looked up at Grevus, and their eyes met. It was strange, but Grevus knew it wasn't him that Cyric saw, but Luther. The shield strengthened, and Grevus pressed further. He waited for another surge, just that slightest bit needed to finally crush through Cyric's defense and put an end to his blasphemous claims. But Grevus sensed Luther's strength wasn't quite complete. A strange pain filled his chest, as if he'd been pierced by a dagger or an arrow. His breathing came shallower, and with desperation he tried to realize the kill.

"No longer!" cried the priest.

Cyric stood, and with a wave of his hand a shockwave rolled out, knocking Grevus back and the sword safely away.

Panic spiked in Grevus's heart, and he knew only part of it was his. He rushed the priest, sword pulled back for a wide swipe. Before he could swing, Cyric pointed a finger.

A tiny ball of darkness shot out, its spherical form outlined with white lightning. It struck Grevus in the chest, punching through his armor and into his flesh. The pain was extreme, and the power flooding through him wavered, the link between him and Luther starting to wane.

"Not yet," Grevus muttered, staggering forward even as blood ran down his armor. Instead of swinging with his blade, he extended a palm, and a blast of energy shot forth, its essence circling with stars and the deep shadows of space. It was the greatest Luther could muster. Keenly, Grevus felt the wounds his priest battled, and how great the strain was to strengthen him. The blast hit Cyric's extended hand. When it broke against his shield like water against a stone, Grevus gave him no time to recover. He lunged forward, sword stabbing for his neck.

Cyric stepped to one side, then reached out with his hands. One grabbed ahold of Grevus by the throat, the other clutched the extended blade. The fire did not burn his fingers, nor did the edge cut his skin.

"How long will you doubt me?" Cyric said, his face inches away. "Will it take death to teach you the truth of my claim?"

"In death we will know all things," Grevus said, and it was his words this time. Already he felt Luther retreating. "But I'll learn nothing of you, save the nakedness of your lies."

Even as the spell enacted around his neck from Cyric's hand, Grevus still reached forward. All he needed was a touch. Fire burned his throat, and he dared not try to breathe. His free hand touched Cyric's chest, and then he unleashed it all, his full fury against the sinful and unrighteous. Ashhur's paladins could cleanse the wounded with their hands. Karak's could destroy the wicked.

Grevus dropped to the ground, Cyric's hand releasing him. Lightheaded, Grevus tried to remain upright on his knees, but his muscles were starting to betray him. His throat was charred shut, and he could not breathe. His lungs burned like fire, but he forced himself to watch, to see the results of his ability. Cyric had staggered back, as if struck in the chest by a mallet. The dark power washed over him, and on a normal man it'd have killed muscle, exploded blood, and shattered bone. But Cyric still stood, and when he looked at Grevus, it was with a smile on his face.

"You would use my power against me?" he asked. "You're a fool, both of you, damned fools."

Forgive me, Grevus, Luther whispered into Grevus's mind. I wasn't strong enough. You are a good man, a faithful man. Greet me when my own time comes.

Cyric knelt before him, cupping his face as if he were a loved one.

"Not yet," the mad priest whispered after kissing his forehead. "You're not done serving just yet."

Grevus could not see him anymore, his vision overwhelmed with red and yellow as his lungs strained repeatedly, desperate for clean air. Blessed darkness started to take him, coupled with a strange lightening of his body and a vanishing of his pain. That sensation suddenly halted, and the wrongness of it left him screaming in his mind, for his lungs could not scream of their own accord. The terrible swirl of colors dissipated. His eyes could see once more, but it seemed they no longer functioned as they should. He could not look anywhere but directly into Cyric's smiling face.

His legs pushed him to a stand. They did so against his will.

"I gave you every warning," Cyric said. "But I will not punish a puppet of Luther. I was similar once, and so I shall show you mercy."

Grevus's lungs did not breathe. His heart did not beat. He felt an overwhelming sense of hopelessness, coupled with a claustrophobic certainty of imprisonment within his own body. No matter what he tried to do, his arms and legs refused to obey.

And then he was walking.

"You'll serve as a loyal man should," Cyric said, staying at his side. "Whenever the sun rises or sets you'll kneel in prayer. With your own eyes you'll witness the unveiling of Karak to the world. I hope that, in time, you will open your heart to the truth. I'm trying to save you from an eternity of fire, Grevus. You may not believe me now, but I have time, paladin, so much time…"

Deep inside, Grevus screamed and screamed as he joined the ranks of the other hundred, and to his horror, he realized he could hear their screams as well, pleading for freedom, for forgiveness, for death.

15

—◆◆◆—

Jerico stood before the crumbled remains of the Citadel. He saw the broken stone and billowing dust with a clarity and certainty of his dreaming status that he knew himself in no ordinary dream. The sun was high, the grass green and blowing in a smooth summer wind. The stables were crushed, thick sections of stone wall having collapsed on top of them. Toward the river was the rest of the former structure, toppled as if the very foundations had been thrown up from the dirt. A deep crater remained where the Citadel had once stood, like a wound on the land.

While he once might have felt fear or despair walking toward such a scene, Jerico now only felt a timid sadness. Was this what awaited him should he finally have the courage to travel south? Was this the scene that would confirm his earlier dreams?

And then the clouds swirled, and Darius stood before him. He wore the same armor as always, except now made of gold, and with a silver symbol of the mountain carved into the chestplate

"Darius?" Jerico asked.

Darius smiled, and did not confirm nor deny.

"You'll soon be betrayed," the dream apparition said. "Show no fear, no anger, and no surprise. Into the hands of the enemy you must go."

"What?" Jerico asked. "Why? If I'm to be a martyr, just say so, and I'll do it gladly."

"Not a martyr," Darius said, shaking his head. "Just remember, you are never alone. Even among the lost there are men of faith. Do not hate them. Let go of your sadness and pride, and above all...trust me."

Darius turned and began walking toward the river, his royal blue cloak billowing behind him.

"Wait!" cried Jerico.

Hearing him, Darius turned, and he gave the paladin a smile.

"Go easy on Kaide, too," he said. "There's hope for him yet."

A white dove flew over him, and its feathers billowed in the wind, multiplying with unnatural means until all Jerico saw was white.

And then he woke to the warnings of a rider approaching from the Castle of the Yellow Rose.

Two hours later, long after the rider had left, Lord Arthur summoned Jerico to his tent. Jerico, left uneasy by his dream, made sure he was in his full armor, his shield on his back and his mace clipped to his side. Getting to the tent involved traveling through a large group of Kevin Maryll's troops, and the icy glares they gave him made him wonder. The guards at the entrance looked tense, but they let him in without attempting to take his weapon.

Inside, Jerico found Arthur and Kevin waiting for him. Arthur sat at his small desk, and he looked greatly troubled. Kevin, meanwhile, had a smile on his face that made Jerico want to punch him. No reason in particular, other than to see his fist wipe away that smirk and replace it with shock. But that was a juvenile thought, and Jerico chastised himself for it.

"I saw the rider," Jerico said when neither seemed ready to start the conversation. "What word from Sebastian?"

"The rider was not from my brother," Arthur said, leaning back into his chair. "No, it seems that priest, Luther, has done what you feared. He defeated Sebastian and his men and then seized control of the castle."

"Then your path is clear," Jerico said. "If Luther's claimed control, send word to all the other lords of Mordan, and to the King himself. This outrage will not…"

"There's more," Arthur interrupted. He glanced to Kevin, whose smirk grew.

"Sebastian's still alive," Kevin said.

Jerico frowned.

"I don't see how that changes things."

Kevin rolled his eyes, all too eager to make the paladin seem unintelligent.

"Luther has offered a trade," he said. "He'll turn over control of the castle, as well as spare the life of our lord's brother. In return, he asks for only one man's life."

Jerico felt his breath catch in his throat. No matter how unintelligent Kevin might think him, it took very little imagination to know who Luther requested. Kevin realized it too, and his hand drifted down to his sheathed sword. From all around the tent, Jerico heard the movement of armor. They were surrounded by men loyal to Sir Maryll, no doubt. Again the words of the dream haunted him, and he looked into Arthur's eyes. A dozen things he wanted to ask, but instead he kept his voice calm.

"Will you say yes?" he asked.

Arthur met his gaze despite his obvious guilt.

"Leave us," he ordered Kevin.

"Milord, he is a dangerous…"

"I said leave!"

Kevin bowed low, and then he left, his hand still on the hilt of his sword. Arthur mumbled after his leaving, then grabbed a cup of ale and downed it all in one gulp.

"Damn it, Jerico, couldn't you at least yell at me?" he asked.

Jerico remained silent.

"Luther's messenger said they'll kill Sebastian by the end of tonight," Arthur continued. "There's no time to send word to anyone, no time to rally an army large enough to storm the walls. They claimed to have a thousand men loyal to Karak, and after what I saw at my own castle, I find that believable enough. My brother's life may not be worth much, but he's still family. And more importantly, Luther's promised to hand over the castle. I can retake all the North without a single drop of blood spilled."

"Other than my own, of course," Jerico said. "Why tell me this?"

"Because I want to know if it's the right thing to do," Arthur said. "You'd follow your conscience, and I'd follow mine, is that not what we promised? And right now, my gut screams this is wrong, screams it loud enough I'm surprised the rest of my army can't hear it. But you know how strong an army we face. This isn't just Sebastian's pathetic remnants. Luther's men could storm out of those gates and kill every last one of us, without need for towers and ramparts. We have no hope here, none. Kevin practically threatened treason if I turned down this deal, saying he wouldn't risk the lives of his men just to save yours. What choice do I have, Jerico?"

Jerico closed his eyes, and he begged Ashhur for calm. No fear, he thought, no anger. When he opened them, he saw Arthur watching, waiting. He was on the edge, he knew. A single word, even a harsh look, and he would cancel the entire plan, even at risk of his brother and his soldiers.

"Your brother's a scoundrel," Jerico said, and he forced a smile. "But your men aren't. Promise me you'll be a good lord for the North, and I'll go."

"I'm not sure it's a promise I can keep," Arthur said, standing. "Would a good lord hand over a man who's been faithful to him without reason, and whose courage has saved his life numerous times?"

Jerico stepped close and accepted the man's embrace.

"I go willingly," he said.

With that, he turned and exited the tent, where Kevin and his men waited. Jerico unclipped his mace and tossed it at Kevin's feet.

"Shield too," Kevin said. "I've heard what you can do with it."

Jerico did so, and one of Kevin's men scooped up both. Lifting his hands high, the soldiers grabbed him, yanking his arms so they could bind them behind his back.

"Your life for the life of a lord and the control of a castle," Kevin said, shaking his head. "Such strange games you men of gods play."

They were two miles out from the wall surrounding the Castle of the Yellow Rose, and they made Jerico walk it, the rest of them mounted. There were over fifty of them, their chainmail rustling with each step of their horse. Kevin himself held the rope that wrapped around Jerico's chest before looping through the knot binding his hands. At one point he ushered his horse to a trot, and Jerico ran behind, his heavy platemail rattling. Annoyed, Kevin raced faster, so that Jerico had to sprint. At last he lost his footing, and the rope dragged him along. The hard dirt jostled him in his armor, and his face scraped against rocks that left him bleeding.

When the horse slowed, Jerico stumbled to his feet, spat a bit of blood, and then grinned at Kevin.

"Always enjoyed a good run," he said.

Kevin only shook his head in disbelief.

At the gates of the wall waited a group of dark paladins, all with their weapons drawn. The sight of the fire made the men around Jerico nervous, and he felt an odd compulsion to calm them.

"Just keep me alive, and you'll be safe," he said.

A few gave him bewildered looks, and Jerico just shook his head and chuckled.

"Greetings," Kevin said as they rode up before the paladins. "I am Sir Kevin Maryll, and I bring the prisoner your priest and master requested."

One of the paladins strode forward, sheathing his sword to show he meant no harm. Maryll's men parted to give him way. The paladin was a hard man, his face wrinkled and his eyes a crystalline blue. He took Jerico's face in his hand, lifting him so they might get a better look.

"Are you him?" the dark paladin asked.

"Probably not," Jerico said, still grinning. "Just Jerico."

The man struck him across the mouth, then nodded to Kevin.

"Your master has upheld his end of the bargain, so we will uphold ours."

Waving his finger in a circle in the air, he strode back toward the gate. Curiously, the stone around it looked old and burnt, as if it'd been struck by fire, but the gate itself looked new. With a rumble of metal it opened, and from it approached two priests and a paladin. A haggard man walked between them. His wrists and ankles were bound together with chains, and he shuffled with what little slack they gave. His eyes were blackened, as if he'd been beaten, and his lips were cracked and bleeding. Jerico looked to him, saw the pathetic remnant of a man that had been Sebastian Hemman.

"He is battered, but will live," said the old paladin as one of the priests took out a key and unlocked the chains.

Sebastian said nothing as he walked unescorted to Kevin. Meanwhile the dark paladins pushed Jerico forward to the gate. As he and Sebastian walked past each other, their eyes met, and Jerico hoped the man might realize the incredible fortune granted to him. They'd ridden to the castle to take his life, yet now he would find safety in their arms.

"Keep an eye out for Kaide," Jerico said, unable to hold back completely.

A fist struck his cheek, but before it did, Jerico caught a bit of fear in Sebastian's eyes, and it made him grin through the pain. Not that he wanted to see Sebastian afraid. It was that he finally saw a sign of life in the man for whom he was giving his own.

They did not chain him, nor take off his armor. One of the paladins accepted his shield and mace from Kevin's men, and another held the rope that tied his arms and hands. They walked in silence through the gate, and as it shut behind him, Jerico winced against his will. Despite the grin on his face, he knew that sound was a death sentence. Whenever Luther abandoned the castle, assuming he even did, Jerico knew he would not be coming with him. Not alive, anyway.

"At last I see fear in your eyes," the old paladin said, who walked beside him.

"Not fear," Jerico said. "Guilt. You realize how many of you I'll have to kill to escape? No man should have that much blood on his hands."

"Stupid words. Brave, but stupid. I'd suggest keeping your tongue in check when you stand before Luther."

Jerico expected another smack to his face to punctuate it, but was proven wrong. Instead one of the other paladins jammed the hilt of his sword against his side. The pain was searing, and he stumbled along, refusing to fall.

They crossed the rest of the distance between the wall and tower in relative silence. To Jerico, it felt like a strange sort of ritual, all of Luther's men staring straight ahead without talking to one another. Jerico wished he could know what they were thinking, then decided he'd rather not. It might crack whatever resolve he had left.

"Ready the army," the old paladin said when they reached the castle doors. Several of the others departed for the rows of tents pitched about the commons, shouting orders to the mercenaries. Jerico quickly counted their numbers, and from what he saw, Luther had not exaggerated in his letter when he claimed a thousand followed him.

Into the castle they took him, tugging on the rope as if he were a reluctant dog. Passing through the great hall, they hooked a right, climbing stairs that wound up one of the castle towers. Jerico knew right there was his best chance to escape, but just as he thought of it, he saw the old paladin had his hand on the hilt of his sword. The moment he resisted, he'd have that blade shoved through his throat. Trusting Ashhur's command, he kept still. At last they reached a door, and after knocking, they entered.

Within sat Luther on a bed. Instead of his robes he wore a thin tunic, which had been cut to give easy access to the many bandages wrapped around his chest. Seeping through them was a hint of red. Before the bed, waiting for him, was a plain wooden chair. Luther started to stand, then thought better of it.

"Untie him," Luther said.

The old paladin hesitated at first, then obeyed. As they cut the ropes, Jerico glanced around the room. It was small, quaint, with but some books, a bed, and a washbasin. More

befitting a librarian than a lord, thought Jerico. Seeing
Luther there, Jerico felt his pulse increase with his growing
rage. Here he was, the man who had killed Sandra without a
second thought, the man he had sworn vengeance upon.

"I would have your word," Luther said to him.
"Promise you will not escape, nor attempt any harm against
me."

His response burned his throat. More than anything,
he wished for his mace so he could crush Luther's skull.

"I promise," he said.

"Good." Luther looked to the others. "Leave us."

Reluctantly they filed out, until only the two of them
remained, Jerico standing, Luther sitting on the bed. With a
sigh, Luther leaned back against the stone wall.

"I trust you to understand the harm that'd befall you if
you tried to escape."

"You look like you can barely stand," Jerico said. "I
understand, even if I don't believe it. But I gave my word.
Consider yourself lucky for it."

Luther chuckled.

"Always joking, aren't you? But this is not a time for
laughter. We must talk, Jerico, and you must hear things
that will pain me to speak, especially to a child of Ashhur."

Jerico stretched his arms, trying to work out the knot
in his back before sitting in the chair provided for him. His
rage was subsiding, however slowly. He hoped within an
hour or so the urge to throttle the priest with his bare
hands would be minor.

"Speak then," he said. "Tell me whatever speech you
have planned. Let me hear whatever justification you'll use
to go against your promise to Lord Arthur and take the
lives of his men."

Luther shook his head, and he looked genuinely
insulted.

"There's more going on in the North than this petty feud between brothers," he said. "And I have no intention of keeping this castle, nor attacking Arthur's army. My goals for a nation unto Karak must be put on hold, for both our holy orders face a threat greater than ever before."

Jerico scratched at his chin, struggling to believe what he was hearing. Ashhur granted him the ability to know truth from lie, and so far, every word the priest spoke rang true. Whatever threat he faced, he believed it as dangerous as he claimed.

"What threat?" he asked.

"A former pupil of mine by the name of Cyric. He has gone mad, and declared himself Karak's mortal vessel come to conquer the world. Already he has overthrown Sir Robert at the Blood Tower, and with an army of wolf-men he now marches south. His power is greater than mine, Jerico. I tried to stop him, and failed. The next time, I cannot fail, or a great many will suffer."

"What do you mean you tried to stop him?" Jerico asked, honestly baffled. "How can two servants of Karak battle? If this Cyric is claiming he's a god, he's speaking blasphemy. Why has Karak not struck him down, or denied him power?"

"He hasn't," Luther said. "And he won't."

"Then is he right? Is he really Karak?"

"Of course not," Luther snapped, and the sudden shout caused him to double over hacking. He coughed until blood was on his fingers, but at last he regained his breath.

"No," he said. "That is the great mystery, one I have long suspected and only now understand fully."

Jerico lifted his hands in surrender.

"Then explain it, Luther, because I do not."

"I will," Luther said. "But promise you will listen with an open mind. What I say may sound like blasphemy to you. Perhaps some of it is, but it is the truth, so far as I know it."

"Say it then," Jerico said. "I'll try to keep my mouth shut."

"The rules of our gods are strange," Luther began, his wet voice painful to listen to. "The power they grant us, be it the fire and light on our blades, or the spells we learn to cast, they are all granted by our faith. Our faith makes them manifest, and our faith decides their power. But it is faith, and only faith, that grants the power. I am beginning to believe that so long as there is faith, Karak and Ashhur will grant that power, whether they approve of the wielder or not. Perhaps they must. There is no way to know."

Jerico felt his hands tighten into fists. Luther was right. To claim either god was helpless against those who took power in their name…surely that was blasphemy.

"What of Darius?" he asked. "He told me of Karak's betrayal, and how he yearned for a restoration of his faith. Yet he was denied it because his beliefs no longer matched your god's dark design. How does that fit into your ideas of gods being slaves to humans?"

"Doubt is a cruel lion. Often it attacks without us ever being aware. From what I know, Darius spent many months in Durham with you, and even counted you as a friend. Your words affected him, though he might not have realized it at the time. His faith was shaken by discovering a second truth, which I will tell you now. He lacked wisdom to understand it, to reconcile with it as I have. You see, Jerico, our gods have changed."

It took all of Jerico's willpower to remain silent.

"I see your anger," Luther said. "I understand it too, for you have forever seen Ashhur as the unchanging mountain. But when our gods first warred, Ashhur was not as you know him now. His tendencies to mercy, forgiveness, compassion…he did not practice these weak compulsions as you now preach. He was a god of Justice. Karak was a god of Order. In a way, their goals were the same. They both wanted a civilized world for Dezrel, a land where men did not murder, steal, and rape, and women did not sell their bodies for a scrap of coin. But my god was all about the ends, whereas yours kept focused on the means. That they warred is no surprise, as much as many in my order like to claim otherwise.

"But the Karak I read about does not quite match the Karak our paladins profess. Ever since our brother gods were imprisoned by Celestia, what we preach has slowly evolved. The miracles change, the demands of our gods shift, and suddenly these two deities of Justice and Order are so very different than they began. What I wonder, Jerico, did our gods change, or did we change our gods?"

Luther believed it, all of it, but that didn't mean it was true. Jerico tried to understand, to know what it was he himself believed. It'd take time to think on these things, time he didn't currently have.

"You said Cyric is our greatest threat," Jerico said. "Tell me why."

"Because the Karak I worship, the Karak I teach to my pupils, is not the Karak others would have him be. No doubt Darius realized this as well, and his faith was broken for it. Can the same god have multiple faces? No, one must be true. One must win out, and the history of our order is full of men in conflict about our god's true nature. The worst of them is the prophet, the man with a hundred names and a thousand faces. Over the centuries he has always been. His words drip with war, and his fingers are stained with the blood of sacrifice. There have been those of my order who have mistrusted his presence from the beginning, for death refuses to claim him. The Council of

Stars even denied his authority over us. I was just a young man then, but I was one of the loudest speakers there. So often I've felt myself fighting a losing battle, but never did I think it would come to this."

"Cyric is like the prophet," Jerico said, piecing it together. "Like him, but worse. He doesn't think he's just a prophet."

"Far worse," said Luther. "He thinks he's a god. His faith in Karak is unbelievably strong, for his belief is now in himself. An older man might doubt or know his limitations, but Cyric's young and inexperienced. With each passing day he'll trust his power more, and wield it with greater skill. Should the North begin to fall to him, he'll be unstoppable. And with him he'll bring about a faith in Karak that I have long attempted to quash. He'll bring back the blood sacrifices, the rituals, the destruction and unbending rules of the old ways. The ideas of choice and free will mean nothing to him. Faith will be little more than chains, and he'll use them to enslave all of Dezrel if he can."

The thought was a horrifying one, even worse than the idea of the priesthood having control of the North's lands and laws.

"You wish for my help," Jerico said when Luther lapsed into silence. "But why give up the castle? You destroyed Sebastian's army, then took the Yellow Rose from him. Did he refuse to play a part in your game?"

Luther chuckled, but there was a furious bitterness to it that made Jerico slide his chair away from the bed.

"No, Jerico. My victory here was a heartbeat away, but I could not continue. I will not be a hypocrite. I will not condemn Cyric for attempting to create a kingdom sworn to Karak while I do the same. My wayward pupil has ruined everything, all because I am not strong enough to stop him. My last best chance failed. That is why I need you, Jerico. I want you at my side, Karak and Ashhur, together crushing a man who would render faith in either of our gods irrelevant. Because if our gods can change, and all of Dezrel comes to worship the cruel god of Cyric, then I fear I will have no place left in this world."

It was such a strange proposition at first, but Jerico remembered when he and Darius had stood side by side defeating the wolf-men threatening to destroy their village. Was it so crazy to think something like that could happen again?

"I don't how much of what you say I believe," Jerico said. "But what you say of Cyric is true. He must be stopped, and if it is within my power, I will stop him."

Luther nodded.

"Very well. Consider yourself no longer my prisoner, but my guest. Open the door. Xarl should be waiting on the other side. I trust him to have heard every word."

Jerico opened the door, and sure enough, the old paladin stood before the door, arms crossed and a frown on his face.

"Follow me to your room," Xarl said. "You can stay there until we march."

Jerico did, but not before looking back to Luther, who lay on his bed, coughing profusely. Even among the lost there are men of faith, he'd been told in his dream. Do not hate them. Jerico knew he shouldn't hate, he didn't want to, but lying there was the man who had killed the only woman he'd ever loved.

And yes, he hated him.

"What does the old Karak think of you killing Sandra?" Jerico asked him as Luther continued coughing. "And would Cyric agree?"

He followed Xarl down the steps, letting his hatred and anger hang in the air of Luther's room.

16

Sebastian's arrival at the camp was full of raucous joy. To Kaide's ears, it was the jubilation of betrayal. He'd not been consulted on the offered agreement, nor been informed of the coming trade. Only now, from the whispers of soldiers closer to Arthur than he, did he hear of the proposal. The loss of Jerico was unpleasant, but with it ending the war, Kaide understood. But what of Sebastian's fate? He knew what should happen. He knew that Arthur should thrust a dagger into his brother's chest and put a worthy ending to their battle. But that wouldn't happen. Deep down, he knew Arthur had a weakness in his heart. His reluctance to openly war against his brother for so long was proof enough of that.

So Kaide gathered his men together, those who had been with him from the beginning, and gave them his orders, to be followed whether he lived or died. And then he marched into Arthur's tent, just behind the escort that brought Sebastian.

Arthur stood before his brother, his hands at his sides. Kevin Maryll was also there, with several of his men. At Kaide's entrance he was given a cursory glance, then ignored. Something hidden was going on between the brothers, a dialogue of long looks, met stares, and twitches of the face. It'd be settled by the first words either spoke.

And then Sebastian kneeled.

"I wronged you," he said. "I put our kingdom at risk. Whether you believe it or not, I sacrificed my life, and the life of my men, to save it. I don't know why they let me live. I don't know who that man was they traded me for. But if the North is now yours, I rejoice. Forgive me, Arthur, if you feel it right to do so. Take my life if that is right as well. I will accept either without protest."

Kaide held his breath as the moment lingered. This was it. Sebastian had cast his life at Arthur's feet. Would he find succor, or a blade?

Arthur stepped forward, and he put a hand on his brother's shoulder.

"By your bent knee, I am now ruler of the North in name and deed. I will not have my first act be the spilling of my own brother's lifeblood. Stand, Sebastian. By gods it's been too long since I looked upon your face."

Sebastian did, and Arthur embraced him. That embrace sealed Kaide's actions.

"Forgiven by you," he said, turning their attention his way. "But not by me."

Unchecked by the guards upon entering because of the fervor around Sebastian's arrival, Kaide still had both his dirks tucked into his belt. He drew them, and like an arrow he lunged forward. One of Kevin's men managed to draw his sword in time, and another flung his body in the way of the two lords. Kaide spun around the man, and the dirk in his left hand parried away the desperate chop. His feet touched the ground, and then he lunged again.

The tip of his dirk slid into the flesh of Sebastian's throat, and as the blood poured across Kaide's hand, the relief was everything he could have ever dreamed of. He imagined the souls of his parents, his siblings, his poor dear Sandra, all settling deeper into their graves, satisfied at last with death. Kaide twisted the dirk, then yanked it out. The blood splattered with greater ferocity, and when Arthur grabbed his brother it splashed across the front of his shirt.

Soldiers reached for him, pinning his arms and tackling his legs. Kaide gave into them willingly. They forced him to his hands and knees as Kevin drew his sword and pressed it against his neck.

"Let me have the honor," Kevin said.

"Do it," Kaide said, "and all of you will die."

The blade at his neck tensed, and Kaide closed his eyes, waiting.

"Wait," Arthur said. "If any man will kill him, it shall be me."

The blade vanished, and then a hand grabbed Kaide by the hair and pulled up to expose his throat. He looked into Arthur's eyes, saw the sadness there. Was it for him, or his brother? Kaide didn't care. He'd warned the man. There'd be no mercy, not from him.

"Not brave enough to take your brother's life, but you'll take mine?" Kaide said. "Of course. Who would weep for the loss of a vagabond rebel without a home? Oh wait, I think I know."

As if on cue a soldier barged into the tent. He stopped, stunned by the sight before him.

"What is it?" Arthur asked, barely containing his anger.

"There's fires spreading along the eastern camp," the soldier said. "The people are chanting for Sebastian's head."

"So many men pledged to me," Kaide said, their attention turning back to him. "How do you think they'll react when it's my head you present to them instead of Sebastian's? You might win, Arthur, but you'll have a riot on your hands. Hundreds will perish. In the chaos of a riot, anything can happen. Anyone can die…"

Arthur stood there breathing heavily, his hands shaking with rage. He put his sword below Kaide's neck, using it to lift his head higher so they might stare eye to eye.

"I once counted you as a friend," he said. "No longer."

Arthur turned to Kevin, and he handed him his sword.

"Take the head," he said. "Use it to quell the riots. Sebastian died by my order, do you understand?"

"I do," Kevin said, kneeling down to begin the grisly work. Kaide watched, thoroughly satisfied with the sight of that skinny, pompous asshole having his neck chopped apart, his stiff face lifted into the air by the hair. Better than he ever thought possible. Jerico had filled his head with unreasonable ideals. Mercy? Forgiveness? Better the cold corpse and a severed head.

Arthur put away his sword and knelt before him. Reaching out, he grabbed Kaide's right hand and took one of his fingers. He said nothing, only wrenched it back until it was out of place. He moved onto the next finger, and the next. Kaide felt his fury rise, not because of the terrible pain, but because the pain ruined his pleasure of watching Sebastian's body mutilated. Somehow, he knew Arthur also realized it, and again and again his fingers were wrenched and twisted, until his hand was a horrible mess of bruises and swelling flesh.

"Look at me," Arthur said, grabbing Kaide's face with his hand. Kaide struggled to focus through the pain. "Look at me, you bastard. Sebastian tried to escape, and when he did, he broke your hand. It is then I ordered his death, and it was my sword that took his life. That is the story you'll tell, no matter how drunk you get around the midnight fire. If you ever say otherwise, to any man or woman, I'll have you executed for treason. Have I made myself clear?"

"Perfectly clear," Kaide said, a grin on his face.

"Good." Arthur stood. "Return to your camp, and make sure the rabble spends all day and night celebrating. Tomorrow, when I move into my brother's castle, you'll disband them. You've found your revenge. I hope it sates you. Return to your forest. Find a place to call your home. It won't be Ashvale, either. Step within twenty miles of there and…"

"…and you'll hang me for a traitor," Kaide said. "I'm not an imbecile. Is there anything else you'd like to tell me before I go? Any other promises you'd like to break?"

Arthur reared back, and his fist struck him in the face. Tears ran down the lord's eyes, but the sadness did not reach his voice.

"My brother also punched you before he died. Now get out of my sight."

Kaide stood, and then struggling to hide the pain he felt, he bent down to retrieve his bloody dirks. Cleaning them off on his shirt, he shoved them into his belt, then bowed low while the rest of the soldiers tensed.

"Such a great day for a party, wouldn't you say?" Kaide asked before stepping out.

He pushed his way through the guards surrounding the tent, not caring for their glares. Winding his way east, he found Adam and Griff waiting for him at one of the fires, the two burly twins standing with their arms crossed over their beefy chests.

"Whose blood is that on your shirt?" asked Adam.

"Sebastian's," Kaide said, and the words put a grin on their faces.

"Hot damn," Griff said. "Arthur's got balls after all."

Kaide drew out a dirk and stabbed it into one of the logs set before the fire, then sat down beside it.

"No," he said. "He doesn't. I killed him against his wishes. We've been ordered to celebrate today, then disband. Someone will soon come parading around Sebastian's head, and we'll toast to his roasting in the Abyss. But come tomorrow…"

"Tomorrow we do nothing," Bellok said, joining them from the mob. "For what else is there to do?"

Bellok was Kaide's wizard, though his skill was marginally higher than an apprentice at the craft. He was cranky and bitter, but often Kaide's most trustworthy advisor. The only person he'd trusted more was his sister, but Luther had taken her from him.

Luther...

"This is my fight now," Kaide said. "There's no reason to put any more of you at risk. Luther will march out tomorrow, and wherever he goes, I will follow. I won't let him escape, not even if he goes to the far ends of the world. But as for you all..."

"Stuff it," Adam said, interrupting him. "You think you're the only one who misses Sandra? She was like a sister to me."

"To both of us," said Griff.

"You have families to return to," Kaide argued.

"Well I don't," Bellok said, running a hand through his white hair. "Or did you forget why we took up arms with you in the first place?"

Kaide looked to the men, and despite his humiliation at the hands of Arthur, despite his fury at such betrayal, he couldn't help but feel proud of everything he'd accomplished.

"Thank you," he said. "But you four only. My feud with Luther has nothing to do with the rest. They wanted a new lord for their farms and villages, and they've gotten it. Let them escape without any more bloodshed. As for us...Luther's not a king or a lord. We need no army to take him down. Just the right moment."

"He's powerful," Bellok said. "And king or not, he still commands a fearsome army. I hope you have something clever in mind."

"There's times for brute force, and times for a clever mind," Kaide said. "I only need to know which one is right for us at the time."

"All and good, but right now's a time for neither of those," Adam said, procuring several mugs of ale that seemed to be magically flooding the eastern half of the camp. "Right now is a time to get completely, fully, thoroughly shit-faced. Sebastian's dead. May he never rest in peace."

"I'll drink to that," Kaide said.

"To the dead," said Bellok.

"Both now and yet to come," Kaide said, and despite the terrible pain of his hands, he lifted the cup and drank.

Redclaw stood in the center of the manmade road, and he let the soft night breeze blow through his ember fur.

He breathed in, and he tried to enjoy the scent of his prey before him. The presence of the priest sapped away all the joy. His wolves would not be allowed to tear through the human ranks with the wild abandon that made them such dangerous warriors. They couldn't howl and feast, the blood of their victims on their tongues. They had to obey rules. They had to obey their god, Cyric.

"You know what must be done," Cyric said to him. "Do it."

With Redclaw's howl, the rest of his pack approached, filling the road and the fields to either side. At his charge, they followed, storming into the dark streets of the village. The defenses were meager. No wall, no soldiers, just a few men who patrolled for thieves and brigands. Redclaw raced ahead of the others, determined to take what little sport there would be that night. He found one of the few wielding a sword and leapt upon him, opening his throat with a single slash. There was no satisfying splash of blood, his claws so hot they cauterized the wound as they cut. Redclaw's disappointment was crushing. Putting his teeth to the man's neck, he bit down, and at last he tasted the blood he craved.

Through the straw huts ran the rest of his pack, smashing open doors and dragging out men, women, and children. Some were bitten, others slashed, but nothing lethal. They had to obey their god. Redclaw stalked through them as the work was done. The village was small, maybe two hundred people. Compared to his thousand wolves, they were nothing, and in minutes the entire town was gathered in the square. They stood huddled and sobbing, rightfully frightened by the great mass of wolf-men that formed a living cage of claw and fur around them.

And then Cyric went to them with open arms.

"I come to you as the living embodiment of your god," he said. "I am Cyric. I am Karak made flesh. Kneel, profess your faith, and live."

Redclaw watched, trying to fight his frustration. His wolf-men were hungry, he knew that, for he was hungry as well. But what they were about to receive didn't feel right. It didn't feel like a hunt. Of the two hundred, all but fifty knelt. Redclaw snorted. No matter how sincere their worship sounded, he doubted even a sliver of the kneeling actually believed Cyric was who he claimed he was. Mankind was a cowardly race, terrified of death. Why would they not bow to spare their lives?

To fight, of course, yet the ones who remained standing were not fighting. They only stood there, shivering, and it made no sense to the wolf.

"Those still standing, step forward," Cyric called to them.

They did. Redclaw saw old people, young, even a few children clutching their parents' hands. He waited, knowing what was to happen next. Calmly Cyric walked to them, and he pulled out five healthy men and women, guiding them to stand separate from the others.

I will claim the faithful, Cyric had told him. *As for the unfaithful, their souls are mine by right, but I will give you a tenth.*

Without a word, Cyric gestured to the five, and that is when the pack descended upon them. They tore and bit at one another, fighting to get at the bodies that were quickly shredded to pieces. Redclaw watched, careful to show no disapproval. It wasn't a hunt, he kept thinking. They were being fed scraps.

Amid the sobs and cries of the rest, Cyric turned on the remaining forty and lifted his hands.

"Your faith is lacking," he said. "But across the tides of time you will repent, and your souls will be spared torment. Know that I do this out of mercy. I do this out of love."

From his hands shot dark fire and lightning, and it tore through their ranks, killing them in ways Redclaw could only guess. Many doubled over, coughing blood, others shaking so violently he thought their bones might break. It was a brutal spectacle, lacking the pride of a claw tearing into flesh. Such strange strength Cyric possessed, but he could not deny it. Within moments the forty-five were dead.

They did not stay dead for long.

"They are not enough," Redclaw said as he rejoined Cyric's side.

"Brick by brick we build the kingdom," Cyric said. "Not wall by wall."

"No," Redclaw insisted. "Them. We are a thousand, and you give us five? My wolves starve."

His god finally looked his way, and something dangerous was in his eyes.

"This village will have many cattle in the outlying fields," he said. "Slaughter half. I trust that will be sufficient until the next village. And if not, see if they have goats as well."

"Goats?" roared Redclaw. "Cattle? We were promised the blood of man, not beasts!"

"Lower your voice," Cyric said.

Redclaw looked away, and though the furious pumping of his heart did not slow, he at least kept his rage in check.

"If you insist," he growled.

"You lose your temper when you are hungry," Cyric said as the wolf-men dispersed into the fields, not needing to be told that they might take the cattle. They would take them anyway. As the remaining people of the village bowed, Cyric walked among them, blessing them, telling them to pray.

"When might I be hungry no longer?" Redclaw asked, thinking the question phrased safely enough to ask.

"We are in the far reaches of Mordan," Cyric said. "These small villages may not satisfy you, but soon we will come to cities whose walls stretch as far as even your fine eyes can see. You will have armies to feast upon, and men whose long blades and heavy armor will give your claws a chance to flex. I have broken no promise to you, so do not blame me for the meagerness of the wilds. Would you eat any better in the Vile Wedge?"

"No," Redclaw said, dipping his head. "We would not. Forgive me."

"You are forgiven," Cyric said. "Now go, be with your kind. I must preach a new wisdom to the converted."

Redclaw thought to return to his pups in the far outskirts, too small to partake in battle, but then changed his mind. He wanted solitude for once, to be away from the enormous pack. As he left, he looked back at the humans gathered at the feet of the priest. It'd be at least two hours before he stopped his preaching and let them return to their homes. Perhaps longer. Such a shame there'd been so many willing to kneel. They might have dined far better otherwise. But there was always another town nearby. It seemed the one truth he knew about humans. There were always more, and for once, it did not frighten him.

That night was the ninth village they'd overtaken, and Redclaw prayed there might be hundreds more.

17

The group of leaders gathered around the map in Tower Silver, and none were pleased with what they were hearing, Darius included.

"It is hard for me to know for certain," Valessa said, looking it over. She tapped Tower Silver, then traced her finger northeast. "But my best guess is that Cyric is somewhere here, leading whatever army he might have."

Darius leaned over in the cramped room, and he shook his head as he counted villages within the vicinity, as well as ones Cyric might have passed through on his way there. The number was frightening.

"At least twelve, if not more," he said. "His progress isn't being slowed in the slightest, either."

"Of course not," Daniel said. "He's fighting unarmed farmers, women and children. But those last three villages we managed to evacuate. The river's letting us stay ahead, and truth be told, it doesn't seem like Cyric's in that much of a hurry to catch up."

"It's not those by the river I'm worried about," Valessa said, turning their attention back to her. "What of those further out?"

Darius could tell what bothered her. A mile from Tower Silver was the town of Wheaton, which they'd already evacuated. But seven miles beyond that was another village by the name of Cade's Rest. They'd sent a single rider to alert them, but so far he had not returned.

"If what you say is right, the mad priest will be here within twenty-four hours, and that's if we're lucky," Daniel said. "We need to move out before nightfall if we're to maintain our separation."

"But what of the town?" Valessa asked.

"If they get here in time, they'll come with us on the boats. Otherwise…" Daniel shrugged his shoulders. "There's not much else to do."

"They won't come," said Livstrom, the soldier in charge of Tower Red. He was an overweight man, and he looked stuffed into the armor he wore. "The people of Cade's Rest are a stubborn bunch, especially the man who leads them. His name's Martin Reid, and even if you showed up with the king's army you'd be hard pressed to make him abandon his lands. Best leave them to their fate."

"No," Darius said, hitting his fist upon the wooden table. "Not acceptable. They're not that far out. I can get them back here in time before Cyric arrives."

"Half the day would be over before you got there," Daniel argued. "You don't have time, even if you can convince them."

"Only if you leave come nightfall," Darius said. "Wait until morning. Give me that. I can convince them. Send a few of the boats south if you must, but we have the time."

"Assuming her guess is right," Daniel said. "She's going off a star in the sky. Forgive me if I'm not so trusting when she puts her finger on the map. And you still haven't told me how you'll persuade them."

"I'm a persuasive guy," Darius said, grinning at him. "After all, you're going to tell me yes, aren't you?"

The older man sighed.

"Gods help me, I think I'm losing my mind…"

Within ten minutes Darius was saddling up the finest gelding Tower Red had to offer. As he started to mount, Valessa joined him in the stable. She wore her plain gray shirt and trousers, and her arms were crossed over her chest.

"You're to go alone?" she asked.

"Seemed to be the plan," Darius said.

"It's a bad one."

"Those seem to work out best for me. If you'd like to come with me, just ask. No need to drug me and steal my horse."

"I had nothing to do with that," she said. "I merely went along with it when I was asked."

"Of course you did," Darius said, and he smiled at her to show all was forgiven. "After all, that was a good plan. Hurry up and saddle another horse, and be careful about it. Your presence seems to make them skittish."

Valessa shook her head.

"You seem to forget, paladin, that the world doesn't hold the same grip on me as it used to…"

Hours later Darius pulled back on the reins of his horse. Less than a quarter mile ahead was the outskirts of Cade's Rest. He'd hoped to see signs of preparations, maybe some wagons loaded up for departure, but instead the village was the same casual bustle that he'd grown accustomed to in the North. So far he'd not encountered any sign of Matt, the rider Livstrom had sent, and his fear for the man's safety grew. Lifting a hand, he waved to the sky, then waited. A moment later a large white dove landed in the road before him, then morphed into Valessa, who stretched her arms and legs.

"I could fly up there for hours," she said.

"Good for you, but I need you down here at my side. That, and I wanted to give you this."

He felt trepidation in doing so, but Darius also knew it was the right thing to do. Reaching into his pack, he pulled out a heavily wrapped bundle of cloth. Within was the dagger Valessa had wielded in Willshire, abandoned when she'd fled with Cyric. He'd kept it from her ever since her return, but no longer.

"It's yours," he said, and he could tell from her hesitation she knew what was inside the thin cloth. "Take it."

She reached out, then stopped.

"I'm not sure I should," she said. "It is an evil blade."

Darius frowned, and gently he unfolded the cloth to expose the dagger. Its blade was dark steel, its hilt expertly crafted. From the blade pulsed a soft red hue. The sight of it made Darius's stomach uncomfortable, as it did whenever he looked upon it.

"The blade is not evil," Darius said. "I do not believe stories and fables. No blade is evil. No blade is good. It is only blessed by the wielder."

"Then it is truly an evil blade," Valessa said. "It used to be mine."

"Then take it back," Darius said, offering it to her. "Make it good."

Like a child reaching out to pet the muzzle of a wolf, Valessa slowly moved to take the dagger. With a sudden burst, as if afraid she might change her mind, she yanked it free of the cloth and held it before her. Immediately the illusion of her vanished, and Darius saw the swirling mass of light and dark that made up her form. The two entities danced, always interlocking, each unable to overwhelm the other. Where her hand touched the hilt, the darkness gathered deeper, swelling like water at the bottom of a well. Darius remained on his horse, not wanting to interfere, but he could see she was struggling. At last he leapt off.

"Stay back!" she screamed, both hands now clutching the hilt. The blade itself was shining a vicious red. The glowing white essence, which ran like veins through her face, across her chest, and spiraled through her arms and legs, was steadily dimming. She fell to her knees, knees that splashed light and darkness as if they were liquid. Darius ignored her impassioned cry, and despite his own fear, he reached out to wrap his hand around hers. His hand sank through to touch the hilt of the blade. Immediately he felt a jolt to his chest, and a sense of fury beyond anything he'd ever felt before. It was the rage of Karak, and whether it was directed at him or Valessa, he did not know, nor did he care.

"Be gone," Darius said to it. "You're wanted no more."

The dagger shook, a tremor building inside it. The rage grew, and for a moment Darius thought he would black out. A ringing filled his ears. He begged Ashhur for strength, and when he heard Valessa screaming, he knew he had to be stronger. He had to be better. Standing firm, he channeled every bit of his own rage into that blade, the betrayal he'd felt, the loss and isolation as everything he'd ever known had been revealed to be a lie. He remembered the loneliness, and then against Karak's rage he flung the sheer joy he'd felt when Jerico reached down his hand and told him to stand.

The ringing vanished, replaced with a sudden, explosive silence. The dagger fell from both their hands, now just an ordinary piece of metal. It landed in the road.

"I've changed my mind," Darius said as his breath returned to him. "Some blades really are evil."

Valessa regained her form, skin shimmering back over her essence.

"Next time you'll listen," she said, picking up the dagger and then sliding it into her belt. How it stayed there, Darius had no idea, nor did he want to know.

"Next time?" he asked. "You think there will be a next time?"

"For that, no," she said. "For listening to me? I hope so. Now what are we to do here?"

Darius turned his attention back to the village.

"First we find out what happened to the rider," he said. "Then we get the town to move."

"And what of Martin Reid? What if he causes trouble?"

"Well," said Darius, grinning, "that's why I gave you your dagger."

They walked into the town, and much to Darius's chagrin, it seemed no one appeared the least bit panicked. The words of the messenger had fallen on deaf ears. Passing through the rows of wood homes and thatched rooms, the people shot them glances but said nothing. Darius didn't like it one bit.

"Not much for hospitality," he said to Valessa, who shrugged.

"Your armor doesn't make you look like the most welcoming of men."

"True. Perhaps you should put on your silver armor and purple cloak. Might as well match me."

She snickered at him but said nothing.

Halfway through town they met a group of five coming from the other way. Four of them were big men, with burly arms and heavyset chests built from long hours in the fields. The fifth was a small man, balding, and he wore a long black robe.

"Really?" Darius muttered as he came to a halt. "Livstrom couldn't bother to say Martin was a priest?"

"Welcome, friend," said the priest. "My name is Martin Reid, and this is my village of Cade's Rest. We do not see travelers often, but I assure you our accommodation will be welcoming, so long as you bring no trouble."

"And if we do?" Valessa asked.

Martin's beady eyes narrowed.

"Troublemakers are not welcome here, nor liars, thieves, murderers, or any other sinners."

"The only village without sinners is an empty village," Darius said. "We've come looking for a friend of ours, a rider from Tower Red named Matt. Might you have seen him?"

Martin frowned, and Darius didn't like the way the other four men tensed and looked at one another.

"A man by that name came here," Martin said. "He spoke lies in a feeble attempt to rob our village. He suffered punishment for it. If you so desire, you may return his body to Livstrom at the Tower Red for a military burial."

Darius's jaw dropped open.

"Matt was sent here to warn your village of an attack," he said, feeling his anger rising. "An attack that is still coming! Everyone here must take what they can and head east toward the Gihon."

Martin crossed his arms.

"These lands are mine," he said. "They have been in my family for three generations, and when I took the cloth of Karak my duty to these people only grew, for now I must supply not only their earthly needs but their spiritual as well. Your armor is not of the king's, but of Ashhur. What authority do you have to speak to me in such a way? Who are you to order me?"

The arrogance was astounding. Darius reached for his sword, and the other men drew theirs, fine shortswords that were cleanly polished. Martin stood there, waiting. Darius glanced at Valessa. So far she looked bored. The men could do nothing to her, but if the priest had any sort of power, then he was a threat. If Darius eliminated them quickly, perhaps targeting the priest while Valessa took out the men…

No, he thought, shaking his head. He let his hand fall to his side, not once touching the hilt. Coming in, shedding blood, and then demanding the people obey him felt too horribly similar to what he'd witnessed Velixar do to Durham.

"My name is Darius, and I speak for Daniel Coldmine, lord of the Blood Tower. The message I bring is true, and I will have no man question it. A madman is coming south with an army, and he will kill every man, woman, and child here. We must flee, now. If this village is yours, as you say, then give the order."

"Darius?" asked Martin, and the excited way he said it put a pit in the paladin's stomach. "Darius, the betrayer? Last I heard you carried a bounty on your head. Now you come claiming to speak for the man who put a warrant out for your death in the first place?"

"This is getting ugly," Valessa whispered into his ear.

Darius glanced around and saw that villagers were gathering, all wielding crude weapons of some kind. Over fifty surrounded them. Darius swallowed. He'd come to save their lives. Slaughtering half their village to do it felt like a mockery of such a goal.

"You won't kill me, Martin," Darius said. "Far better men have tried. If you will not believe me, then give the choice to the others. Let me speak my piece, then leave. No one needs to die here, not by my hand. What comes beyond, though, will not be on my head."

"No one leaves," Martin said. "And if you do not throw down your weapon and surrender, it will be you who dies today."

"I have a better idea," Valessa said. She strode toward Martin without making a single threatening motion. Martin tensed, and he lifted a hand.

"Stay where you…"

In a single smooth motion Valessa drew her dagger, thrust it into Martin's heart, then spun. Blood spurted as the dagger came free, and without a care to the remaining four, she walked back to Darius's side. The whole town stood stunned silent, and the men that had been Martin's bodyguards were clearly frightened by the speed Valessa displayed.

"We have words to speak," she shouted to the crowd. "Listen well, then make your choice."

It was a moment before Darius snapped out of his daze and addressed the villagers, warning them of Cyric's approach. Most stood shocked still, a few coughing or heckling at his warning.

"You have one hour," he told them. "Then we must depart. Take only what you can carry. Bring food, clothes, and blankets. Your life is not worth your possessions, now hurry!"

A few rushed away, and many others shared looks, no doubt wondering if they should believe him. Frustrated, Darius pointed to one of the big men.

"You," he said. "Lead me to where Matt's body is."

They found him hanging from a post on the opposite side of town. He'd been stripped of his armor and hanged naked from the waist up. Carved into his chest was a single word. Liar. Darius stared at it as he felt his blood boil.

"He came to help you," he said, turning on the man who'd brought him there.

"Martin swore he was a brigand who stole the armor he wore," said the man.

"So you killed him without proof?"

The man shrugged.

"Martin owned the lands my crops are growing on. Would you give up your home and crops for some stranger? Besides, Martin said he spoke for god."

"Indeed he did," Valessa said, staring at the word carved into Matt's chest. "And such a loving god he is."

They sent the man on his way, then cut down the body. Darius knew he couldn't transport the body back, so he asked about until someone loaned him a shovel, and then outside the village limits he began to dig. Valessa sat on the grass and watched him.

"Why?" she finally asked.

"Helps pass the time," Darius said as he jammed the shovel into the dirt.

"I mean why give the people a choice? You know those who remain here will die, or meet a fate even worse than death. Without the priest, no one here can stop me. Give the order, and make them obey."

Darius chuckled.

"The thought's been on my mind this whole while, Valessa, but every time I think to do it my stomach ties itself into knots. I'm not going to kill people while claiming to save them. That's something Cyric would do. That's something I might have done once. No longer. Now help me with the body."

They'd arrived in the late afternoon, and once Matt's body was buried, Darius and Valessa waited at the eastern exit of town. He'd planned to leave after an hour, but at the pitiful few that gathered there, he let time stretch, and twice more he cried out to the town. Of their three hundred, only sixty came.

"The sun's setting," Valessa said to him when he came back from a third attempt to bring more.

"I know," he said.

"We have to leave."

He sighed.

"I know."

They had two carts pulled by horses, and they put as many children in one as they could, their supplies in the other. Many of the adults looked embarrassed to be there. They thought he might be lying, Darius knew. They thought in a week or two they'd return to Cade's Rest, shamefaced and terribly behind in their work in the fields. The worst of it was that Darius wished they were right. Far better that than there being no one left to return shamefaced to.

Valessa walked at the front of the sullen band, and Darius joined her side as the town steadily drifted into the distance.

"How far is he?" he asked.

"Thirty miles or so," she said, staring at the sky.

Darius bit his tongue to hold in a curse. They had seven miles to travel on their own just to get to the Blood Tower.

"Cyric's been traveling at night, hasn't he?" he asked.

Valessa nodded, souring Darius's mood further.

"Just perfect. Then we travel at night as well."

The miles passed, and when the sun set, thankfully the sky was clear. Under starlight they followed the road to Wheaton, from which Tower Red was but a mile. Darius moved through the ranks, talking to them, encouraging them, but found words difficult.

"What do I do?" Darius asked Valessa after the first hour. "Reassuring them they made the right choice is the same as telling them the friends and family they left behind are dead."

"Then say nothing, if you're so afraid the truth will hurt them," she told him.

Darius looked to the distance, and Cade's Rest.

"We needed more time," he said, letting out a sigh.

When they arrived at Wheaton, most of the children had fallen asleep in the cart, and the others looked tired, their emotions frayed. Darius stopped them at the edge of the village, for in the past few minutes he'd felt a strange urgency in his mind. It was foreign to him, but the closer he got to Wheaton, the more certain he became that it was a warning from Ashhur.

"Something's not right," he told Valessa.

They stared into the village, waiting, and then they saw the first of the shadows moving.

"A scouting party," Valessa said.

"How far away is Cyric?" he asked.

"Five miles at least," she said after a quick glance at the stars.

"Then we have a chance." He stood beside the cart with the children and called the others around him. "Stay close," he said. "I fear a small force of the enemy is already here. Wake your children and keep them alert. They might need to run with you should things turn ill. Remember, always go east to the river, and from there to Tower Red."

He watched the panic bubbling beneath the surface of the crowd, but they remained strong. Darius drew his sword, and as the soft light bathed over him, he felt himself calm.

"I'll draw them to me," he said to Valessa. "Stay in the rear, and take them out quickly while they're still overconfident."

Valessa drew her dagger and nodded. With a wave, Darius led the two carts into the village. Wheaton had been completely deserted, so through empty streets they walked. Darius kept his head on a swivel, checking either side of the road as they passed. With their numbers, and him leading the way, he hoped whatever creatures serving Cyric might decide to not take them on.

Valessa drifted toward the back of the group, looking no different from the others. The surprise would easily be worth a kill or three, thought Darius. Several times Darius caught glimpses of shadows moving around them, and from the gasps of others he knew he was not the only one. After a minute, Valessa returned to the front.

"Wolf-men," she whispered into his ear. "At least ten."

Darius nodded.

"Bloody fantastic," he said, thinking of the horde that had attacked Durham. Alone they'd been deadly. With a mad priest leading them? He didn't want to think about that. Urging the people along, he bade Valessa back to her place of ambush, then lifted his sword high. The light shone upon them all. Let the wolves see who protects them, thought Darius. Let them know the death awaiting their charge.

If they knew, they were not afraid. A sudden cacophony of roars heralded the wolf-men, ambushing from a dozen various buildings. They leapt from the alleys, they leapt from the rooftops. Darius screamed for the people to run, his voice lost amid sixty others crying out in panic. Only two attacked him from the front, and he rushed at them like a madman. No time, he had no time. The first to lunge had its belly opened. The other tried to use its greater size and weight to bury him, but Darius's blade stabbed through its chest, and a twist sent it toppling to the side instead of crashing atop him. He had only the briefest moment to notice the way the wolf-man's black claws shimmered red before he turned around to the people of Cade's Rest.

They fled along the road as he'd bidden them, but from what Darius could tell, nearly fifteen wolf-men had joined in the ambush. There were too many of them, and they slashed and cut through weak, unarmored flesh with a wild frenzy. Darius rushed into the gore and death, and he prayed Valessa would match him kill for kill. The first wolf-man he neared was too busy gorging himself on the innards of a dead man to notice. His sword lopped off its head with a single swing.

"To me!" Darius screamed. The people fled, and the wolf-men heard his challenge and rushed to meet it. A heavyset gray was the first to near, his mouth already smeared with blood. He held the arm of a man in his left hand, wielding it like an obscene club. The horror didn't seem to register to Darius. He felt furious yet strangely in control. He felt powerful, yet helpless to prevent the deaths happening all about him. More than anything, he saw the wolf-men and wanted to stop their killing. His sword lashed out, cutting through the severed arm. His foe dropped it and bared his teeth. They too shimmered with red. In answer, Darius shoved his sword into the mouth, pushing all the way through the creature's skull.

Four dead, yet far too many left. Corpses were everywhere. Two more wolf-men rushed him simultaneously, and with a cold stare Darius met their uncontrolled rage. Claws swiped toward him, and he stepped back, and even parried one paw as if it were a blade. Instead of cutting through, the sword sparked at the mere contact against those glowing claws. He seemed just as surprised as the wolf-man, but he recovered faster. His sword shoved through the muscular chest and pierced the heart.

Too deep, thought Darius, struggling to pull the blade out in time. The other creature struck him across the chest, the claws punching deep grooves into his platemail. The force of the impact knocked the breath from his lungs.

Unable to hold onto the sword, he fell back as another swipe cut across his arm. He felt blood drip down to his elbow, and it spiked with pain.

Unarmed, Darius had no way to hurt the monstrous creature. His foe howled at the top of his lungs, then tensed for a leap. He never got off the ground. Valessa landed atop him, repeatedly stabbing his eyes with her dagger. The wolf-man let out a stinging howl, then collapsed. Valessa stood atop the corpse, her body strangely still. A normal woman would have shaken with the adrenaline of a kill, and blood should have covered her from the fight, but she was clean as always.

"How many?" Darius asked, clutching his left arm and trying to decide how bad it was.

"I killed four," she said. "Five if I count yours. The rest fled."

Darius bent down to retrieve his sword. Putting a boot against the wolf-man's chest, he yanked it free with a sickening plop. With a heavy intake of air, he stood to his full height. Grunting against the pain in his chest, he lifted the blade high into the air. The light shone far, and he hoped those who fled through the city would see it and know they were safe.

"How many?" he asked again.

"I told you, five."

"No," Darius said, shaking his head. "How many of ours?"

Valessa put away her dagger, and her hesitance in answering was enough.

"At least half," she said at last.

Darius nodded, his teeth clenched tight for he knew nothing else to say. He'd led them there for safety. For that, thirty had died, perhaps more. Valessa reached out toward him, then let her hand fall. Darius saw strange markings on her clothing as she did, and he stepped closer.

"Are you all right?" he asked.

In answer, Valessa lifted her arm again, let him see the claw marks that shone red against her ribs, refusing to change like the rest of her. Liquid shadow dripped from them, intermixed with a light that shone like silver as it bled to the ground.

"Their claws," she said. "Cyric has blessed them."

He could just barely hear it in her voice, but it was there. Fear. Taking a step closer, he yanked off one of his gauntlets and then pressed his hand against her face, which she kept firm so he might make contact. Neither said a word, but they understood each other. They were both vulnerable now. They both bore wounds.

"You won't die to them," he promised. "You'll die on your terms, and only after Cyric, not before."

"Don't make promises you cannot keep," she said.

"It is a promise I can keep," he said. "If you'll help me."

Two hours before dawn they rode up to Tower Red, just a pitifully small band. Daniel's men welcomed them warmly despite the early hour. Many were led to the docks without a moment of rest, to board boats kept waiting all that time.

"Was it worth it?" Daniel asked Darius as he met him at the gates.

"Worth it?" Darius said. "Thirty will live that might have died. Yes, it was worth it."

"Funny, then, that you don't look so eager to celebrate."

"I said it was worth it," Darius said. "I never claimed it was easy. Get us to a boat. I want to be miles from here when Cyric comes with his damn wolf-men."

Daniel clapped him on the back, eliciting a groan of pain.

"You try to do too much, paladin," he said. "It'll get you killed one day."

"Better to die trying for too much than dying old having done too little," Darius said, earning himself a chuckle.

"You'll get your chance," Daniel said as they approached the docks. "Once we hit Tower Silver, we'll be abandoning the river, instead making a run toward the Castle of the Yellow Rose. I'm sure you'll get plenty of opportunities to die along the way, you and your demon girl."

18

They marched out at dawn, and Jerico felt like a sheep among wolves as they passed by Lord Arthur's camp.

He kept his armor on, and his mace clipped to his side. Against the glares from the other priests and paladins it was meager protection. He touched his shield often, and only from its soft light did he receive comfort.

"Help me out here," Jerico muttered to Ashhur. "I think I'm in way too deep."

Luther had made it clear he was a guest, so he walked to the outskirts of the camp and waited. Many men saw him, and it didn't take long until Arthur himself arrived.

"Jerico!" he called out, and the relief was palpable in his voice. Amid it was guilt, and despite everything, it made Jerico smile.

"Rule well," he said. "Rule fair."

And that was it. He gave him no other wisdom, no other knowledge of why he lived or where they were going. He'd thought briefly of trying to enlist Arthur's aid in fighting Cyric, but Luther appeared insistent on dealing with the mad priest on his own. Was it pride? Jerico didn't think so, but then again, he couldn't pretend to know Luther all that well.

"I will," Arthur promised as he walked away. "I would have you proud of me."

Luther's army marched along the road, well-disciplined and well-supplied. Jerico knew without a shadow of a doubt it could have crushed Arthur's army, without need for walls and castles. Luther's plan had been flawless, and after

Arthur's death, it wouldn't have taken long before Sebastian was reinstated as their puppet ruler, always in fear for his life. That all this had been abandoned because of Cyric only reinforced how great a threat he was to the North, if not all of Dezrel.

Jerico kept to the rear of the army, with the rest of the mercenaries. Most paid him no heed other than the occasional glare. Far better that than the aura of loathing he felt from the priests and paladins at the vanguard. When they stopped for their midday meal, a young squire found him sitting amid the grass far from the road.

"My master, Luther, asked that I ensure you have enough to eat and drink," said the freckle-faced boy. As he said it, he offered a waterskin as well as a wrapped package that smelled of smoked meat. Jerico took both and thanked him, and in silence he ate, enjoying the momentary privacy. Before him stretched fields of farmland, stopped only by a distant pine forest. They traveled to the river, and from there they'd head north. Jerico wondered how Darius fared. He'd gone to the Blood Tower in hopes of removing the bounty on his head, and he must have been there when Sir Robert was overthrown. Had he survived? If so, where was he now?

As Jerico wondered, he saw a thin trail of smoke rising from the distant forest. He thought little of it, and then came the call to resume the march.

Come nightfall, Jerico wanted to do little more than stretch out his sore legs and sleep in the soft grass. Instead the same squire returned, inviting him to Luther's tent. With a sigh, the paladin agreed, and to the north of the army he went.

"Welcome," said Luther as he stepped inside. "I am glad you chose to join me."

"The last time I was in your tent I tried to crush your skull with my mace," Jerico said. "Are you sure I should be so welcome?"

Luther lay propped up on pillows, his face pale. When he spoke, each word came out labored.

"I remember," he said. "You promised to kill me, if I recall correctly. That is why you should never promise to take another's life. The gods might decide to amuse themselves."

Whatever wound he suffered was affecting him greatly, and Jerico could tell he was worse off than the day before. He knew he should ask, but didn't want to. Part of him enjoyed seeing the priest in pain, as much as it shamed him.

"What is it you want?" he asked. "Or am I here just to reminisce about good times?"

Luther shifted the pillows so he might sit up higher.

"I have not known many paladins of Ashhur," he said. "But all I met were the same. Men who thought they were good. Men who thought they were better than everyone about them. Most of all, they hated the very sight of me. You were different. Even when you were my prisoner, you did not look upon me with hatred, not that first time."

He shook his head.

"Now you are like all the others. The world will not weep for your passing, Jerico. Not anymore."

Jerico breathed in deep, and he begged Ashhur for patience. There was some truth to Luther's words, however bitter they were to hear.

"You're right," he said. "I should not hate you, and it shames me still. But I don't hate you for what you are, Luther. I don't hate you for the robes you wear, or the god you worship. I hate you for what you've done to me. I hate you for what you did to Sandra. You took her from me, and for what reason? A colder, crueler man I have never known. Ashhur asks that I love all the world, from the sinners to the kings. In this, I fail him. In you I see little to admire, and nothing to love."

Luther listened to this with his head bowed and his eyes downcast. When Jerico stopped, silence lingered between them, broken only by Luther's raspy breathing.

"I have thought often of her since that day," Luther said when Jerico stood to leave. "I never expected to. When I cast my spell, I saw the light in your eyes die. I saw your hope crushed, and it was everything I'd desired. But to see the joy on that woman's face suddenly extinguished...she had never harmed me. No, she didn't even disobey me, for Kaide is far too stubborn a man to listen to anyone, not even his sister. Yet I killed her. I thought I'd teach you, teach Kaide, teach the whole North a lesson. But it was...wrong of me to do so in such a way."

Jerico stood there, lost in a swirl of emotions he could not make sense out of. Looking at the priest, he tried to understand him. Ashhur's gift assured him the man spoke the truth, every word of it. But what did it mean? What did it change?

"You took the life of another, all to torture me," he said. "I strive to not hate you, yet you so openly hate me. What have I ever done to deserve this? Or is the god you serve so terribly cruel? What a joke this is, that we march to stop Cyric as if the Karak he envisions is any worse than the god you serve."

His heart hammered in his chest, and even then Jerico had to fight down his rage. It would be so easy to attack the priest, to give in to his fury. Crushing the skull of a wounded man...what a way to honor Sandra's memory.

Luther breathed in deep, then let out a sigh.

"I do not expect you to understand, but I will try," he said. "There is fire in the Abyss, and who better knows how to avoid it than the god who rules amid it? We preach an ironclad law, a way to live so that men may escape the purifying fire through their works. Yet you paladins of Ashhur would show men a different way. It is easier, to be sure. Weaker. You elevate the sinner instead of condemning him. You cast aside all laws and rituals in favor of a single moment of repentance. You lead men astray, Jerico, how can you not see that? You heal wounds with your hands, but we purify the wretched with fire. We spill the blood of thieves and murderers, and like a gardener we pull away the weeds so the pure may become numerous. You are a destroyer of souls. Your words send men and women to an eternity of torment until Karak's fire can purge away every last bit of their sin. And then you wonder why I hate you. You wonder why we so desperately desire the blight of your faith removed from the world. Is it not obvious? Is it not, even to one of the blasphemers, something so easy to understand?"

Jerico opened his mouth, then closed it. Against such a mind, his words would mean nothing.

"I am not a strong man," Luther continued. "Nor am I a good one. But I am faithful. I pray that faithfulness will lead us to victory in the end. But what I did to Sandra was done out of spite. It was done out of malice. I will not ask for your forgiveness, for it is folly to ask for forgiveness from sinners. Karak's forgiveness is all I will seek."

"Then why tell me?" Jerico asked.

At last Luther met his eye.

"Because you are a good man, and seeing hatred in your eyes sickens me. If only you were as faithful as you were good. To have you at my side would be a wonderful thing. Imagine us together, instructing the weak of this world, and through our strength helping Dezrel become a new kingdom of righteousness."

Jerico felt something in his heart finally give way. Luther's words had helped him, though not in any way he might have expected. He knelt before the priest. Reaching out a hand, he touched Luther's chest, and immediately he felt the wound. Closing his eyes, Jerico began to pray. His hatred, while not gone, was greatly lessened. Instead it had been replaced with pity. White light shone about his hands, and after only a hesitation, he plunged it into the wound. Luther gasped in air as his body straightened. Finished, Jerico stood.

"We save this world by healing it," Jerico said. "Not with fire, not with destruction. I pray you one day realize this, and believe."

Luther touched the bandages on his chest, and when he spoke, his voice was firm, healthy.

"A good man," he said. "But we don't seek to make good men. We seek believers. Go your way, Jerico. I will ensure the rest of my brethren treat you with respect."

Jerico stepped out of the tent into the far reaches of the camp. The privacy was welcome after such a long day amid the mercenaries. For a moment Jerico looked over the rows of campfires and tents, seeing an army sworn to kill, fight, and destroy in the name of Karak. It made him sad, but at least it might accomplish something worthwhile if they stopped Cyric's conquest. As he walked away, he glanced back, thinking of the torn, twisted priest inside.

Shadows moved, and then the tent shook as several men entered.

Pulling his shield off his back, Jerico charged, knowing he had not a second to waste. Through the tent flap he barged. In the confined space he found Kaide standing in the center, his dirks drawn. The wizard Bellok stood beside him, Adam and Griff each holding one of Luther's arms.

The priest himself was gagged, and his face reddened as he struggled to breathe.

"Kaide," Jerico said, for he knew not what else to say. The brigand was at first startled by his entrance, but seeing who it was, he smiled.

"It was a cowardly thing Arthur did, trading you," he said. "But I'm glad you're alive. You should be here with me when this bastard dies."

"Don't!"

Jerico flung himself between him and Luther. The dirks bounced off his shield. Nothing could match the shock and betrayal he saw in Kaide's eyes.

"How dare you?" he asked. "Have you gone mad?"

"Get out of here Kaide," Jerico said. "You don't need to do this."

"I do," Kaide said. "Sebastian's dead, and by my hand. It felt good, Jerico. It felt so damn good, but it didn't last, and you know why? Because Luther is still alive. He killed Sandra. She died in your arms for the gods' sake. How can you defend him?"

With his shield still blocking Kaide, Jerico pulled free his mace and pointed it at the two Irons twins.

"Let him go," he said.

Adam leaned to the side so he could see Kaide.

"We could break his neck, if you'd like," he said.

"No," Kaide said. "No, his life is mine. Move out of the way, Jerico. I don't want to hurt you."

"And you won't," said Jerico. "Last time, get out now. Go to your daughter. Find happiness, but not through this. I traded my life for Sebastian's, yet you killed him anyway? Save yourself, Kaide. Save yourself before it's too late."

The standoff continued, Jerico bouncing his attention between both sides. Either of the twins was capable of wrestling him to the ground, and Jerico had seen firsthand the speed and skill Kaide possessed with those dirks. So worried about them, he almost didn't catch the subtle waggling of Bellok's fingers as he cast a spell.

Jerico shoved his shield in the way. For a half-second he felt a terrible exhaustion clawing at his eyes, but then the light of his shield flared, and the spell broke. The motion stirred the two Irons brothers into action, Adam securing Luther with both hands while Griff flung himself at Jerico. The paladin shifted so the hilt of his mace jammed into Griff's stomach, blasting the wind out of him. Griff was a big man, though, and that was hardly enough to stop him. As his momentum kept him moving forward, Jerico turned and pushed with his shield, flinging him in the way of Kaide's desperate lunge. During the brief respite as the two were entangled, Jerico spun on Adam.

"I'll break him," Adam said, his hands tightening around Luther's neck.

"You won't," Jerico said, and in a single smooth motion he stepped close and struck Adam with the base of his mace. It connected between his eyes, and in his daze his arms loosened, and Luther slipped free.

Kaide, sensing their advantage almost gone, rushed Jerico, and his dirks flashed with blinding speed. Jerico blocked two strikes with his shield, and with a hard counter he sent a dirk flying from Kaide's hand. The move put him off balance, though, and like a dancer Kaide angled about him, avoiding his feeble attempt to block the way. With nothing between him and Luther, Kaide ran, his dirk hungry for blood. Jerico shouted for him to stop but knew it was pointless.

Luther, however, had pulled free the cloth from his mouth.

Shadows pooled before him, forming a shield. Kaide's dirk hit it and bounced off, filling the tent with the sound of reverberating steel coupled with a crack of thunder. The brigand tried sidestepping, but with a twist of Luther's wrist the shadow-shield followed, remaining between them. Jerico moved to help him, but both Irons twins flung themselves atop him, each wrestling control of an arm.

"Wait," said Luther, his voice surprisingly calm. "I would make you an offer, Kaide, if you would give me but a moment to listen."

"Speak," Kaide said, a dirk still dancing eagerly in his hand.

"As I told Jerico, I have wronged both of you greatly in what I did to Sandra. In this, I will make amends. You may face me, Kaide, and me alone."

"A duel?" Kaide said, and there was no hiding his surprise.

"Yes, a duel, a single chance for you to find your vengeance. But not yet. I must stop Cyric, a man who threatens to enslave every last man, woman, and child your army has fought to protect. Come with us. Help us kill him, as Jerico has also sworn to do. When my former pupil's body lies at my feet, then the matter between us shall be settled."

Kaide looked to Jerico, still pinned by the twins.

"Is he telling the truth?" he asked.

"He is," said Jerico. "But that doesn't mean you should agree. Go home. Go back to Beth."

Kaide breathed in deep, then put away his dirk.

"I'll help you," he said. "Though no god will keep you safe if you dare betray me."

"If you say so," Luther said, the shield before him vanishing.

Kaide strode to the tent's flap, and the rest followed.

"We'll be close," he said.

When they were gone, Luther straightened his robes and began to put right his things. Jerico rubbed his neck, which was sore from the awkward position he'd been held in.

"A duel?" he asked as the priest fixed his bed.

"Yes, a duel," Luther said, turning. "Why, would you like one as well?"

Jerico was so stunned by the sour humor in the priest's voice it took a full second before a smile spread across his face.

"No," he said. "I'd like a peaceful night's rest. Good night, Luther. And good luck to you when you duel Kaide. I know I'd never like to be the one facing his wrath."

"You just did," Luther said, grabbing several pillows and piling them back together. "For that, I thank you."

"Didn't do it for you," he said, stepping out into the moonlight. This time, no shadows lay wait in ambush, and he found an isolated spot of grass, set down his blanket, and slept.

19

In the dark of night Cyric stood listening to the cries of his
slaves. No one else might hear them, but he could, and it
filled him with anguish. Were they still so blind to the
dangers their souls faced? All they seemed to know was fear
and anger. So few acknowledged him as the god he was,
instead they were content to curse his name and beg for
either freedom or death.

"For you," he told them, and though he was a full mile
from his camp he knew they would still hear. "I do this all
for you."

Their number was growing, and sadly at a far faster
rate than he'd hoped. Where were the faithful? When his
wolf-men charged into these backwater villages, why did so
many refuse to bend the knee? He didn't desire
enslavement. He didn't wish their souls trapped in corpses,
forced to march behind his army for however many
centuries. What he asked for was faithfulness, for
obedience. What sane man would deny him that? It wasn't
as if he strode into the villages and demanded they sacrifice
their firstborn or throw themselves upon a fire. Obedience.
Faithfulness. How lost Dezrel had grown for these things
to be so rare, to be so frightening.

Beside him flowed the Gihon, and he stared across the
waters to the wild lands of the Wedge beyond. They'd been
following the river south, but as they neared greater
civilization it'd become harder to keep his forces together.
Soon Redclaw would have to rule on his own, in lands far
from Cyric. Who then would create the undead faithful?

Perhaps if Redclaw kept them imprisoned, waiting for his arrival. Or maybe he was deluding himself in thinking he might save so many. The world was a wretched place. It seemed no matter what he did, souls would be lost. Feeling guilt for those he could not save was not proper, not when they had turned their backs on him.

But at least they were just lost children, ignorant of the wisdom of Karak. The same could not be said for Valessa.

Cyric knelt beside the river, and as he stared at his moonlit reflection he watched his face change into a vision of the gray sister. She'd been one of Karak's most loyal. It'd been her place to hunt down and kill those who betrayed the faith. In death she'd failed, and Karak in his mercy had given her a new body and a new chance to wash away her failure. For her to break faith, even when her very life was owed to Karak, was a betrayal of the highest order. He'd thought it only a matter of time before he found her, for day by day more of the North fell under his grasp. Yet his scouts had recently returned, telling of their defeat by her hands, as well as by a man who wielded a shining blade of light.

"Do you feel guilt, Valessa?" Cyric asked the watery reflection. "Do you fear the great retribution you will feel at my hands for all eternity? How you will burn, Valessa. Your very existence is an insult, one that must be remedied."

Yes, his decision was made. As long as she remained, she was a thorn digging into his mind. Finally he would extract it.

Day by day he felt his power growing, the strength of his imprisoned essence flowing into the newly living. With closed eyes, Cyric lifted his arms to the heavens and felt his spirit sour free of mortal flesh. Below him the lands passed in a blur, and then he arrived in the center of the rebel's camp. They encircled Tower Silver, hundreds huddled around fires and beneath dilapidated tents. Nearby was an armed man holding a torch, but Cyric walked past him without fear. The man's eyes were closed to the spirit world. He would see nothing, sense only the briefest hint of his passing. Toward the southern edge Cyric walked, for it was there he could feel Valessa's presence. In his mind's eye she pulsed like a great beacon, like a dying star.

Most of the camp was asleep, but he did not expect Valessa to be. Her gifted form had surpassed such a mortal need. At her tent he gathered his strength. Miles away his body lay unconscious beside the river, but his strength was the essence of his soul. It burned with fire, with faith, for why should it not? He was Karak made flesh, the god of Dezrel come to save them all. Into the tent he stepped, and he discovered Valessa's capabilities for blasphemy had stretched even further than he gave her credit for. In the cot beside her slept Darius, the traitor paladin.

For one brief moment he dared feel fear. He remembered his shame in Willshire, when he'd fled from that glowing blade. But his strength had been like that of a child compared to the power he wielded now. A needed lesson, he told himself. A reminder that his power could indeed be limited if he closed his mind and did not fully embrace his godhood.

"Hello Valessa," Cyric said, focusing his attention on her. He didn't need to introduce himself, for her whole body shimmered with fear at his entrance.

"How are you here?" she asked.

At this, he laughed.

"You stand before your god, yet ask such simple questions. Is that your deficiency? Is that why you so easily gave into fear and cowardice?"

There was no way for her to deny it. Her terror held her immobile. Cyric walked closer, and a red glow shone from every surface of his body.

"You're not my god," she said, but it was such a weak denial. "You're a madman."

"Mad, perhaps," he said. "I am mad when I see you walking free in this world. I am mad when I see others spitting in the face of the one who gave them life. But you're wrong about one thing, Valessa. I am not a man."

He outstretched his hand.

"You no longer deserve your gift," he said. "And so I take it back."

She started to scream, but he silenced it in a heartbeat. Power flowed from his hand, and it tore at her form. He knew she could feel pain, and what she did feel must have been intense, but it was nothing compared to what she'd feel as the eons rolled along and she burned in the purifying fires of the Abyss. The woman crumpled to her knees, and she flashed with shadow and light. Her mouth remained open in a silent, wordless scream. Tears ran down her face, and when they touched the ground they were red like blood. She looked so pitiful, so weak, but Cyric hardened his heart against mercy. This is what he'd come to do. Valessa had been given enough chances to make amends.

"Enough," said Darius, and that single word sent a shiver through the soul-being of Cyric. Chastising himself for his fear, he turned and smiled at the traitor paladin.

"He awakes," he said. "Not that it will change anything."

Darius grabbed his sword from beside the bed as Cyric pointed a hand toward him. From his palm shot a great beam of shadow. The beam struck the light of Darius's sword, and then they battled as Cyric tried to pour more of his power into his attack. Being separated from his body by such a great distance weakened him, but against a faithless wretch like Darius, he knew he still possessed enough. Willshire was an aberration, the mere stumbling of a child learning to walk. Curling his fingers, he poured his righteous fury into the attack. The beam halted, and instead a shadowy sword shimmered into being, striking at Darius from behind. He spun to block, but not in time. The blade passed through his armor and into his flesh. It did not break skin, and no blood splashed. Instead it set his muscles aflame, filling him with spasms that left him gasping on the floor, arms and neck straining into awkward positions. The sword fell from his grasp, the light on its blade fading away.

"Where was I?" he asked, turning back to Valessa. She still knelt, struggling to maintain form. Her skin was translucent, her features hazy and without color. She looked like an unpainted doll. The gift of Karak still flowed through her, and with a wave he beckoned it back. No longer would she profane her god. No longer would her existence eat away at his subconscious.

Shadows bled out of her, from her eyes, her nose, even the tips of her fingers. Her mouth hung open, and she thrashed upon the ground. Then she melted. It was the only way to describe the death happening before him. Her body turned liquid and ran into itself, bones like jelly, flesh peeling away to nothing.

"Stop it!" Darius cried before his jaw locked tight.

Cyric smiled. This was it, the final moments…but then as the last of the darkness was revoked, she still remained. His smile faltered. The skin and hair were gone, Valessa stripped down to her very essence. For a moment he did not see, but then the light shone. He recoiled in horror. What had happened to her? She had been one of the unfinished, a being blessed with a shadowed, shifting life, yet now the light of Ashhur burned within her. Her body reformed, the skin shimmering back over the light. When Valessa's eyes reopened, a fury burned in them far greater than ever before.

"Thank you," she said, but there was only rage in her voice.

Cyric cast a bolt of shadow at her, but she ducked it, instead rushing for Darius's sword. Grabbing the hilt, she shoved it into Darius's hands. The white light shone, and Cyric noticed it did nothing to her now. If anything, it made the life in her skin grow more vibrant. But the curse coursing through Darius's flesh broke, and together they stood to face him.

"What blasphemy is this?" Cyric asked. "Have you so fully abandoned your god that you would turn to Ashhur in your folly?"

"What god is that?" Valessa asked. "You?"

In answer, Cyric pushed his hands together and released wave after wave of pain and torment. There was no blocking it, no avoiding it, and he saw it immediately reflected upon Darius's face. That he stood at all was a miracle. Valessa, however, only stepped closer with a look of maddening calm.

"You're not a god," she said. "You're not even a man. You're a mad dog, Cyric. And we will put you down."

Her hand became a shining blade of light. He crossed his arms, but it punched right through, burning a hole in his robes and leaving a gaping wound in his chest that bled shadow. With a cry he flew back, back across the hills and over the Gihon to where his body lay on the grass, gasping. With a moment of disorientation he plunged into it. The pain hit him then, and he screamed out into the night.

"You bitch," he moaned as he curled onto his knees and tore at the grass. "You would deny me even now?"

Deep in his chest he felt a fire burning. With each passing moment it lessened, but still the ache was unbearable, and greater was the insult it represented. Not a god, she'd told him. Not a man. Who was she to declare such things? She was Ashhur's last resistance, he realized. She and the traitor were the best the failed god could do to protect himself, and both had been stolen from the ranks of Karak. Of course they were stronger. Of course they were dangerous. Twisted faith always was.

"I will show you," Cyric said as he rose to his feet. He stared south, and in his mind's eye the miles were but inches. He beheld the tower, and the many tents alongside it.

"I will show you all. I will not be mocked, nor denied. I am a god, you fools, a god!"

His voice echoed across the camp so that all there heard his proclamation, bearing witness to his fury in the final moments before their deaths. With all his power he clutched the ground. Let the very earth tremble! Let it swallow the cowards, the traitors, the disloyal! And in his hands it did. The sound of a great crack echoed over the hills. Tents shook on their poles, and fires scattered. Greatest of all was Tower Silver, whose stones cracked as its foundation was rocked side to side. All around men and women screamed as it fell. Those within it were crushed instantly, as were many of the tents. Cyric felt exultation at the sight, but he was not done.

"All of you," he cried. "All of you will know only darkness!"

More and more the earth churned. He tried to split it wide, to open a great chasm to swallow them all. A line spread like a spider web through the remains of the tower, but it would not split. Cyric felt himself at a loss for breath, and his vision of the camp blurred the more he pressed on.

At last he pulled back, and with a gasp fell to his knees. The earth grew still.

Close, he knew. So close. With every prayer, every broken village, he felt his power being freed from the Abyss and pouring into his soul. While he wasn't there yet, they'd seen it now. They'd watched their tower crumble, felt the earth rage beneath their feet. Such a shame the two he most desired to die had managed to escape the rubble and quake.

"Time," he breathed as he pushed himself to a stand. "All I need is time. I am the infinite, and you are the dust. You will not escape, Valessa, nor will your bastard lover. Pray for salvation. Pray for mercy. I am coming, and when I exact my glory upon your souls, you will wish for death."

Exhausted and bathed with sweat, Cyric returned to his camp, where the wolf-men waited. He called for Redclaw, and the giant beast came.

"The survivors are by the river many miles south," he told him. "Hunt them down, and stop for neither day nor night."

"And the tenth?" Redclaw asked, his head tilted to one side as he asked his question.

"No," Cyric said. "There will be no tenth, no professions of faith, no salvation. Kill them all, Redclaw, and let your pack feast upon the remains. They are wretched. Let their souls burn."

Redclaw smiled wide, and he reared back and let out a howl. One after another the rest of the wolf-men joined him, and then in a river of fire and fur they ran for the hunt.

20

When Cyric's specter left their tent, defeated by the glowing blade of her hand, Valessa turned to where Darius lay on his back, tears running down his face.

"Do not fight it," she told him, kneeling down. "Breathe in, breathe out. The pain will pass as the spell fades."

He nodded, closed his eyes, and did as he was told. Valessa stayed at his side, a strange peace overcoming her. She took Darius's hand in hers as his breathing calmed, the pain on his face slowly ebbing away. A part of her wanted to think on what had happened, to understand the meaning of what Cyric had done to her, but she dared not. The peace she felt, the comfort, she couldn't risk ruining it. The pain was gone. The guilt was gone.

"Valessa," Darius whispered. He sounded like he'd just run a hundred miles. "I think we need to move."

And then Cyric's cry washed over them, howling in mad fury. The ground shook along with it. Still clutching Valessa's hand, Darius pulled himself to his feet. His arms wrapped around her as they staggered away. Screams of panic and pain filled the camp. Still pushing on, the first of many cracks splintered from the base of the tower. With a groan it suddenly tipped, then fell. Valessa ran faster, nearly dragging Darius away from the shadow it cast as the falling tower blotted out the stars. Mere feet behind them it struck, the impact sending dirt and dust billowing over them. Darius fell forward, rolling as stones flew all about them.

The ground below continued to groan and shake, but the greater fury was spent. Cyric could do no more. Just as suddenly as it began the quake stopped, and in the following silence the cries of the frightened and dying filled the air.

Despite how weak he seemed, Darius forced himself to a stand. He looked to the broken tower and shook his head.

"Thank you," he said, glancing her way.

"For what?"

"Saving me."

He trudged toward the tower, to help the others swarming it in a desperate attempt to locate survivors. Valessa remained behind, and in the momentary privacy she dared banish the illusion of skin so she might see what lay beneath. At the sight of shining light, and nothing else, she quickly brought back her illusion, then went to join Darius's side. At first she stood about, feeling like an intruder, until Darius beckoned her over.

"I know you're stronger than I," he said. "Help us lift the stones."

And so she did, pushing aside pieces of rubble that three men together could not move. They pored over the remains, but of the fifty that had slept inside, only four had lived. The rest of the bodies they piled together, and come the rising of the morning sun, they prepared a pyre. Twenty more bodies joined it, those whose tents had been crushed by the tower's fall.

Daniel Coldmine demanded he be the one to light the pyre.

"I got out just in time," he said, having slept on the bottom floor. "But it should have been me. Those men, they were young. They were loyal. Damn it all, I'm tired of watching the young die."

All around were refugees of the various villages, and they remained respectfully quiet as Daniel stood before them, torch in hand. For a brief moment Daniel looked at Darius, as if the paladin might speak. Changing his mind, he shook his head and flung the torch onto the bodies. They'd been soaked with oil and covered with kindling, and they caught with ease. At the far back of the crowd Valessa watched, and she felt her condemnation of Cyric growing.

Burn the sick branches with fire, she thought. It was one of the axioms they'd been taught. Burn them so the healthy may live. But they weren't burning the sick. Cyric was killing at will, slaughtering anyone that might deny his claims of godhood. If they were to judge by fruits and not by words, then Cyric was not a saver of souls but a butcher of thousands. And there, at the front of the crowd, was Darius, who had counseled all that he could, and had been the last man to leave the crumbled pile of stones. The last man to give up.

She thought once more about the being she was now, and for once it did not frighten her.

If I am a blasphemy, so be it, she thought as she watched the smoke rise. But I see no hope in Karak. I see no life. Gods help me, I think Darius might have been right from the start.

The crowd had begun to disperse, to ready their things for another day's march, when a cry came from the western guard. Valessa rushed to the front, for a vague feeling had plagued her since the early morning. It was faith in Karak, and it rode ahead of the approaching army like a stench. At least a thousand marched along the road toward them, their flags showing the roaring lion. At first Valessa had to calm herself, lest she panic like the many about her. But a glance to the sky showed the black star was far away to the north.

"Are they allied with Cyric?" Darius asked, coming up beside her.

"If they are, then we are already defeated," she said. "Our tower is broken, and we have no walls. Against such a force we have no hope."

Darius touched the hilt of his sword, and despite his obvious exhaustion, there was no defeat in his eyes.

"We'll see about that," he said, leaving to join Daniel. Absently she followed, her mind still on the approaching army. There was a presence with them she recognized, though distantly. It was different from the others, once painful yet now somehow…comforting. It made no sense.

Daniel Coldmine was surrounded by his men, and he shook his head as he listened to them.

"No," he said at last. "They outnumber us, they're better trained and better armed. I'll ride out to hear their terms, but so long as they'll let the common folk live, I have every intention of surrendering."

A few protested, but they were not many. They'd run themselves ragged fleeing from Cyric, and now a new enemy came from the west. There was nowhere left to go.

"Come with me," Valessa said, touching Darius's shoulder. "Something bothers me, and I want you to see."

"If you wish," Darius said. "But we might need to flee, and soon. The peasants might get away unscathed, but I doubt any army of Karak will be happy to let us slip through their fingers."

About five hundred yards from the camp the army halted. The people gathered in groups, fearfully watching for the slightest sign of violence. Daniel waited with his most trusted men, and from somewhere amid the rubble they managed to find a flag of Mordan they might wave. With it high above their heads they went to meet Karak's delegation. Against the twenty red, black, and gold banners of the lion, it looked meek. Just to the side of the crowd Valessa stood, and when the delegation marched out from Karak's army, she pointed, unable to hide her excitement.

"There," she said. "That is who I sense. Do you know him, Darius? Is he who I think he is?"

The group walked closer, and there was no disguising the red hair, the silvery armor, and the giant shield strapped to his back. Darius's grin spread wide, and for the first time that morning both dared hope.

"That crazy whoreson," Darius said. "What in blazes is he doing with them?"

"A captive, perhaps?"

"A captive who keeps his weapons and armor?"

Darius suddenly ran to join Daniel, and Valessa hurried after. She kept herself in the guise of a commoner, not wanting to upset a precarious situation because of her former allegiances as a gray sister. Daniel gave them a glare, and she could sense his worry about what them joining him meant. But then they heard Jerico cry out in surprise.

"Darius?"

Beside Jerico was a priest, who clearly led the army, and when Daniel bowed low to him he bowed in return.

"I am Luther of Mordeina," he said, "loyal priest of Karak."

"And I'm Daniel Coldmine, and I control what's left of the wall of towers. Please tell me you've come to help, not kill."

Before he could answer Jerico and Darius embraced, and they both laughed with joy to see each other again. Valessa watched with her eyes downcast, feeling like an outsider. She stepped back so she might stand behind Daniel, and her presence go unnoticed.

"I've come to kill," Luther said, glancing at the paladins. "But it is not you, so you may stand down your men. Tell me truthfully, Sir Daniel, do you run from the one known as Cyric?"

"We do," said Daniel. "That bloody priest has hounded us all the way from Willshire. Why, is he a friend of yours?"

"No friend," Jerico said, stepping back and smacking Darius across the shoulder. "We're here to kill him."

"Consider us come to your rescue," Luther said, and his smile was ice to Valessa's nonexistent veins.

Redclaw could smell them from miles away. They'd left a trail of fear on their passage south. As he led his pack through the forest that grew alongside the river, he felt his excitement rise. At last they could give in to their every instinct. Leaving the surrendered alive, and being given only a tenth, had worn on even his most loyal. But this was his promise, his land of feasts and blood. A thousand of them ran, in a pack of such strength he'd never seen in his life. Only the rising sun tempered his excitement. What he'd have given to arrive while the moon was still high in the sky, shining down upon them.

They were near now, having run all night. At last they approached the forest's edge. Past that were the humans and their tents, their wagons, and their broken fortress. His pack took up his cry, and with the echoes of a thousand howls they burst from the forest and out into the hills beyond.

Immediately Redclaw knew something had gone amiss. There were far more than he'd expected. With his keen eyes he saw the scattered tents, most placed around a giant pile of rubble. But at the edge, coming in along the road, was a great force of men. They wore dark armor, and above their heads flew flags of lions. Combining their might with the group they'd already chased, Redclaw knew that his pack was suddenly outnumbered by a significant amount.

"Our feast will be great," Warfang said, running beside him with his tongue hanging out one side of his mouth.

"Cyric said nothing of them," Redclaw said, pointing his nose toward the second army.

"Is that piss I smell running down your leg, Redclaw? None can stand. None will stand!"

He let out another howl, and Redclaw's pride had him join in, his legs pumping harder. The two took the lead, the rest veering out behind them at either side. They'd hit like a wave, bury their foes before they could bring their strength to bear. There were no walls to stop them, no river to protect their prey. His footfalls left fire in the grass, and with a great burst of smoke he launched himself at the first of the humans.

There was no contest. The man was unarmored, and he held no blade. Blood splashed across his claws, and the human's head fell from its body. The rest of the wolf-men slammed into the fleeing forces. Redclaw urged his pack on, wanting them to stay together. They swept through the camp, Redclaw leading. It wasn't until they reached the road, and the secondary force, that they encountered true resistance. The humans stood in a straight line, and something about their organization worried Redclaw. He paused only slightly, and Warfang took the lead. Their fur glowed with fire as they leapt against the line, their weight crushing shields, their claws crunching in armor. Redclaw slashed aside a feeble attempt to stab with a sword, then buried his claws in the man's heart. With a cry he ripped it out, let it's blood drip across his tongue.

Then a unified cry rose from the men, and it's sound filled Redclaw with fear and doubt.

"For Karak!" they cried.

For Karak? But Redclaw followed Karak made flesh, the priest named Cyric. Who were these men, and were they foes at all? But it didn't matter, not now. The bloodlust had begun, the battle engaged. Wolf-men pushed forward, but every inch was bought in blood. Redclaw returned to the fray, and against his strength the humans were but pups. Tearing at steel the wolf-men pushed again and again, and he knew that, despite the casualties, they'd still conquer.

But then came those he hated most. Men with blades burning with black fire rushed to the forefront, cutting down his pack. Redclaw watched his wolf-men try to bury them with sheer size, but these were not the same as other humans. Their strength was great, and their blades cut even the wolf-men's muscled bodies in half.

"Press on!" Warfang roared, unafraid. "Do not fear their fire, for we are fire itself!"

It seemed Warfang was, for smoke billowed off him. The swords of the normal humans could barely scratch him, and Redclaw rushed to his side, knowing that only together could they make a stand against the paladins. Their claws slashed against steel, blocking and pushing. What had begun as an easy advance became a crawl. When the men in robes joined in, the crawl became a halt. Redclaw's doubt heightened, for these men dressed like Cyric, and from their hands leapt dark spells that flooded his pack with electricity and broke their bones with bolts of shadow. Even their very presence seemed to sap the strength of his wolf-men. Still Redclaw pressed on, and with sheer pleasure his claws tore through the throat of a paladin, putting an end to the damned fire surrounding his blade.

"Redclaw!" roared a human voice, and he could hardly believe the sound. It couldn't be him. Why here? Why now?

The glowing shield advanced, and at the sight of that red-haired paladin Redclaw knew real terror. This was the human he had failed to defeat in their very first attack across the river. This was the man who had left a score of wolf-men dead at his feet.

Jerico Wolf Smacker pushed to the front of the human forces, and at sight of him the human grinned.

"You've gotten bigger," said Jerico. "And uglier."

One of his pack tried to leap at the paladin, but Redclaw snarled at him, forcing the wolf-man to go around, striking at those who tried to come to Jerico's aid.

"I was alone when you beat me," Redclaw said. "Now I wield the power of a god."

"Whose?" asked Jerico. "Karak's? Look behind me, Redclaw. So do they."

Redclaw's eyes flicked to the many banners, and that was when the paladin struck. His shield led the way, along with that damnable light. It burned into his flesh with a pain far worse than their first encounter. It seemed the embers of his fur faded under its glow, the fire dripping from his claws dimmer and lacking any true heat. As Redclaw crossed his arms against it, Jerico struck with his mace, tearing open a strip of flesh across his wrist.

"No!" Redclaw roared, slamming both his fists against the shield. The blow sent the paladin back a step, and despite the terrible agony it inflicted on his hands, Redclaw struck again, wanting the shield out of the way. Its position shifted, he swung, his claws catching the interior edge and shoving it all the way to the side.

"Die at last," he said, flinging all his weight forward. He'd expected to crush the exposed paladin, but instead a blade slashed through his left arm, cutting all the way to bone. He twisted in mid-air, crashing at the feet of Jerico.

"You didn't forget the Wolf Slayer, did you?" asked Darius, greatsword in hand. In his delirium Redclaw saw it glowed blue instead of the dark fire it once possessed, but he didn't know what that meant. He couldn't think, not with such terrible pain flooding his body. He struggled to stand, but Jerico slammed his shield against his forehead. The blow nearly knocked him unconscious. Clutching his bleeding arm, he thrashed on the ground. His quick glance about saw much of his pack defeated or already in retreat.

Together the two paladins approached him as on either side the rest of the human army surged forward, letting out cries of victory.

"Last words?" Darius asked, pointing his sword at him.

Before he could utter any, Warfang slammed into the paladin's side, flinging him through the air and into Jerico. The two rolled along the ground in a clanking pile of armor. Without any care to be gentle, Warfang reached down, grabbed Redclaw's wounded arm, and yanked him to a stand. Redclaw howled, and he used the pain to focus.

"Run," Warfang told him, and together they did. A howl left Warfang's tongue, subtle in its inflection. A human might not hear the difference, but all the wolf-men there heard the anger and shame embodied in the howl. It was their call to retreat. Some ignored it, giving in to their bloodlust and dying in a flurry of blows against their superior opponents. The rest turned and fled, easily outrunning the slow humans in their armor. Only the spells of the priests gave chase, slaying a few before they could reach the forest.

Within the trees Warfang stopped, turning on Redclaw. Before Redclaw could say a thing, Warfang's claws were digging into his chest, slamming him against a tree.

"You are not worthy of your gift," he snarled. "I smell your fear, you coward. You did not revel in the fight! You did not trust Cyric's power!"

"You want this power?" Redclaw asked, fighting down the impulse to snap at Warfang's neck. "Then take it."

Warfang's eyes narrowed.

"Some gifts can't be taken by force," he said. "And some cannot be given away. Remember your place, Redclaw. Remember who you are."

"Or what?"

The claws dug deeper into his chest.

"Or our god will find a new champion."

With that, Warfang pulled free and then ran. Redclaw waited a moment for his bloodlust to settle, then followed. Without a word spoken between the entire pack they fled back to Cyric's camp, leaving a trail of spilled blood behind them.

21

With the sun well on its rise they staggered into the camp. It had been difficult to count numbers with so many hidden behind trees, but as they stepped into the open, Redclaw saw that nearly half his pack had been crushed in battle. How many humans had they slain in return? Two hundred? Three? At least his arm had stopped bleeding. It seemed the very fire of his blood had sealed the wound.

Most of the pack collapsed at the edge of Cyric's camp. For many, it seemed the run was all that had kept them alive. Redclaw knew the feeling, and with head low he slunk through his pack. All he felt was shame and confusion. Who did he serve? Had they attacked the followers of his own god? Or was he a god at all?

And then Cyric called his name. He looked up, met his eyes briefly, then once more cast them to the dirt.

"Warfang told me of the force you faced," said Cyric. "Fifteen hundred strong, all sworn to Karak. Even more fearsome, you fought priests and paladins as well. Do not be ashamed of your loss. They are the greatest foe we will face in all the North, for they no longer follow the true god of their faith. I would not expect you to defeat them without my presence."

The words helped, but only a little.

"Master," said Silver-Ear, the shaman rushing up to them as fast as her old bones would allow. "I have gathered the wounded. Please, you are our god. I beg you to heal them."

"Of course," Cyric said, smiling at her. "The faithful must always be rewarded."

At the far edge of the camp was where the shaman tended the wounded. Redclaw followed them there, and counted at least fifty that Silver-Ear deemed in mortal peril. Cyric walked among them, scanning their wounds and nodding his head as if privy to a conversation none of them could hear.

"Hold faith," Cyric said at last. "It must be done."

He lifted his arms, and from his hands shone a deep red light. It flared brighter, brighter than even the sun. Redclaw watched one of the wounded beside him, a wolf whose belly was sliced open. He must have run the whole distance while holding in his innards. His mouth was open, and he was gasping for air at a feverish pace. Then the red light shone upon him, and he breathed no more. A quiet sense of terror settled on Redclaw as he saw the wolf-man stand. Intestines roped out, hanging like decorations from a belt. All around stood the rest, their backs straight, their mouths and eyes perfectly still.

"You killed them," Silver-Ear growled, and Redclaw could hear the shock in her voice.

"I saved them," Cyric said. "Their bodies failed them, but now they will fight for me still. Their souls remain, and even now I can hear them praying to me in worship."

Silver-Ear bared her fangs.

"You are not the moon," she snarled. "You are not the giver of life. You bring only death, and then slavery after."

"I am your god," Cyric said, his expression still calm. "Do you dare question me, shaman?"

"Question?" Silver-Ear shook her head. "No. Not question."

She lunged at him, snapping her yellow teeth. In a single smooth motion Cyric waved his arm, and from his palm a single orb of black shot forward. It struck Silver-Ear in the snout, sank into her skin, and then activated. Her body convulsed, twisting in ways painful to watch.

"I will not be doubted, nor questioned, nor betrayed," Cyric said, and he looked straight at Redclaw when he did. "Today we will rest, and your pack will sleep. Come tomorrow you will be my vanguard as we crush those foolish enough to stand against us. The North will be ours, Redclaw. It's only a matter of time. As for you, shaman…"

He knelt down before her. Silver-Ear had finally stilled, her tongue hanging out the side of her mouth as she slowly breathed.

"You are important to me," he whispered to her. "But even without you I can still rule these dogs. Know your place, unless you'd rather join the wounded you cared for."

With a command, the fifty undead wolf-men followed, taking up ranks with the rest of the dead Cyric had marching with him. The sight of his brethren standing side by side with the human corpses was nearly enough to empty Redclaw's stomach. Looking to Silver-Ear's limp form helped matters none, either.

As his pack settled down to sleep, Warfang sought him out.

"When the moon rises, we will have a Gathering," he told him.

"Who has called for one?" Redclaw asked, earning himself a massive grin.

"Why, you did," said Warfang as he left. "At least, that is what I told them."

Redclaw laid down for the day, closing his eyes and trying to sleep. His mind, however, refused to stop churning, and when it turned to the coming Gathering, he felt an idea take root. Its audacity frightened him, but he knew, for the safety of his pack, and the life of his pups, it must be done. Silver-Ear's punishment had been a message, one delivered with both clarity and brutality. To ignore it now would mean to be a fool. Even if Warfang was right, even if he was a coward, Redclaw refused to be a fool. Not anymore.

Sleep did not come for him, so instead he watched his pups as the sun crawled along the sky.

Cyric had stayed up for much of the day, meditating with his body facing the south, so when Redclaw rose for the Gathering they were free of his presence. For this, Redclaw was thankful. They had no mound of bones, no sacred places to meet, but the nearby hill made do for their purpose. The five hundred gathered about it, and in their center burned a small fire, made at Redclaw's demand. The hill, however, he had not chosen. The pack had gravitated toward it, and it was no surprise to him. They were on the side furthest away from the dead that marched in obedience to their god. None of them, whether they were aware of it or not, wanted to be anywhere near those mockeries of life. Their presence was like a thorn in the eye.

Think of your pups, thought Redclaw as his breath caught in his throat when he stepped into the center. Think of them, and act.

"Wolf-men of the Wedge!" he roared, the volume of his voice earning their attention. "I have called this Gathering, and would have you hear me now!"

"We have not come to listen!" Warfang roared back. Redclaw glared at him but was not surprised. Warfang would not risk losing control of the Gathering. He'd had a plan in mind from the start, and through the strength of his personality he would dominate proceedings as he desired. What he didn't know, however, was that Redclaw desired the exact same set of events.

"You would deny my right to speak at my own Gathering?" asked Redclaw, playing along with the farce.

"No," Warfang said, stepping out from the ring to stand beside the fire. "You may speak. I only tell you that none will listen, for that is not why we came. That is not why we gather. We gather so you may be judged."

"Judged? Why am I to be judged?"

"Because you are not faithful! You are weak. You are cowardly. You dishonor our god, and dishonor the gift given to you. I call upon the pack to cast you out and let a new pack leader be chosen."

Warfang was whipping the wolf-men into a frenzy, and never one to let a bleeding enemy recover, he continued.

"You are why we were defeated last day. You are why our strength failed against the armor and blades of the humans. All here with eyes can see it, and all with noses can smell it. Bow your head and run, Redclaw, run from this shame until the moon shines in the day."

They were ashamed of their defeat and at a loss for how to mourn their dead. Warfang twisted the guilt his way, using the Gathering to pin all the blame on him. They howled it all out, demanding blood, demanding retribution. Redclaw let them howl. He wanted their emotions high. He wanted them to remember who they were, and to revel in the old traditions they now invoked. For Cyric would crush every single one of those traditions if he had his way.

"You would have me run in shame before being judged, before speaking my tongue, and before demanding a challenger?" Redclaw bared his teeth at Warfang. "You seem to forget our ways. You are all too eager for power. I demand a challenger to face me before I accept judgment from the pack."

Every wolf there knew who the challenger would be, but they cried out the name anyway.

"Warfang! Warfang!"

The enormous wolf-man grinned.

"They have named him," Warfang said. "I am the pack's champion, and I call you coward. I will serve our god truer. I will serve him as he should be served."

"And that is where you are wrong," Redclaw said. "Cyric is not to be served at all. Wolf should never serve man!"

The last cry was like a thunderbolt, and the following silence was delicious to Redclaw's ears. He'd startled them now, awoken them to the truth that had been naked before them all along.

"You would deny the moon made flesh?" asked Warfang. He didn't have to roar. His voice carried with ease in the calm.

"I deny Cyric," Redclaw said. "I deny the moon. I deny everything we bow to, for we should never bow. We are strong. We are proud. But that human would make us slaves. We follow orders. We slay armies for lands we will never have. We die for a god who is only a man. This ends tonight. I am your pack leader. I am your champion. Hear me now, and listen. Let us, this night, declare ourselves free."

"And go where?" asked Warfang. There was no hiding his incredulousness. "Would you have us flee to the Wedge? Would you have us give up all we might have?"

"Our numbers are too few. I would have us live, even if it must be in the Wedge."

The first of many growls and calls came from the wolf-men around him. Convincing them to obey Cyric in the first place had been a difficult task. To now revoke their fledgling faith? Dangerous. Unpredictable.

"You, his champion, the one blessed with his power, would deny him?" Warfang asked. "You would have us all die rather than serve. That is what you say. Your shame is great, Redclaw, greater than your pride. You do not deserve that power."

"No," Redclaw said. "And I do not desire it. If you would have it, Warfang, then take it. I give it to you. Step into the fire, and know Karak's blessing."

Warfang clearly sensed a trap, but the eyes of the pack were upon him. Could he act afraid, now that he had lorded over Redclaw so mightily?

"Promise me," Redclaw whispered so he might calm his fears. "Promise you will let those who follow me escape without giving chase."

The other wolf-man slowly nodded.

"Very well," said Redclaw. "You heard my command. Step into the fire."

As the five hundred howled and stomped the ground, Warfang put a foot into the fire that burned in the center. It was small, the flames no higher than Warfang's knee. Still, it was enough to burn, and with considerable control the wolf-man ignored the pain. The other foot stepped inside. Flesh cracked, and with clenched teeth he looked to Redclaw and demanded the promised gift.

"I would say you would not enjoy it," said Redclaw. "But that is a lie. Go to Cyric. He is the perfect mate to your bloodlust."

His right arm lashed out, his claws digging into Warfang's chest. The other wolf growled, believing betrayal, but then the power hit him. As Cyric had promised, Redclaw had gradually gained control of the gift he'd been given. And then, all throughout the night, instead of sleeping he'd been practicing the removal of it completely, of rejecting every bit of the gift that made his fur burn like embers and made his blood feel like flame. And now, with his claws embedded into flesh already blessed by Cyric, he banished the rest of it.

The exit was pain and torment, and it left a great feeling of emptiness in his chest, but overpowering it all was a sudden, intense sensation of freedom. Redclaw stepped back, gasping in air. Standing in the center of a fire that could no longer burn him was Warfang, even taller than Redclaw, his arms rippling with muscle.

"Let a judgment be made," Redclaw cried out before Warfang might act. "Not by pack, but by every wolf here. Those who reject Cyric as god come with me. We will find ourselves a home. Beyond that, I make no promises but one, that we shall be free of all gods, and never again slaves to man."

Redclaw held his breath and waited. This was it. Would he slink away without a pack at all?

The first were his two pups. They ran on all fours to join him, and he took them into his arms. For once, he could hold them without fear of burning. Next followed Silver-Ear, limping to his side with her head bowed in respect. More came, first a trickle, then a flood. Of the five hundred, a fifth stood with him in the center. When it was clear no more would join, Redclaw turned to Warfang, who had watched silently.

"Hold to your word," Redclaw said.

"I will," said Warfang. "And you are right. This power is of a god, Redclaw, and I will enjoy it greatly. You are a fool to have rejected it."

"We shall see."

"Run fast," Warfang shouted to the small pack as they turned north. "If Cyric demands your heads, I will not deny him!"

Nor did Redclaw expect him to. But with his hundred, he would grow. He would build a pack to rival all packs.

The shamans were right, he saw that now. The human lands would not be conquered, not by a mere tribe. Not with so few. And even at Cyric's side, they could conquer the entire world yet never have lands of their own. Forever they would be slaves.

"No," Warfang said when Redclaw turned to go. "Not you."

"You promised..."

"I promised those who followed you would live. I never said you."

Redclaw met his eyes, saw the mockery and death in them.

"Come to me, my pups," he said. They did, and to Redclaw's relief Warfang gave him that shred of honor. The first he licked across the forehead, then ran a claw along the back of his neck.

"Manfeaster, I name you," he said. To the second he did the same. "Moonslayer, I name you. Now go. Go!"

They ran to Silver-Ear, who beckoned them.

"I will raise them," she said, standing as tall as her old back allowed. "They will honor you in their time. Not Karak. Not the moon."

The pack left, and so many cast frightened looks seeing their pack leader remaining behind. Warfang towered over him, a gleam in his eye.

"I will not fight," Redclaw said. "I give you no sport."

"I don't want sport. I want blood."

Warfang's claws slashed out, ripping the flesh of his chest and slicing open his belly. To his stomach he collapsed, nose striking the dirt. Far ahead of him he saw his pack running. His pups did not look back, and for that, he was proud. As he felt chills spreading throughout his body, he arced his neck so he might stare up at the sky.

"Forgive us," Redclaw whispered to the moon. "But even you will no longer have our worship. We are free. Free…"

And free they ran, to the prison made for them by man, as Redclaw bled until he died.

22

There were so many wounded, and with only Jerico and Darius to tend them, the day passed long and tiring. At last, when Jerico's eyes were blurred and his head pounded hard enough to make his stomach ill, they finished. By then night was fast approaching, and the combined armies would make no march.

"You've done us a miracle," said an older man who had tended the wounded while they waited for the paladins to come heal them as they lay on the bloody grass. He was the surgeon for the mercenaries traveling with Luther, and while the rest of Karak's faithful had treated the two with disdain, the surgeon had welcomed them gladly.

"No miracles, not by my hands," Jerico said, nearly losing his balance as he stood. "Through them, maybe."

"Whichever way makes you feel better," said the surgeon.

"You need to rest," Darius said, grabbing Jerico by the arm to steady him.

"And you don't?"

Darius grinned.

"A strong wind will blow me over, yet you look like you don't need even that to fall on your ass."

Jerico let out a chuckle.

"If you insist. Food does sound good right now, though…"

An hour later, after they'd drunk their fill of water and ate the salted meats Daniel's men brought them, Jerico stripped off his armor and lay before a fire.

"Looks like Daniel's keeping his men with the rest of the refugees as they head southwest," Darius said, sitting across the fire from him. "We'll be going after Cyric alone. Well, not alone of course, but not exactly in friendly company. We'll have a nice army of mercenaries, priests, and paladins marching with us."

"And Kaide."

"Aye, him too. But him at least I'm not worried about killing me in my sleep."

Jerico grunted at the word.

"Speaking of which," he muttered.

Darius stood.

"Not quite ready to turn in," he said, "so I'll leave you be."

"Much appreciated."

Jerico listened to the gradually retreating footsteps of the paladin, and then, bathed only in the sound of the crackling fire, he tried to sleep. He could not. With a sigh, he gave up and pushed himself to his feet. All around were a hundred campfires, but he knew he wouldn't find who he needed at them. Beyond the camps he walked, to the far west where a group of four sat around their own secret fire.

"Welcome, Jerico," said Bellok as the paladin joined their camp.

"You look like shit," said Adam. "Well, you always do, really. But shittier than normal."

Jerico smiled, but was too exhausted for it to remain on his face. He looked to Kaide, who so far had kept his eyes on the fire instead of his newly arrived guest.

"A moment," Jerico said.

The other three waited, and after a nod from their leader, they stood and departed for the greater camp. Jerico felt his heart skip as he tried to think of what to say.

Honestly, he didn't have a clue. But he knew what was bothering him, and he had to try something.

"Kaide…"

"I know what it is you want to say," the brigand said, interrupting him. "And I have heard it all before. From you, actually. So save your breathe, return to your campfire, and get some sleep. Gods know you need it."

"You would dismiss me so easily?"

"Would you prefer I make you leave the hard way?"

Jerico grinned at him.

"Are you so certain you could?"

Kaide gave him a look, then shook his head.

"You're a stubborn one, I'll give you that. It'd be easier to move mountains. More pleasant to talk to as well."

Jerico took a seat next to him, and he thought of what to say. Strange how the greater the weight on his heart, the harder the words came. It was as if he feared he might fail at the very first word spoken.

"Luther deserves death," he said at last. "He's hardly the first, and he won't be the last. But you shouldn't be the one to kill him."

"Fearing for my eternal soul, paladin?"

"I fear for a man I once considered a friend. Revenge is wrong. You have to know this."

"Do you?" asked Kaide, glaring across the fire. "Strange coming from a man whose mace has taken more lives than my blades."

"I kill in defense," Jerico insisted. "I kill to save others, to preserve innocence. Should I strive for vengeance, then I've lost my way."

"Then what of when he attacked Sandra? Would it have been right to kill him then? Why then but not now? Why is it right for your hands to be covered with blood but not mine? Nothing else matters if the end is the same."

"I would kill to protect, to keep others alive. I fight for life, but what of you? You would kill because of vengeance, because of hatred, because…"

"Because I want her to live! Is that so hard to understand? If only I could perform the miracles your hands can, but I can't. We both kill for life. It's just mine's coming way too damn late."

Jerico's fingers dug into the dirt as he struggled for the words.

"No," he said. "I don't believe that. I don't believe you. I'm begging you, Kaide. I loved her, I still do. I would give anything to have acted faster, to have pulled her behind my shield. In my dreams, I sometimes do, but even then my shield breaks, and the spell hits, and I can't do anything. I can only watch. I can…" He took a deep breath. "Kaide, you're so close, so very close. You're a good man, a great man. And one step farther, you'll fall off a cliff, and all of Dezrel will see just how far down you go. Don't honor Sandra by becoming a man she'd hate. Be the brother she loved, that she still loves."

"Don't you dare," Kaide said even as tears filled his eyes. "Don't you feed me this shit. I won't hear of clouds and angels and loved ones watching over us. You're wrong."

"And if I'm not? As she looks down and watches, who does she see? Who do you want to be, Kaide? Please, let it go, let it out. I'll shoulder the burden if I must, but don't let it consume you like this. I see the death in your eyes, the rage in your fists. You can stop it. You still can."

Kaide opened his fists, and he stared at them as if he'd never known they were clenched.

"Will you stop me?" he asked, his voice suddenly quiet. Jerico let the question hang in the air, let it have the gravity it deserved.

"I'll pray for you, Kaide. And I'll be here for you. But I won't stop you."

"It'd be wrong to stop me."

Jerico shook his head.

"That's not why. I won't stop you because I trust you. That's all. This world is dark, and we'll always need swords, but hatred is no such need."

"Are you really so free of it yourself?" Kaide asked.

Jerico cast his eyes to the dirt.

"No," he said, his voice hoarse. "Ashhur forgive me, I'm not. But I love my enemies as much as I hate them, and hate myself as much as I love my friends. Luther doesn't deserve your hate, only your pity."

"Pity?" asked Kaide. "You would offer your pity to such a pathetic man? His cruelty surpasses anything I've ever done. He's sick, he's mad, he's ruined me, ruined everything. Let me hate him, Jerico. Why can't you just let me hate him? What does it matter if I live or die trying to kill him? I must, damn it, I must."

Jerico could see him, his strength, could see the iron breaking. It was a man wishing for death, almost begging for it.

"You insult your daughter seeking death so openly," he said. "Go to Beth. Live. Don't make me go to her, and tell her of her father's death. She'll ask me why. She'll ask what happened, and what will I tell her then? Your rage against Luther was more important? Your love for Sandra greater than your love for…"

Kaide slugged him, his knuckles splitting his lip open across his teeth. Blood splattered, but Jerico did not react, nor move to strike back. Instead he stood there, letting the blood drip down his lips and neck.

"You bastard," Kaide said. His face was red, and he openly wept. "Is this what you want? Do you want to break me and send me in pieces back to my daughter? Live, you say, as if it were so easy. Live, as if the world would be so kind. You know why I can't go back to Beth? Because whenever I hold her in my arms, all I'll feel is dread. All I'll feel is sorrow. Every shadow will be Luther ready to take her away from me, to make me feel that same pain all over again. You think revenge will be what ruins me? I'm already ruined. I'm already broken. I'm a dead man, and Luther prevents me from coming back to life. Let me kill him. Revenge isn't my doom. It's my salvation."

"You won't find salvation with a blade through another man's heart."

"You won't find it eating the flesh of another, but I did it to live. I've done so many terrible things to live, Jerico, and this won't be the worst. You tell me to live, and I shall, and the way I have always lived. You have nothing to offer me."

Slowly Jerico stood, and it felt like all of his limbs weighed a hundred stone.

"I would love you," Jerico said. "Despite all you have done. All you will do. I would have you forgiven for it all, and sleep through the night without guilt, without nightmares. I would give you peace. Strike me again. Scream, cry, beg, I don't care. And then go home without a splinter in your heart and without blood on your hands."

The seconds crawled along. Jerico held his breath.

"I can't go home. Not yet." Kaide looked up, cutting him off when he saw Jerico was to speak. "Not while Cyric is still alive. If he's the threat you say, you need my help. I won't let Beth be forced to kneel before that bastard and choose slavery or death."

"And Luther?"

Slowly Kaide let out a breath.

"I make no promises. Now leave me be."

And so Jerico did, returning to his camp. By his fire he tried to sleep, yet the hours crawled, the stars shone, and sleep did not come.

Warfang watched until Redclaw's band of cowards was beyond even his excellent sight. Then he ordered his pack to rest, for tomorrow they would fight their most important battle yet. Despite his own orders, Warfang could not sleep. The power coursing through him was too new, and along with it came an excitement coupled with dread. What they had done, they had done in the shadow of their god, hidden from his eyes. What would Cyric say when he saw who now led his chosen warriors instead of Redclaw?

More importantly, would he give him the pleasure of hunting down the cowards and ripping the tendons from their bones?

And so at the edge of Cyric's camp he waited, until just before the dawn the moon-made-flesh came walking, and his face was without emotion. Even his scent did not give away his true thoughts.

"I see my champion before me," Cyric said, crossing his arms. "But he is not the champion I remember. Where is Redclaw? Did you kill him?"

"Redclaw was weak," Warfang said. "He denied you, and had those who are afraid, those who are like toothless pups, flee back to the Wedge. Yes, I killed him."

Warfang thought such words would elicit anger from the priest, but instead he remained calm. If anything, he looked curious.

"He denied me?" asked Cyric. "Do you know why?"

"Redclaw was stupid and weak. Why does it matter?"

"I asked," Cyric said. "Therefore it matters. I would know where Redclaw failed, so I might know if I should fear the same failure from you."

The very idea insulted Warfang, and he had to struggle to prevent it from showing.

"Redclaw lost what it meant to be wolf," he said. "He never understood. He was strong, he was smart, but he was also fearful. To kill, to tear into life with our claws and taste blood on our tongue…that is what we are. That is what we were made for. Redclaw dreamt of kingdoms, of packs and families and cubs. He dreamt a lie. You give us power, and tell us to kill. You are the true god we have always served."

"Are you stronger than Redclaw?"

"I have not forgotten my bloodlust. I have not lost my love of killing. I will use your power far better than Redclaw ever could, for I am who it was always meant for. Give me prey, my god, and I will serve."

At last Cyric smiled.

"Prey," he said. "We do not chase after rabbits, Warfang. We chase after the most dangerous prey imaginable. We chase after men of faith and men in service of money. They wear expensive armor and wield weapons of light and shadow. Can you face them, even after being defeated once?"

Warfang let out a roar, and its thunderous noise awakened the rest of his pack. The second one was taken up by them, and their howls echoed throughout the hills, across the river, and into the Wedge beyond.

"We were led by a coward," he snarled. "But I do not know fear. I will not be beaten."

"No," Cyric said. "You will not. My dead are ready to march. Prepare your pack, but do not let them eat. I want them hungry. Today the faithless of my order will meet their god, and at last they will open their eyes…or they will fall to your claws."

Warfang lowered his head, and at Cyric's dismissal he stormed through his pack, nipping and snarling to get his fellow wolf-men ready.

"Up, up," he cried to them. "This day, under this sun, we will feast!"

23

Jerico looked up from his prayer, felt the warm touch of the morning sun on his face, and smiled.

"Amen," he whispered, standing. Sleep had not come, but he'd passed the final hour in prayer, and now come the light he knew at last he would face Cyric. He didn't know if they'd stop him. He didn't know if he'd live. But Jerico always preferred his challenges before him instead of looming on the horizon.

And since the sun was up, it was finally time to move. But first...

"Where is Valessa?" he asked Darius when he found him. Darius looked up from his breakfast and frowned.

"She's frightened of Luther," he said. "Cyric was nearly able to kill her with a thought. I think she fears he will do the same."

Jerico's brow furrowed.

"I don't understand," he said. "We are no more loved by Luther than she is, yet we are safe."

"Aye," he said. "And look at how safe we are."

Jerico could see he was troubled, and he sat down, unwilling to let it go.

"What is it really?" he asked. "What's bothering you so?"

Darius put aside his bowl.

"Luther doesn't know she even exists yet. She said now is the time for her to flee. She could go and make a life, without fear of the priesthood hunting her down."

"Like they hunt us," Jerico said. "Don't be upset with her, Darius. We walk among lions. I don't blame her for not wanting to be eaten."

Darius chuckled.

"I don't blame her. I just thought she'd stay with me, regardless the demons, the lions, and the mad priests. But I have a feeling she'll be watching. Perhaps she knows better what is going on than we do."

"I wouldn't doubt it. Finish up, then come with me. Right now, Luther's the only one keeping us safe, so we might as well find out where he wants us."

Luther ordered that he and Darius march at his side, to both of their surprise. When they joined him, they received many dreadful looks from the other priests and paladins, who slowly dispersed among the mercenaries ahead.

"Do not mind them," Luther said. "They see your presence among us as a blasphemy, and they are all too set in their ways to be convinced otherwise."

"Is it not a blasphemy?" Darius asked, and his smile didn't hide the seriousness of his question.

"Blasphemy?" Luther said with a laugh. "Even the lion and the lamb will run side by side when chased by fire. Do not worry about them."

"I'm not worried about right now," Jerico said, thinking of the cold glares the paladins had given him. "It's after."

Luther nodded, and his silence was enough to show he shared such fears.

"Will you tell them of the enemy they face?" Darius asked as they traveled along.

"The less they know the better," Luther said. "Cyric is dangerous, and a blasphemer. Any knowledge beyond that only invites heresy."

They marched alongside the river, following it north. When a forest appeared in the distance, Luther gave orders for them to slow, and then with it a mere hundred yards away they came to a halt. The mercenaries scrambled about, setting up lines.

"Why here?" Darius asked.

"Wolves are creatures of the forest," said Luther. "Let them come to us."

"Will they, though?" Jerico asked. "We crushed them when they had far greater numbers."

"That is true," Luther said, his attention focused on the forest. "But now they have their god with them. They will come."

Despite the sun, there was a darkness lurking in the trees, something ominous the light could not penetrate. Jerico pulled his shield off his back and took comfort in its glow. When he heard the first of the howls, he readied his mace, and then eyes shone out of the darkness, coupled with afterimages of hulking bodies wreathed in soft flame.

With a cry they charged, hundreds leaping from the trees. When Jerico took a step forward, Luther gently grabbed his arm, stopping him.

"No," Luther said. "Let the mercenaries take the brunt of the first charge. Your energy must be saved for the true threat."

"You'd let them die?" Jerico asked.

"Better this death than the life they'd have known without us, raping and pillaging for coin. Now their lives are sworn to Karak. Let them honor that vow. Whether they live or die is irrelevant. All that matters is Cyric."

He glanced at Darius, who shook his head.

"Not our army," he said.

The mercenaries formed a disciplined line, shoulder to shoulder, shields up and weapons braced. They'd faced the wolf-men before and held firm, so there seemed no reason to expect them to fail now. But Luther was right. This time they had their god with them.

From the forest sailed a thousand arrows, their tips gleaming purple, their shafts like obsidian. High into the air they arced, then fell like a dark rain.

"Hold!" was the communal cry of the mercenaries, and to their honor, they did. They fell by the dozens, and regardless of Luther's cry, Jerico could not stand idly by. The line in tatters, the wolf-men slammed into them with renewed fury. At their forefront was a beast that towered over the rest, so similar to Redclaw, yet not him.

"Take him down," Jerico heard Luther cry after him. "The rest will scatter."

He risked a glance back, saw Darius following, and allowed himself a smile. Together the two paladins crashed into the conflict, right in the center where it was most chaotic. No longer outnumbered, the beasts clawed at the armor of their foes, and the unholy strength of them left black grooves in the metal. Against this Jerico flung his shield, and with each hit the wolf-men fell back, howling in pain. Darius's sword soon followed after, cutting off limbs and opening huge gashes across their chests and bellies.

Worst, though, was Cyric's new champion. He was bigger, stronger, and fought with a ferocity that he'd never seen matched. Together Jerico led them closer, trying to push through to where the wolf-man shredded their lines. It seemed they were to break, but then Luther called forth the rest of his army. The dark paladins filled the gaps, their burning weapons more than a match for the beasts. The priests remained back, and when another volley of black arrows sailed from the forest, they were ready. A shield appeared over the battlefield, protecting both friend and foe. The arrows hit it, sparked like flint, then vanished.

"Hurry!" Jerico cried, smashing in a wolf-man's face before spinning to put his shield in the way of a charging beast. The wolf-man slammed into the shield hard enough to shatter his own skull, yet with a flare of light, Jerico slid only a small space backward.

"Trying!" Darius cried back, parrying away a flurry of blows from a smaller, nimbler beast.

Barely twenty feet away, the champion snarled and tore into the last of the mercenaries, and amid them Jerico saw Kaide and his band prepared to hold firm. Translucent daggers flew from Bellok's palm. Their blades broke against the molten hide without shedding a single drop of blood. Again and again Jerico slammed forward, trying to reach them and trusting his platemail to protect him from the strikes he missed. Adam and Griff stepped between the champion and Bellok, and they swung their giant clubs with enough strength to shatter the skull of any mere human. The clubs broke.

"Get back!" Jerico screamed at them, ignoring the pain of a claw slashing open his cheek. Griff crossed his arms in a futile defense. A single swipe stripped them down to bone, and a second broke his neck. Before Adam suffered the same fate, Jerico stepped between them, and he let out a cry as the champion's claws scraped across his shield.

"About time," said Kaide, using him as a screen for his own attack. His dirks sliced across molten flesh. Burning blood dripped to the grass, but it was so little it seemed a mockery. Dashing away, Jerico covered his retreat with a strike from his mace, followed by another blow with his shield. The enormous wolf-man took a step back, as if to reevaluate his opponent.

"I know you," it snarled.

"Can't say the same."

"I am Warfang!" the beast roared. "I am your better."

Jerico braced his shield.

"Let's see," he said.

Warfang lunged, and his strikes against Jerico's shield felt like sledgehammers. Jerico shifted side to side to prevent him from curling around, and then Darius arrived, his sword cutting into Warfang's bicep all the way down to the bone. Warfang let out a cry, then hurled the paladin back. Jerico, seeing Darius vulnerable, flung himself into an attack, his mace striking the beast's mouth twice.

"Warfang?" he said. "Better? You amuse me, wolf. Redclaw was better than you."

The insult cut far deeper than he expected. Warfang leapt into the air, and when he landed atop of Jerico he ignored the pain of the holy shield to crush Jerico into the dirt. Jerico gasped for air, struggling to free his pinned mace. Before Warfang finished the kill, a bright flash blinded him, released from Bellok's hands. Another followed. The weight left Jerico, and then came the scream as Bellok had his chest torn open. Kaide assaulted immediately, crying out his rage. His dirks were a flash, and for a moment Warfang crossed his arms and accepted them, his burning blood dripping down, and then he lashed out, catching Kaide across the face with the back of his paw.

Jerico staggered to his feet, ignoring the pain in his chest. Kaide weaved side to side, trying to avoid the giant beast's attacks, but his balance was clearly lost from the blow to his head. Two wolf-men leapt in Jerico's way, and he barreled through. Before they could chase, Darius attacked from behind, buying Jerico time.

"To me, you coward, to me!" Jerico cried at Warfang, but he was ignored. With terrifying speed Warfang reached out, grabbed Kaide by the front of his tunic and lifted him into the air. His other claw pulled back, but before he could go for the kill Adam flung himself onto the arm. The fire of the wolf-man's flesh burned into him, and Adam screamed, but still he hung on, wrestling the champion despite his size and strength. Warfang hurled Kaide back, spun, and buried his claws into Adam's eyes.

"I am the fury of our god!" Warfang cried to them as he flung the corpse aside. "I am the fire and death that will consume you all!"

Jerico swung his mace, but Warfang slammed him back as if he were insignificant. Bracing himself, he found his backwards flight halted by Darius's arms.

"You're a dumb, stupid wolf," Darius said to Warfang as he stepped forward, the light of his sword shining. "Look around you. Your pack is dead, and I don't see any god to stop me."

It wasn't quite true, for there were pockets of scattered fighting everywhere, but in that sliver of time Warfang glanced about Darius thrust his blade. Warfang tried to turn it aside, but it was too late. The tip pierced through ribs, punched through his heart, and then burst out the other side. Warfang convulsed, drool and blood spilling out of his mouth as the power granted to him fled in an instant.

"So much for his fire and death," Darius said, yanking the blade free and kicking the corpse aside.

"Not quite over yet," Jerico said, catching his breath. "It looks like the god has come to play."

From the trees marched a horde of undead, shambling bodies with rotted flesh and haunted eyes. With most of the mercenaries scattered or dead, only the paladins and priests remained to face them. The paladins formed a line, a mere fifteen against the thousand that approached. The few mercenaries who remained joined either side of the line, looking haggard and afraid. Behind them the priests made ready, their hands glowing with the dark light of their spells.

Jerico readied himself, for he would not fall, not to the mockeries of life that Cyric had created. No matter the horrifying way they moved toward him, without sign of breath or thought. No matter the rot in their teeth and the blood dried on their hands.

Behind them came Cyric. He wore his priestly robes, a smile on his face, and atop his brow burned a crown of fire that did not consume.

"Why do you resist me?" he asked them, his voice rolling across the plain. "I come offering power. I come offering freedom. The true faith, the faith you all serve, will blanket this land. We'll know peace. We'll see an end to chaos. I am your god, you fools, yet you would still stand against me? Everything you've dreamed of, every prayer for this world you've prayed while on your knees, I've come to fulfill. No one need die. Not now. Not today. All you must do is kneel."

Jerico looked to the paladins around him. There was a power in Cyric's words, and the approaching dead only added danger to his message. Would the others listen? Jerico had heard no speeches or warnings from Luther, no explanation of the foe they fought beyond him being a heretic to the faith of Karak and a threat to all of Dezrel. Or did keeping them in ignorance protect them from Cyric's twisted wisdom?

"Send the dead back to their graves," Luther called out to them. "And do not listen, do not obey. Kill him, my brethren, for the sake of your souls, kill him!"

The dead were near, and Jerico lifted his shield.

"Burst through," he told Darius at his side. "Cyric is all that matters."

"Then lead the way."

The undead hit their line. Flaming swords cut them down, slicing through rotted flesh with ease. But they were so many, even with each swing taking two at a time the paladins were nearly overwhelmed. Jerico let the light of his shield flare, and all about the abominations staggered and moaned, the magic holding them together threatening to break. In their weakened state he slammed through them, shattering them to dust with his shield and crunching bones with his mace. Darius followed after, his sword spinning side to side to finish off the undead who tried to close around their rear. By the dozens they fell, and then the paladins were beyond them, rushing across the space between Cyric and his army.

Risking a glance back, Jerico saw the dark paladins holding their own, but just barely. A few of the priests helped them, but the rest hurled arrows of shadow and bolts of black flame over their heads, each one aimed at Cyric. It felt like they were rushing a besieged castle, but instead of high walls it was only one man, who stood with his arms out. A translucent shield shimmered before him, and against that shield broke the bolts and arrows.

"Paladins of Ashhur?" Cyric asked as they neared. "Truly my brethren are lost if they have enlisted your aid."

The priest clapped his hands together, and a shockwave rolled outward. All magical attacks against him ceased to exist, and then the force slammed against Jerico. He struggled, and it wasn't until he placed his shield before him that he felt the pressure vanish. Darius kept his sword up, arms braced, as he screamed out with every painful step he took.

"Can't you do better?" Jerico said.

No more attacks by the other priests followed. The dark paladins were overwhelmed, and only their spells kept them from falling. Jerico and Darius were alone.

"Trying," Darius said through clenched teeth.

A great funnel of fire burst from Cyric's hands. Jerico took a step back, and he let his shield absorb its heat. Darius did the same, swinging his sword so the light about it banished the magic. Free of the resisting force, Darius rushed Cyric, who only grinned at his attack.

"You beat me, once," Cyric said. "Not again."

From his palm tendrils of shadow burst in all directions, growing upward and outward for several feet before turning downward and punching into the dirt. The ground rumbled, and then all around Darius the tendrils surfaced, lashing at him, curling around his ankles, wrists, and neck. Darius screamed, and he hacked at them, but each one he cut became two, and even faster he lost the mobility of his arms and legs.

"Let him go!" Jerico cried. He flung himself forward, shield leading, mace at the ready to crush the priest's skull. With his free hand Cyric reached out as if to greet him, but his skin was like that of a ghost. When it touched Jerico's shield, his progress halted, and a great thunder shook the battlefield. No matter how hard he pushed with his legs, he could not close the distance.

"The others will serve," Cyric said, and though he smiled, Jerico could see the strain wearing at him. "You, however, will die. There will be no salvation, not for you. My order has tolerated heathens long enough."

"Heathens?" Jerico said, and he couldn't but laugh. "Your words hurt, Cyric. Let me return the favor."

He shifted his shield to the side, and around it he swung his mace. It connected with the palm the tendrils grew from. Blood splattered as the flesh of Cyric's hand tore, and all at once the tendrils vanished. From behind him, Jerico heard Darius let out a gasp of air. Before Jerico could feel too proud of himself, Cyric shoved his wounded hand his way, splashing blood across Jerico's armor. With a snap of his fingers, it ignited, covering his armor with flame. Jerico screamed. Despite his urge to roll to the ground to put out the fire, he stepped closer and swung his mace. It should have connected with Cyric's head, but instead it struck the fire of his crown and halted.

"See how little you are to me," Cyric said, and with a flick of his fingers Jerico flew backward through the air. When he hit ground the air blew from his lungs, and he silently screamed as he rolled along the dirt. When he came to a halt, Darius was there, reaching down to grab his arm and pull him to his feet.

"Least that put out the fire," Darius said to him, and Jerico grinned, despite the terror of their situation. Still laboring for breath, he looked to Cyric, who approached with his arms at his side, his crown glowing so fiercely that even in the daylight he looked like a vicious red star.

"You are nothing!" Cyric cried to them as Darius's eyes drifted to the sky. "Nothing to me, nothing to a god! You are mortal, human, pathetic."

"Perhaps we are," Darius said. "But how do you feel about birds?"

And then from the sky plummeted a white dove, its left wing malformed. Mere feet away from Cyric's head the dove transformed, becoming the silver-armored, long-cloaked, furious Valessa. Her hands were white, and they shone with brilliance as they slammed against Cyric's head. With all his power he screamed, denying her, and against that Valessa flew, her body twisting so that she landed not far behind them.

The crown broke, and all across Cyric's face and forehead there was blood. On his knees he crumpled, and his whole body shivered. Behind them, the undead collapsed, marked with heavy sighs as their souls found relief. It blew across them like wind.

"If you're a god, then I'd rather be human," Valessa said as she struggled to her feet, fighting through the magic of Cyric's attack.

With his crown broken, his undead crumbling, panic flooded across every feature of Cyric's body. Jerico raised his shield, the light shining over the mad priest, mocking him. But Cyric, god or not, bleeding or not, refused to admit defeat. He stood, and with a particular strength given only to the frightened and the fanatical, he let his power roll.

"I am Karak!" he cried, a wellspring of rage and fury bursting. "I am your god! Now kneel!"

It hit them all like a wave. Even Jerico felt the impulse, an irrational desire to fall to his knees and beg for mercy. He resisted, for never would he bow to Karak, not an imposter, not even the real deity if he stood before him with blade raised. He took a hesitant step forward, then glanced over his shoulder. Only two others remained on their feet: Darius and Valessa. The other paladins and priests knelt, some weeping, the rest crying out in anger or confusion.

With his domination incomplete, Cyric turned and ran into the forest. Jerico gave chase, and each step made it feel like bricks were falling off his legs. Valessa soon caught up with him, having shaken off Cyric's blow. Darius was not far behind.

"Give him no respite," Valessa said. "His power is still great."

As they stepped into the cover of the trees, Jerico saw many catching fire, the mad priest no doubt burning them to stall his pursuers. Weaving through the smoke and flame, they ran until stumbling upon Cyric on his knees, his back to them. Blood covered his body, and around him was a ring of fire. Most frightening of all, he was laughing.

"Do you understand now?" Darius asked between labored breaths. "You're no god, Cyric. You're just a man. Now turn and die like one."

Cyric glanced back, and the madness in his eyes was in full control.

"No," he said. "I'm no man. But I bleed. I hurt. I understand now. I cannot be Karak, not in this pathetic mortal shell. The demon legions will not tremble before me, the Abyss will not worship its true ruler, until I assume the proper form."

His skin rippled as if boiling water bubbled in his veins. His hair burned, and the bones in his body began to shift and break.

"Darius?" Jerico asked, taking a step back.

"No idea," said the other paladin. "So kill it."

Jerico rushed forward, but the ring of fire surged into a towering wall. Jerico staggered back, and Darius had to shift aside to avoid him. Only Valessa passed through the flame unharmed, but she came flying back out, having been struck by something great. She flew through a burning tree, then fell through the ground itself, her momentum carrying her far below the surface. Jerico held his shield before him, its glow the only thing keeping him from losing himself completely to terror.

Cyric grew taller as words streamed off his tongue, each syllable painful to hear. Their rhyme and rhythm put a deep sense of wrongness into Jerico's chest. Cyric's bones twisted, his flesh darkened, and then cracks of fire burst through his molten skin. Larger and larger he became, his fingers extending into claws, his muscles molten rock, his eyes twin chasms of burning coal. Any unlit leaves about him curled black and fell. This beast that had been Cyric took a step forward, and the footfall sent a tremor through the dirt.

Suddenly Jerico's shield seemed rather puny compared to that.

"Jerico…" Darius said, his sword before him as if he might ward off the demon with it.

"Do you still doubt?" asked Cyric, his voice rumbling like deep stones knocking together. "Look upon me and know that I am God."

Jerico knew Darius was looking to him, needing him. Against such a thing, easily twice their height, they were but mere mortals. But the army beyond the forest knelt against its will. If Cyric was not stopped now, he would never be. What arrow would pierce his side? What sword would break through that rock? Who else would not bow before such power? Darius, Jerico, they were both about to break, to succumb to the fear that rolled over Cyric's body in waves. But Jerico couldn't give in. Darius looked to him for strength, and somehow he'd give it to him.

"We are the light shining in the deepest pit," Jerico said, reciting a mantra of his order. "We are the hope that lets the fearful sleep. We are the strong that kneel before the weak."

Cyric reared up, his fist billowing smoke and fire. Jerico lifted his shield.

"We are the stone that will not shatter. We are the mountain all may climb. We are everything good, everything joyful, that must never die."

A sword formed in Cyric's fist, its blade as long as Jerico was tall. The edge shimmered with lava, the hilt cracked with black obsidian.

"We will not break," Jerico cried as the sword descended. "We will not break!"

Sword hit shield. The shockwave rolled as the ground shattered beneath Jerico in all directions from the force of his stand. Branches blew outward, the fire on them nearly dying. Sparks flew, metal groaned, but the sword could not break the shield.

"Now!" Jerico screamed.

Darius lunged, the light of his blade gleaming. It cut into Cyric's side, and from it flowed blood that burned from contact with the air. The demon swung its sword toward him, but Jerico was there, putting himself in the way of the attack. Again it hit his shield, and he screamed at the pain in his arm. When Cyric pulled back for a third strike, Darius slipped in, cutting another gash along the inside of his arm before bouncing away. The molten blade struck the earth but not flesh.

Jerico gave him no time to recover. He flung himself forward, his shield leading. It was his weapon, his defense, and with its light he would burn away everything Cyric represented. The shield slammed into Cyric's chest, and it hit with a heavy crack. Cyric bellowed in pain, and he twisted his sword to stab Jerico's neck. Before he could, Valessa leapt from the very earth, her arms twin blades of light. They slashed up Cyric's back, spilling burning blood. When the demon cried again, she looped her legs around his neck, spun, and then slashed at the arm holding the blade.

Cyric struggled, his body assaulted from both high and low. It was amid that struggle Darius stepped forward, let out a cry to Ashhur, and then sliced through Cyric's knee. The beast crumpled, Jerico fled back, and Valessa leapt off. Together the three faced Cyric as the demon pounded the earth attempting to stand.

"Follow my lead," Jerico said. He raced forward, and when Cyric lashed out, the sword struck his shield, knocking him flying. His back hit a tree, and he gasped for air, but the way was clear. Valessa danced, her speed incredible, her hands slashing across Cyric's stomach before plunging deep into his wounded leg. Cyric roared out his pain in a bellow of breaking rock and madness personified.

Darius cut off his head, ending Cyric's cry forever.

Before a single horn on the demon's skull touched ground, the body had broken into fire and smoke.

"I think…" Jerico winced, stumbling off the tree with bits of bark sticking to his armor. "I think we won."

Darius jammed his sword into the dirt and smiled at Valessa.

"I think we did."

"Praise Ashhur," Valessa said, returning his smile as the demon's body consumed itself, leaving only a black scar upon the land where the mad priest had once been.

24

Darius and Jerico stood there, both exhausted, both gasping in air, as they watched Luther approach.

Valessa, however, hid behind one of the burning trees just outside Darius's line of sight. It seemed she didn't want to be seen. After everything, Darius did not blame her. So far Luther likely didn't know she existed.

"He is dead?" Luther asked as he stepped through the flames.

"He is," Darius said, and the relief was palpable on Luther's face.

"You have done something all of Dezrel should thank you for," he said to them. "Though I fear they might never know your names, nor understand the peril you saved them from."

"What now?" Jerico asked. "Will you leave us be?"

Luther shook his head sadly.

"No," he said. "I cannot. There are too many of my order who desire your death. You're the last of them, Jerico. You are too great a prize, and too dangerous a foe, to let live."

Darius laughed.

"How else would Karak reward loyalty and aid?" he asked. "We've done your dirty work. Now to dispose of the corpses, correct?"

Luther's neck flushed.

"It does not have to be this way," he said. "Darius, you were once a most faithful paladin. You know the law that must be given to this world. And you, Jerico, your order is crushed. Your brethren are gone. But you can still aid this world. Have you not seen what we can accomplish together? Bring your teachings of mercy and forgiveness to the Stronghold. Help me mold our understanding of Karak into something men of all faiths might embrace. Come with me. Both of you, join me. It is not too late."

Darius looked to Jerico, and the answer was clear on his face.

"Give us a moment to consider," Darius told Luther. "I would talk with my friend."

Luther bowed low.

"Of course," he said before trudging off.

"Talk?" asked Jerico when he was gone. "What is there to talk about?"

"Plenty," Darius said. He beckoned Valessa to come out of hiding. "We can't win this, Jerico. They are too many, and even if we could cross the river, it would only be a matter of time before they hunted us down like dogs."

"I will not sell my soul," Jerico insisted.

"And I would not have you do so, either. No, you need to run. I have a plan, desperate perhaps, but I think it will save you."

Jerico began shaking his head, immediately protesting.

"No," he said. "No, I won't. I won't leave you, Darius, listen to me, I'm not leaving."

"You have to," Darius insisted. "You're the last, Jerico, and you're the best of us. I owe you everything, so for this once, let me pay you back."

"You would have me run like a coward?"

"I would have you live," Darius said. "Is that so terrible a request?"

Jerico flung his shield onto his back, and he glanced about the burning forest. His eyes settled on Valessa, who stood quietly beside him.

"And you?" he asked her.

"My place is with him," she said, nodding toward Darius.

Jerico bit his lower lip, and then at last he gave in.

"So be it," he said, stepping forward and embracing Darius. "May we see each other again."

"In this life or beyond," Darius said, and he did his best to smile. "Now get out of here."

Slowly, reluctantly, Jerico clipped his mace to his belt and turned to the river.

"Promise me something," he said before he left.

"What is that?"

"When you see Luther again, don't hate him. I've never seen a better man so horribly lost."

Weaving his way through the fire, he vanished amid the smoke. Darius watched him go as he felt his stomach harden into a stone. Valessa touched his arm.

"I know what you're thinking," she said.

"Do you?" he asked, and when he looked into her eyes, he saw she did.

"I do it for you," she said. "Is he worth it?"

Darius looked to the river.

"I hope so," he said.

They turned and waited for Luther's return as the fire around them spread. Into that growing inferno came Luther, a dozen priests and paladins with him. They halted just beyond the edge of the trees, and Luther stepped forward.

"I would have your answer!" he cried.

Darius drew his sword and looked to the side. Valessa was there, but she wore the heavy platemail of a paladin of Ashhur. Her hair was long and red, and on her back was a tower shield. Her face, though, was still her own when she spoke to him as they stood before the ring of flames.

"Feel no guilt," she said. "No one will weep for my passing."

"One person will," Darius said softly as her face became Jerico's.

"An answer!" cried Luther.

"You would have an answer?" Darius said, jerking his attention back to Karak's followers. His sword rose high in the air. "His life is not yours. You will not have him. You will not kill him. He is beyond you now."

Down came his sword, crashing through Valessa's neck. Light flashed, and then she collapsed into the fire before her, the flames obscuring the decay of her body as it dissolved into white mist that was soon lost amid the smoke. Darius felt a sob catch in his throat, and he prayed they would not see the tears in his eyes as he turned to face them.

"All you have is me," he said. "I hope I'll suffice, you sick bastards."

Luther's mouth hung open, and he seemed at a loss for words. Those behind him knew what they wanted, though, and they readied their weapons and magic. Darius tensed, and he dared let a grin show. Him against them all in a desperate battle to the death. What more could he possibly have asked for?

With a cry, he charged, the light of his sword shimmering bright. Dark paladins swarmed around Luther, bringing their weapons to his protection. Darius swung, pouring into it a reckless energy. His sword connected with a large blade akin to his own, and sparks showered across the grass from the contact. Darius was the faster to recover, and he thrust for the man's neck only to have it blocked by another. An elbow struck his forehead. Staggering back, he swung again, hitting only air. Two priests leapt forward, hands extended. Shadows shot forth, and at their touch he screamed as his nerves ignited with pain.

Fully surrounded now, Darius continued to swing, constantly turning in a vain attempt to prevent a sneak attack. A sword thrust pierced his side, slipping through a crease in his armor. It wasn't deep, but it was enough to steal his balance as the blood ran free. Another man caught him, slammed his helmet into his face. To his knees Darius fell as all around he saw the blurred faces of men who hated him.

"That..." he gasped, "that all you can do?"

He tried rising, but a heavyset man lifted a great mace with both hands and swung. It smashed into Darius's leg, and he felt bones shattering. He screamed. Unable to stand, the others held him, pinning his arms. When he refused to be disarmed, they pulled and twisted until his elbow snapped. His sword fell to the ground before him. More spells shone from the hands of priests, sapping his strength.

Helpless, Darius watched as Luther slowly approached.

"You could have been our greatest," he said, pulling a dagger out from a hidden pocket of his robes.

"No," Darius said, defiant to the last. "The greatest of you is still so much less."

"Less?" asked Luther as those around him laughed and mocked. "You're beaten, Darius. You're abandoned. You are the unloved. At least accept this one last truth before you die."

The words were muffled in his mind, but one sliced through his delirium and pain.

Unloved...

Unloved...

Luther stabbed the dagger just below his chestplate and into his stomach, but Darius never felt it. Instead, an anger grew in his breast, and it contained such fury it terrified him. The pain in his limbs started to fade, and with vision suddenly clear he looked up at Luther.

"Unloved?" he said. "Who are you, Luther, to deny the love I know?"

The words were his own, but not. He heard ringing, he felt power, and then from his back spread wings of silvery light. Their edges sliced through the armor of the paladins that held him, and when blood splattered, it refused to stain the ethereal feathers. Darius cast off the men and grabbed his sword. Immediately the metal vanished, overwhelmed by a blade of purest light, as weightless as the feathers stretching from his back. The wounds in his body were closed. When he pivoted, his knee felt stronger than it had in years.

In a single swing he killed three, the blade of light cutting through their bodies like they were stalks of wheat. Turning, the paladin with the mace lifted it up to block, but Darius cut right through, splitting him in twain from forehead to sternum. Spinning, he caught two priests trying to curse him. The wings stretching from his back folded protectively, and the spells hit without the ability to penetrate. Spreading wide, Darius rushed them, with two flicks of his wrist severing their heads. Faster and faster he moved, nothing able to satisfy his rage.

They were panicking now, and one dark paladin moved to guard Luther. The black flame around his sword was great, and when Darius swung the man blocked with a great cry to his god. The blades connected midair, releasing a shockwave that felt like a pale imitation of when Cyric's sword had struck Jerico's shield. As the other paladin stood shocked, Darius pulled back and swung, the second blow shattering the steel. Helpless, the man could do nothing as Darius cut through one side of his waist and out the other.

To his left a priest gathered shadows on his fingers. Feathers from his wing lashed out, and to the ground fell those same fingers. Another beat of the wing, and the priest fell with them. Blood pounding in his ears, Darius turned and turned, his sword cutting down all who would face him. A single beat of his wings and he leapt on those who tried to flee.

And then, quick as it began, it was over. Only one remained, and the tip of Darius's sword hovered just shy of his throat.

"Tell them what you saw," Darius ordered Luther as he felt the rage in his chest slowly subsiding. Luther had not moved, had only stood and watched from the moment the wings had burst through the armor on Darius's back.

"I will," he said, taking a careful step backward, then another. When it was clear Darius would not kill him, he turned and ran from the forest as fast as his old bones would allow.

Darius stood there watching until he was gone. The moment lingered, and he did his best to enjoy it. It was the calm after a storm, the peace of a quiet morning. The light of his wings dimmed, and with each beat he felt them losing their luster. The moment gone, the presence of Ashhur vanishing at last, Darius turned and began to walk. The wings faded from his back, shimmering away like soft white smoke upon the wind. His direction was not aimless, and he passed through the fire without a thought to its danger. With each step his exhaustion returned, the rage he'd known slowly draining into an emptiness in his chest that refused to fill.

"Was it right?" Darius asked as he felt the wound in his side reopen. "Was it right to let him live?"

Luther would return to Mordeina and inform the rest of Karak's faithful about Jerico's death. If they hunted for anyone, it'd be him now. Jerico was free. He could go and live, wherever, however, and perhaps make a life for himself. But was it worth letting such a terrible man like Luther escape? He didn't know. But he'd killed enough that day, and he'd made Jerico a promise.

Jerico...

"Let him find some happiness," Darius said, feeling a fever starting to burn in his face and neck. "Let him find some peace. Can you do that for him? If that's possible. If you're even in this world anymore. It's so dark, Ashhur. So terribly dark."

His breath grew weaker. Blood trickled down his face and neck. Step by step he pushed onward. The sword he'd held, once light as a feather against Luther's neck, now felt like it weighed a thousand stone. It dragged behind him on the ground, the tip bumping against the dirt.

"Will she be waiting for me?" Darius asked, forcing his body to move forward. "Will Valessa..."

He screamed as he felt the bones in his right arm shatter and break. His sword fell to the ground, and he left it there. Staggering, he screamed again as the torn muscles of his chest pulsed with fresh pain.

"Please," Darius said, his voice ragged. "Please, Ashhur, please. I don't want to die."

Another scream, this time when the bones in his left leg snapped, just as they had from the dark paladin's mace. Every cut, every break, he felt them returning, the pain fresh as it had been when first inflicted upon his body. Unable to walk, he collapsed onto his stomach, his blood painting the grass below him red. But he wasn't done yet. He wasn't there. With shaking hands he dragged himself along.

"Was it enough?" he asked, straining to look ahead. Before him was the river, and he crawled to it on his knees.

"All those people. Oh god, the family. The town. I watched them die. Was it enough? Will they be waiting too?"

Another inch closer he dragged his broken body, even as he felt the stab of a dagger through his stomach. He thought of their faces, of the terror he'd brought them. A family praying to Ashhur, killed to prove his faithfulness to Karak. The prophet's words were poison, but he'd believed them anyway. He'd stood in Durham and watched it burn. Why? What madness had possessed him? Again and again he saw their faces, frozen in pain and fear.

"Will they be waiting?" he asked. "Will they forgive me? I slew your faithful, Ashhur. I slew them. So many…"

His fingers dipped into the water. It was cold, and he splashed some across his face, wiping away the blood. With that same water he washed away his tears, and then he rolled onto his back, his hands above him, still in the river. Could it really be that easy? Could he just kneel and plead for forgiveness, and it'd cleanse it all away? But it didn't wash away the death. It didn't erase the damage. The pain he'd caused would always be there, festering in the lives of others, sown like seeds that would sprout only thorns.

Unworthy, thought Darius, and he dreamed of meeting those pained faces in a shining land. He dared hope they would greet him with smiles, and when he fell to his knees before them, they would reach out and tell him to stand. It would be a poor eternity spent in a place that could harbor bitterness and blame.

"What's it like?" he wondered aloud, his tongue so dry it was starting to burn. Would it be streets of gold as they said? He hoped not. For some that might be their vision of beauty, but Darius liked to think himself a simpler man. He wished for fields of grass, for tall mountains capped with snow, for forests and animals. There'd be large gatherings of friends, maybe a cool lake where he could wait for Jerico to join him, where they could embrace and forget the torment they'd suffered on Dezrel. More than anything, he wanted peace. He wanted there to be no more need for someone like him, no more need for the sword he'd left behind.

The river flowed across his hands.

"I hope she's waiting," Darius whispered with lungs slowly starting to fail him. "I hope she's…"

The wind blew across him, and a smile blossomed on his face.

"I see," he said.

And then he died.

25

Away from the forest staggered Luther. He felt baffled by the display, and in awe of the strength that had humbled him. Over and over he thought of that moment, when Darius had lifted his sword high above Jerico's neck.

"His life is not yours," the paladin had said. "You will not have him. You will not kill him. He is beyond you now."

And then the sword had fallen. The moment left Luther sick. He'd hoped the two would listen. They could have joined him, come back to learn. Why would they do such a thing? Why were they so willing to die? In stabbing Darius, he'd taken pleasure in punishing Jerico's murderer. But then Ashhur had shown his presence, and what a presence it was.

The smoke billowed into the sky behind him, the fire slowly spreading along the riverside. Luther saw none of it. Instead he saw a man waiting for him, his two dirks in hand. The land beyond the forest was smooth grass, and it rippled in waves as the wind blew. Without fear Luther approached, even though his strength was sapped and his head ached. All around them were the corpses of men and monsters.

"I see you survived," Luther told Kaide, stopping ten paces away and standing to his full height.

"And you as well. It will take more than a few wolf-men to lay me low."

The wind howled. Their eyes met, and they shared a stare that dragged on and on.

"Is Jerico dead?" Kaide asked.

Luther nodded. The motion made the brigand's whole body tense. An attack was imminent. Luther knew he would not survive.

"Did you kill him?"

Kaide's voice was like ice, and there was no disguising the loathing.

"No," Luther said. "No, I did not. I would have had him live. The choice was taken from me."

The dirks lifted. Luther closed his eyes, and he prepared himself to meet his god. But the hit did not come. He heard a slow exhalation of air, and when he looked, he saw Kaide jamming the dirks into his belt.

"I do not understand," Luther said.

Kaide shook his head, and his eyes swept across the bodies of the battlefield.

"No," he said. "I doubt you would."

"This is the promise I made to you. Here I am. Strike me down."

"I want to," Kaide said. "But I will not honor Jerico's memory that way."

He turned to leave, but Luther had to know. He called out, stopping him.

"Tell me first, do you honor the man, or what he believed?"

Kaide turned his head to the side. His gaze remained firmly on the ground, as if ashamed of what he needed to say.

"He begged me to let you live," said Kaide. "He loved Sandra as much as I, yet still he begged. It wasn't to protect you. I hope you realize that, Luther. He didn't put himself in the way of my dirks for your sake. He did it for mine. I honor Jerico for everything he ever was, and you're a fool if you think you can separate the man from what he believed."

With that he trudged off. Luther watched him go, his bafflement growing. This was a man prone to murder first, a man who knew only hatred. Yet now he let it all go, and for what? To honor a dead man? Men didn't change like that. He'd seen it a thousand times before. A man was what a man was. To put his back to him, to walk away...

Luther looked to the burning forest, and he heard Jerico's words echo in his ear.

We save this world by healing it. Not with fire, not with destruction. I pray you one day realize this, and believe.

Kaide had been a man of fire. He'd been a man of destruction. No longer.

Luther's eyes, for the briefest moment, dared open to a world of possibilities that frightened him. On his knees he fell, and the lion named Doubt roared and roared.

Epilogue

In the morning light Jerico approached the grass-covered remains of the fallen Citadel. Wind blew through his hair, and it felt good. Alongside the river he saw scattered remnants of the boats that had once patrolled both the Gihon and the Rigon, keeping the lands beyond the Vile Wedge safe. It looked like many had been scavenged over the past few months. The heavy stones, though, they remained. As he neared, he saw the bulk of the tower had collapsed upon its eastern side, and the pile of stones there was enormous. Drifting through, he found bits and pieces of clothing, beds, broken hilts and templates for shields. No doubt people had scavenged their remains as they had the boats.

"We protected you," Jerico said aloud, thinking of the people coming in from the south. "And when we fell, you came to pick our corpses clean. Did you weep for us? Did you shake your heads and mutter as you walked among the bodies?"

Now he made his way over the uneven terrain of the foundation. In its center was a great crater, and a crack in the earth as if the very world had deigned to break the building. What could have caused that? A man of Karak had led the attack, that was all Jerico knew. He'd seen the collapse many times in his dreams, and what he saw before him matched perfectly. But lately the field before it was barren. No fighting, no siege, no demons or prophets or last stands for his dead brethren. Just the Citadel shaking, crumbling, then falling on its side. What did it mean? Jerico

wondered. Long they'd been told the destruction of the
Citadel would herald the ending of the world, a ceasing of
all things good and pure. But he knew that wasn't true. His
order was not yet done, and there were still many good and
pure things left in Dezrel.

"What is it you want from me now?" Jerico asked
aloud. The empty field was so quiet, so serene, he could
almost imagine Ashhur standing there, listening. "I've done
everything I thought was right, and it resulted in death.
Must I watch more of my friends die? Must my very
presence put them in danger?"

He felt a pain stab him in the chest.

"Is Darius with you?" he asked the rubble, and the
only answer he was given was in the blowing of the wind.

Slowly Jerico put his back to the broken pieces of his
order and began walking across the tall grass fields. He
wondered about the children there, if they'd been destroyed
with the rest. Perhaps they lived? Or maybe there were still
more paladins out there, cowering in cellars and temples in
the far corners of Mordan and Neldar. So much he didn't
know, and as he walked he left the one place he'd hoped
would give him answers. But now he knew. He was alone,
all alone.

He stepped on something hard and uneven. Glancing
down, Jerico found the hilt of a weapon hidden in the
grass. Reaching down, he lifted up a splendid mace. The
flanged edges shimmered with power, and the balance of
the weight was perfect. Inscribed along the shaft in gold
was the weapon's name, Bonebreaker. Jerico remembered
the man who had wielded it, a faithful paladin named
Jaegar.

"Is this a gift?" Jerico asked, and he laughed despite
himself, laughed until the laughter was replaced with an
impotent rage. "The lost weapon of a dead man…is this all

you would have me do? Kill? Slaughter? Is the pain worth this, the murder, the loss, all in vain hopes of hearing your voice? Is that what I am to this world now, just a way to shed blood? What would you have me do, damn it, what? What?"

I would have you live.

The remembered words struck him with their softness, their simplicity. Jerico fell to his knees, and before the ruins of the Citadel he wept, the weapon still in his hands. A noise startled him, and he looked up to the see the landing of a dove, her feathers white and pristine. The left wing, however, was withered and uneven, yet still the creature flew, and still it was beautiful. The message was clear, and with a heavy heart Jerico stood.

"I will," Jerico said. "I promised Darius I would. But I'm not strong enough just yet. My faith is shaken, and I would not have it break. Permit me an exile, Ashhur. I think you'll understand."

Casting aside his old mace, Jerico clipped the new one to his belt and then began walking north. Not far from the Citadel was a shallow crossing, one he would use to leave the mortal kingdoms of men and instead venture into the wild lands of the Vile Wedge. In there, he would hurt no one. In there, no dark paladin would come to kill him, and he would kill none in return. Perhaps it was cowardice, but he knew his time there would only be fleeting. Live, commanded his lord, and so he would live.

And just perhaps, when death came for him, he might meet it with a shred of the bravery Darius had shown.

The sky was clear and blue, and the wind through his red hair felt like an affirmation.

Still amid the ruins, the dove with a broken wing watched him travel north, head and shoulders bent with a heavy burden, yet his step lighter than when he first arrived.

"Live," said the dove before flying away.

Note From the Author:

Normally I write this section after some separation from the novel, most often the day before they are published. Not this time. I'm writing this immediately after finishing the last chapter and the epilogue, so I can try to keep whatever emotions I'm feeling about it fresh. It only seems appropriate enough for Darius.

Speaking of…for three novels, whenever I expected him to die, he lived. Now, when I fully expected him to live (and anyone who's read the endnote in Blood of the Underworld knows this), he goes and does…that. Is it an ending befitting him? I don't know. But it's his ending. I've killed plenty of characters before, even some very beloved ones, but I'm not sure I've ever given them such a death, if I've ever stripped them so bare in their final moments. There's a lot of me in Darius, and a lot in Jerico as well. When it comes to their doubts, their questions, their desperate hopes, they so often mirror mine. If I'm given such a moment, I also hope I have the same courage. I also hope I have a few people waiting for me with open arms.

This is pretty much the end of the Paladin series. If you're curious about Jerico, he's re-introduced in the third book of the Half-Orcs, Death of Promises, while he's still in exile in the Wedge. Luther will be causing trouble in Blood of the Father, the next up on my agenda. I have a feeling Valessa might be there as well. As for the events Jerico's hinting at, I do think at some point I will write that novel. The Fall of the Citadel was the first full novel I ever wrote and completed, and it's still in a shoebox in my closet. Should I rewrite it, it'll be a standalone, or perhaps just Paladins #0. Either way, it'll be awhile. I've got some half-orc brothers to get to before that.

I hope you all have enjoyed this series. I've poured my heart into it, be it dark or light, and more than anything I'm proud of this particular book. It might not sell as well as the assassins, but that's okay. A smaller audience means more intimate stories, right? I wanted an uplifting ending to this series, a nice triumphant moment for these paladins. I don't know if I gave it to them. Right now, I have no clue. I can't tell if they're exultant, happy, depressing, lost, hopeless, what. But it's the right ending, damn it. It's an honest one.

If you'd like to send me an email, fire one off to ddalglish@yahoo.com. I promise to get to it eventually, though I'm falling behind, so consider this a plea for patience. You can also check out my website at ddalglish.com, and if you want to keep up on whatever bizarre project I'm planning next, you can find nearly every update at www.facebook.com/thehalforcs.

Again, thank you for making it this far. Thank you for your time, your patience when I screw up, and your sharing with others when I do something awesome. God Bless.

David Dalglish
July 5th, 2012

Made in United States
Orlando, FL
19 May 2022

18011387R00162